"I'm going to call the doctor."

"Don't," Jane said. "It would cost money, and I don't have any."

Duncan took her small hands in his. Her hands were cold, and his touch warmed them.

"I'll pay for it. I want to," he said.

"You don't even know me," she whispered, amazed that he would take care of her, that he even seemed to *want* to take care of her. "Why don't you just let me go?"

He studied her for a long moment. She had an idea that he was used to being in charge, and that she was now someone he considered his responsibility and therefore not to be dismissed lightly.

"I doubt that you have anywhere to go," he said.

The truth of his perception staggered her. So far she had fooled herself that she was preserving the fiction that she was a real person with a real place to be.

ABOUT THE AUTHOR

Pamela Browning lives with her husband and two teenage children in South Carolina, where she occasionally reviews books for her local radio station.

Pamela loves to travel and finds inspiration for new books whenever she does. A trip out West that included a visit to a llama ranch led to the idea for *Until Spring*.

Books by Pamela Browning

HARLEQUIN AMERICAN ROMANCE

HARLEQUIN ROMANCE

Don't miss any of our special offers. Write to us at the following address for information on our newest releases.

Harlequin Reader Service
901 Fuhrmann Blvd., P.O. Box 1397, Buffalo, NY 14240
Canadian address: P.O. Box 603,
Fort Erie, Ont. L2A 5X3

Until
Spring
Pamela Browning

Harlequin Books

TORONTO • NEW YORK • LONDON
AMSTERDAM • PARIS • SYDNEY • HAMBURG
STOCKHOLM • ATHENS • TOKYO • MILAN

Published June 1989

First printing April 1989

ISBN 0-373-16297-9

Prologue

The woman dozed west of Rawlins, Wyoming, her head lolling against the back of the seat.

She would be pretty, thought the truck driver, if only her face wasn't so thin. He jammed his foot on the accelerator. When they reached Rock Springs, maybe he'd find out what the rest of her looked like. It was hard to tell if she had much of a build underneath that tacky old coat.

She stirred and mumbled something, and then her eyes jarred open, the pupils widening as she tried to place him. There was something spacey about this chick, no doubt about it. It wasn't anything he could pin down, only a wariness or a wildness or something; he wouldn't know how to describe it. Right now she was retreating into the corner of the truck cab, almost as though she disliked him intensely. Heck, that was crazy. Females usually flocked to him; all he had to do was crook a little finger and they'd come running.

"You hungry?" he asked her, none too gently. She'd riled him by acting so standoffish.

She nodded a cautious yes, but didn't speak. Her eyes were huge in that tiny face.

"We'll pull into a truck stop outside of Rock Springs," he said.

"I don't have any money for food," she said in a faint voice.

He lifted an eyebrow in her direction. He fancied that this expression gave him a devilish look. "It don't matter," he said. "I'll feed you—if you're nice to me."

His meaning was unmistakable. He had meant it to be. He watched her, keeping one eye on the road.

"Let me out," she said. Her voice was weary, not feisty. That was too bad, because he liked feisty women.

"I can't put you out here," he said. "It's starting to snow, and there's no place for you to go."

"Stop the truck," she insisted. She drew her tattered garments tightly around her. The cat—he had forgotten about the cat—uttered a faint mew from somewhere inside the voluminous folds of the coat.

"Hey," he said in a jocular tone. "What's wrong with you and me having a little fun? Two strangers keeping each other warm for the night—it could be nice." He touched a placating hand to the knob of her knee, which was barely distinguishable under the coat.

"If you don't stop this truck immediately, I'm going to jump," she said, reaching for the door handle.

"Don't do that," he said, becoming alarmed.

"I mean it," she said. She shot him a look of pure determination.

He slowed the big rig to a stop at the side of the road. "Hey, listen, lady," he began, but before he could say anything more, she had opened the door.

It happened so fast that there wasn't anything he could do to stop her. A mixture of snow and sleet swirled inside, and the woman, no bigger than a bundle of rags, tumbled out into the darkness.

"What the—" he exclaimed, jumping down from the cab. He couldn't see much of anything in this weather, and there wasn't a sign of her. With a muttered curse he walked back along the road, but it was as if she had vanished into thin air.

It confounded him that she had proved feistier than he'd figured. He felt a grudging admiration for her spunk. He peered down the snow-covered highway embankment, trying to make out footprints or some other evidence, but didn't see anything.

He would have called her name, only he'd never asked her what it was. Finally, when ice started to form on his eyelashes, he decided to cut his losses and give up the search.

"Dumb broad," he muttered with a quickly passing regret as he walked back to the rig. He had offered her a meal and a bed, and if she was too stupid to take him up on it, she could just freeze to death out there. Serve her right, too.

2

A SNOW-COVERED LOG REARED UP to trip her when she started down the embankment beside the road, and when she fell, she hit her head on something hard. She rolled to the side to avoid crushing Amos, then lay stunned for a minute or two before using one of the branches on the log to help pull herself to her knees.

Amos the cat, who had somehow stayed snugly bundled inside her coat when she fell, stirred and sank his claws into her midriff. She winced, but clutched his scrawny body even closer. She was determined to hold on to him at all costs. Amos was all she had.

She waited until the obnoxious truck driver who had picked her up at a gas station near Elmo climbed back into his truck and drove away. Then she swayed light-headedly to her feet.

She should have known that the guy would be a problem; he was young and cocksure and his eyes shone with a predatory gleam. She usually rode with older, more settled types or married couples, if possible. At the time, though, she had seized upon his offer of a ride as a refuge from the frigid January gale that had roared unexpectedly out of the north.

It was so cold that her feet were numb, so cold that she couldn't feel her nose. Her right shoulder and hip ached where they had taken the brunt of the impact of her fall.

The terrain here was deceptive. Previous snowfalls had filled in the hollows, and sometimes her feet crunched through the thin surface layer of ice, so that she found herself wallowing in knee-high drifts. It was hard getting up, but she knew that she couldn't lie there, even for a minute. She had to find shelter, and soon.

She paused, trying to establish a sense of direction in the darkness. The sleet and snow were turning into a blizzard, she realized with a pang of apprehension. She saw no welcoming lights in the distance and understood bleakly that the truck driver had been right. There wasn't anybody here to help her, perhaps not for miles around.

She turned back toward the highway. Under the circumstances, it would be better to try to hitch a ride with anyone who happened along. The truck driver wouldn't be back, so intent was he on a hot meal and whatever other warmth he might find in Rock Springs.

But where was the highway? She blinked, but her eyes refused to focus in the whiteout conditions. She didn't hear any cars or trucks passing, but maybe there weren't any. Why would anyone go out on a night like this?

"We'll make it, Amos, don't you worry," she said out loud to the cat, cradling him close. He didn't answer, and his warmth felt like a deadweight in her arms. With a feeling of dread, she opened her coat to make sure he was all right. Suddenly Amos, feeling the full impact of the cold, struggled to free himself.

"Amos," she said, but he fought her restraining arms and leaped down into the snow.

"Amos!" she called frantically. She couldn't lose Amos! Where was he?

She stood uncertainly, not knowing which way he'd gone. Although she called him repeatedly, she heard no plaintive meow in reply.

Stupid animal! Why had he chosen this time and this place to wander away? Didn't he realize that she needed him? Didn't he know he was all she had?

She cast about, taking a few steps this way, a few steps that way, all the while calling his name. She headed in what she thought was the direction of the highway but soon realized that she was hopelessly lost. Her knees giving way beneath her, she sank into the snow.

It wasn't smart to rest, she knew that, but oh, how wonderful it felt. If only she were warm, sitting in front of a fireplace perhaps, or a wood stove, or beneath an electric blanket. She tried to imagine the heat spreading upward from her frozen toes to her equally frozen legs, fanning out through her body like a warm little blue flame, heating her from the inside out....

She startled herself awake, knowing that she had to get back on her feet, if she was to survive. She fought to pull herself to a standing position, but all she could manage was to push herself to her hands and knees in the snow. She wasn't wearing gloves, and her fingers ached.

"Amos?" she called, her voice barely a whisper now. "Amos?"

All she heard was the howl of the wind.

She thought she saw a flick of his ginger-colored tail out of the corner of her eye and oriented herself toward it, bowing her head in deference to the cutting wind. Slowly she crawled toward the cat, listening for his plaintive meow.

She was conscious only of her own plodding determination to propel herself through the snow. Tears froze upon her cheeks, and sleet gathered on her eyebrows, but still she pressed on.

Amos ran just ahead of her, the little imp, twitching his whiskers in that sassy way of his. Funny, but he, who had looked so bedraggled and forlorn a month ago, now sported a luxuriant coat, and he feinted and scampered playfully in the snow.

Amos, you crazy cat, I'm going to catch you now, she thought gleefully. Then she lunged for him and fell through a doorway into a place where it was blessedly warm and dry.

Chapter One

"You're not planning to go out tonight?" Rooney asked skeptically.

Duncan Tate pulled the saddle cinch tightly around old Flapjack's middle. "You bet I am," he said.

Rooney walked around the horse and stood watching Duncan as he checked the contents of his saddlebag.

"I wouldn't if I was you," Rooney said. "There's a storm brewing."

"I want to find Quixote. I've got a feeling that this is a real bummer of a winter storm." Duncan didn't add that if Rooney's ten-year-old granddaughter, the incorrigible Mary Kate, hadn't left the door to Quixote's stall open, he wouldn't feel compelled to go anywhere in this weather. He'd stay home by a crackling fire instead.

"Quixote can take care of himself. Llamas are used to the cold."

"All I need is for my prize stud to fall and break a leg, and there goes my herd."

"All *I* need is for *you* to fall and break a leg, and that leaves me to manage this llama ranch all by myself. You're our most valuable asset, Duncan, not Quixote."

Duncan ignored this and heaved himself up into the saddle. "I'm not going to take any chances with the weather, Rooney. You know me better than that. I'll just ride down valley a bit and try to get a feeling for where Quixote might be. I'd like him safe and warm in his stall on a night like this.''

He urged the reluctant Flapjack out into the night, knowing that once they were free of the barn, his reliable old mount would get into the spirit of things. He was right. Flapjack headed down valley, exactly as Duncan wanted him to. They'd take a look at the far pasture, then aim toward the highway. Maybe they'd even manage a look-see around the old mine, if the snow held back a while longer.

No sign of Quixote in the far pasture, so they proceeded toward the highway. Duncan would give almost anything to find Quixote tonight; with his woolly coat, the llama was well protected, but Duncan didn't like to think of him wandering around the ranch. He was almost ridiculously attached to each member of his llama herd, and he knew that Quixote had a tendency to be a bit too adventurous for his own good.

During a previous escapade, this one also engineered by Mary Kate, the llama had turned up on a neighboring spread. Somehow Quixote had managed to cross two streams and a small mountain all by himself, and during the four days it took him to do it, Duncan had given up all hope of ever seeing Quixote again.

A few snowflakes sifted from the sky, and then the wind picked up some bite. Duncan reined in Flapjack before deciding to go ahead and check out the area around the abandoned mine. If he didn't, he knew he wouldn't sleep all night for worrying.

Before he was halfway there, he knew it had been a mistake to go on. Sleet stung his face, and the wind began to howl like a coyote on the prowl. Maybe that fool llama had managed to get inside the old mine; the door had been hanging from its hinges last time Duncan had been there, and he'd meant to have it repaired. As long as he'd come this far, he might as well check it out.

He dismounted in front of the ledge of rock that sheltered the mine entrance, slapped Flapjack on the flank by way of reassurance, and mentally chastised himself for not repairing the door before this. The wind had torn it from two of its hinges so that it hung crazily to one side, and the mine was open to the elements. He unclipped a flashlight from his belt and trained it inside the opening. His nostrils twitched at the familiar smell of the mine, musty and dank and still faintly scented from Duncan's boyhood camp fires. This had been one of his favorite camping places.

"Quixote?" he hollered as loudly as he could, thinking that the animal could have wandered down the long curving tunnel, far from where he stood.

His voice echoed back at him, but there was no answering movement within. He was about to turn and head back for the ranch when a cat, blinking warily at the bright light, detached itself from a bundle of rags on the floor.

Surprised to find a cat there, Duncan stopped and let the animal rub against his hand. It was a skinny creature, scarcely bigger than a kitten, and an ugly ginger color. Still, it had a winning way about it, butting against his hand and purring loudly.

"Guess maybe I'd better take you home with me," he said. "We could probably use another cat around the barn." Rooney would have a fit, he knew. If there was one thing they didn't need at Placid Valley Ranch, it was another cat. He started to pick up the cat, and then, from the bundle of rags came a soft moan.

It might have been the wind, but Duncan played the flashlight beam over the rags and they moved. Not much, but slightly. It was enough to make him drop the cat and spring into action.

He knew immediately that he was dealing with a serious situation. He saw a hand, white and wet, so he turned the pile of clothing over—to discover a small, pale face framed by wisps of wet blond hair that were escaping from a felt hat pulled low over the forehead.

He could see that it was a female, because no boy had ever had such fine bone structure or such long eyelashes. He knew that she was at risk from exposure to the cold. He also mistook her for a child.

Her eyes opened slowly. They were blue and void of expression. She tried to speak, but couldn't.

"Don't worry, I'll take care of you," he said gently, but at the sound of his voice, the look in her eyes turned to panic and she tried to pull away from him. It was no use, though. She was too weak.

He didn't stop to wonder why she was in the abandoned mine; all he knew was that he had to do something for her— and fast.

She was conscious; that was a good sign. From the look of the melting snow around her, she hadn't been in the mine for very long, maybe less than a half hour.

He always kept a small survival kit in his saddlebag, and he headed outside to get it.

"Please," she said in a faint voice, then coughed a deep, wracking cough.

He knelt immediately. He should have let her know that he wasn't going far.

"I have to get something," he told her, stroking back the wet hair from her forehead. He realized suddenly that she had thought he was leaving and not coming back.

She managed a small nod of her head, and seeing that she understood, he swiftly went out to Flapjack, who was leaning stoically into a rip-roaring wind. When he realized the strength of the blizzard, Duncan began to have serious doubts about heading back to the ranch tonight.

The least he could do at the moment was to get Flapjack out of the wind. "Come on, fella," he said, leading the horse inside the mine. The opening was narrow but tall, and Duncan had an idea that they'd be grateful for the added warmth of Flapjack's body heat in the small space.

When he returned, he saw that the girl had tried to pull herself to a sitting position and that her hat had fallen off to reveal a mass of pale curly hair. She slouched motionless as he checked her hands for frostbite. Miraculously there was none, although they were pretty scraped up. He quickly removed her shoes, which were only a pair of old Nike running shoes, and her socks, of which there were two pairs. No frostbite on the toes, either.

"You sure picked a rotten night to go out for a stroll," he told her.

Her eyes opened, then drifted closed again. They jolted wide when he started to remove her heavy coat.

"We have to get you warm," he explained. "Water-soaked clothes against the skin can be deadly when you've been out in weather like this."

She made a little grasping motion at the edge of her coat and pulled away from him, but she was so feeble that she only slid down the wall and lay coughing on the floor of the mine.

He didn't care about her sensibilities or her protests; he only knew that she might die if hypothermia got the better of her. She already showed the signs of this dread reaction to cold. She seemed to have no judgment, no reasoning power, and had little control over her hands. She was barely surviving in a half-conscious stupor, and after collapse, the next stage of hypothermia was death. He was sure that she had no idea of the dangers.

Despite her weak cries, he stripped the coat from her body. The coat, although old, had once been a good one; it was made of pure wool. It was soaked clear through, and so were the clothes she wore underneath it: an inappropriately thin cotton shirt and a pair of blue jeans. He stripped those off, too, working methodically and scarcely paying attention to the fact that this was no girl, but a full-grown woman.

He pulled off his own coat and wrapped it around her, covering it with a thin Mylar survival blanket, which took up only a few inches of space in his saddlebag but served admirably to conserve body heat when unrolled and wrapped around a victim. Then he found a couple of heat tablets, lighted them, and melted snow in his tin cup. By the

light of one of the candles in his survival kit, he dropped a
bouillon cube into the hot water, keeping an eye on the girl
all the while. She lay on her back on the rock floor, her chest
rising and falling regularly. He was afraid that she might
suddenly stop breathing or experience heart failure. Both
were possibilities.

"Do you think you could drink this?" he asked gently,
holding the cup to her lips. She managed a few sips, then
turned her head away. He understood. She was offended
that he had so unceremoniously stripped off her clothes.
Didn't she understand that he had only been acting out of
kindness?

He found a few oily rags in the cubbyholes near the mine
entrance, and lacking anything more suitable, fashioned
them into a cushion against the rocky floor.

A particularly strong gust of wind delivered a surge of
snow deep into the interior of the mine, and Duncan hurried to the entrance to see if the storm was worsening. It
was; visibility was zero, and he felt sure that the outside
temperature had dropped. It would be foolish to try to make
it home in this storm. He knew the old mine well enough to
know that the temperature inside ranged in the low sixties,
no matter what the weather outside, but also knew he'd
better repair the door, if they were going to be there all
night. He dragged it across the opening and wedged it shut
with a rotting two-by-four.

When he returned to the girl, he found that she had rolled
over on her side into a fetal position. Despite his coat and
the survival blanket, she was still shivering.

"We have to get you warmer," he said, and he knew she
understood his words because she curled herself into an even
tighter ball, as though to shut him out entirely.

He started to unwrap the Mylar, but she held it fast. Losing patience, he rolled her over and dragged her out of it.
The look she gave him was one of pure resentment. She
must be feeling miserable, and yet she cared more about

proprieties than saving her own neck. Still, her lips were blue.

As carefully as he could, he pulled her arms out of the coat, and then, looking at her naked body as briefly as possible, he wrapped his coat around the two of them and rolled them both in the Mylar blanket. Her body was so tiny that she reminded him of a bird, and he felt her heart beating wildly against his. Shivers wracked her body for a long time, but finally, gradually, they stopped.

Her head rested against his shoulder; her legs warmed between his. At last she slept.

Flapjack whinnied, and Duncan spoke to him calmly. The girl didn't wake up. Outside the wind keened and whistled, and after the candle flame flickered and died, Duncan dozed off, wondering just before he did so whatever had happened to Quixote.

Chapter Two

She woke up carefully, letting the feeling flood back into each stiff limb one by one, not yet daring to move. Once she could feel her arms and legs, she was sorry. They were stiff and sore. Her throat hurt, and she stifled a cough.

She smelled his scent before she felt or heard him. It must be a throwback to caveman days, when humans depended on sense of smell much more than they do now; when in danger, she knew to rely on it again. He smelled musky and of the outdoors. It was a decidedly male smell, and her first reaction was to panic.

She forced her fear to subside because her well-honed intuition told her that he was safe. He had helped her when he found her here. She might have died if he hadn't.

His arms held her close, and his legs were wrapped around hers. Her head was cushioned from the stone floor by his shoulder. And she was naked. She closed her eyes, trying to block from her memory those few minutes when he had undressed her. It didn't work.

Was it morning? She couldn't tell. It was dark in this place. She heard a whinny and a scuffle. A horse, then. She didn't remember the horse.

She felt something furry brush against her cheek. It sank against her chest and began to purr. Amos! He was all right!

Carefully she pulled her arm free of the coat, meaning to curve it around the cat, but the Mylar survival blanket crackled and the man stirred. She felt him waking up and held her breath, hoping that he would fall asleep again. Unfortunately he didn't. Instead she felt him pushing himself to a sitting posture. He removed his legs from around hers and she lay motionless, scarcely daring to breathe as he left the shelter of the blanket and coat. She pulled the blanket tightly around her and huddled against the cat.

She heard him fumble in the dark before he struck a match. It flared and illuminated his face, which she didn't remember from last night. His cheekbones were high and pronounced, and his skin was tanned and lined. A web of fine lines fanned out from deep-set eyes. His hair was dark. He turned inquiringly toward her.

"So," he said conversationally as he lighted a candle, "you're awake."

She said nothing, but he seemed to expect nothing. He spoke a few words to the horse, which stomped its feet a few times, and then he tugged a board away from a door and pulled it open.

The glare of sun on snow made her wince.

The man surveyed the scene outside before looking back over his shoulder to address her. "Well, it looks like we'll be here for a while. I doubt that Flapjack could make it through those drifts." The storm had evidently passed, and Flapjack, she surmised, was the horse.

Her rescuer used a board to clear the snow from in front of the door and led the horse outside.

"There's a rock overhang here," he explained when he came back, stamping the snow from his boots. "It protected the entrance from the snow. It looks as though we'll have to wait for Rooney to bring the snowmobile and save us."

She only stared at him. Evidently he had decided to make her his responsibility. She wasn't sure she liked the idea, but what choice did she have? If she wanted to get out of here, she'd apparently have to depend on him. She knew that the snowstorm the night before had been a whopper.

Her eyes darted around the room, if that was what it was, looking for her clothes. She saw them hanging from a spike in the wall. She inched her way up the wall, meaning to edge toward them little by little.

His back was toward her, and she was able to make some progress before he wheeled and saw what she was doing.

"You want your clothes, do you? I'll check to see if they're dry." He reached out and tested her shirt and jeans for dampness.

He tossed everything but the coat in her direction.

"Here, I suppose you can put these on if you like. They're dry enough. The coat is still soaked."

She scrambled to collect her clothes and drew them under the blanket. She eyed him warily, wondering if he expected her to dress in front of him.

His eyes softened. "You can go around the curve in the tunnel to put those on," he said. He indicated the dark passageway beyond.

Still grasping the Mylar blanket close around her, she rose painfully to her feet. She cast a fearful look in the direction he'd indicated. A yawning black hole seemed to stretch infinitely into the rock. It smelled damp and dank.

"Go ahead. There's nothing back there. This is an old mine. The tunnel curves a bit, then splits off into passageways. Did you think you were in a cave?" His eyes invited a reply, but she merely stared at him. He seemed kind and considerate, but you never could tell. Sometimes those were the very ones who insinuated themselves into your good graces, showing their true natures only after you learned to trust them.

"Here, you can have the flashlight," he said. He took several swift steps forward, startling her so that she faltered and almost fell.

"Hey, I'm not going to hurt you, okay?" he said. The light in his eyes was warm.

She reached out a hand from under the blanket and grabbed the flashlight, then scuttled around the curve in the tunnel until she was out of his sight.

She set the flashlight on the floor, and with shaking fingers pulled on her still slightly damp jeans and shirt. There was a huge bruise on her right hip and a corresponding one on her right shoulder. She'd hit the ground harder than she'd thought when she tripped over the log.

She picked up the flashlight and inspected the tunnel. Little sparkly flecks of mineral in the rock walls glinted back at her. The passage wasn't wide, but it was about five and a half feet high, which gave her plenty of room to stand upright. The man who had rescued her would have had to crouch in here. She estimated his height at about six feet.

Amos slipped up on her and twined himself around her ankles. She bent to pick him up and rested her cheek against his warm fur.

"Don't worry," she said to him. "It'll be all right. We'll be on our way in no time." She said this only to reassure herself. Amos, she had discovered, was happy anywhere that he could nestle close to her and keep warm. He didn't care whether they reached California or not.

When she had dressed, the flashlight beam preceded her into the front of the mine. The man had put his coat back on and was boiling water in a tin cup. He spared her a glance and said, "You'd better wrap back up in that survival blanket. It'll keep the chill off. I'd give you my coat, but I want to step outside and take care of my horse. I'll also look around and see if I can find a way to get out of here. I hate to wait for Rooney if we don't have to."

He seemed to assume that she knew what he was talking about. She didn't, but his advice to wrap up in the blanket was a good idea. She wrapped herself tightly in the Mylar, leaving a hand free to push her hair out of her eyes. Her hair was matted together and could have used a good brushing. She'd carried a purse when she jumped out of the truck, but she must have lost it in the storm. It had held everything she owned in the world, which wasn't much, but had included a brush and comb. She dismissed the idea of her appearance from her mind. She wasn't trying to win any beauty contests.

"Would you like chicken or beef bouillon?" the man asked.

She blinked at him.

"For breakfast. I have chicken and beef bouillon cubes. Which would you like?"

She realized from the patient way that he spoke that he was trying to decide if there was anything wrong with her mental faculties. This gave her the impetus to croak, "Chicken, please." It definitely wouldn't do for him to think she was a mental case. What they did with people they suspected were mentally incapacitated was to call the authorities. Then someone came in a van and took you away to an institution.

"Here, you can hold this while the bouillon cube dissolves." He handed her the cup, and she cradled it in her hands. The heat was welcome.

He crouched beside her, and she wished that he'd go away. She felt uncomfortable with the way he gazed at her with such concern.

"My name's Duncan Tate. I live on a ranch near here. You were in pretty bad shape last night." He waited for her reply.

She bit her lip and looked away. He had certainly been in a good position to know exactly what shape she was in last night, right down to her bare skin. She didn't want to think about it.

"How about telling me your name? It looks like we're in for a long morning together." He smiled, and the smile tugged the wrinkles beside his eyes upward. It was a pleasant smile, full of sunshine.

But how could she tell him her name, her *real* name? She didn't even know what it was. Despair settled over her. She didn't know what to say, so she said nothing. This clearly displeased him.

"Has it occurred to you that you're being rude?" he said in an exasperated tone. He got up and walked over to the cubbyholes lining the wall. He rummaged around in one and closed his fingers over a saddlebag, from which he pulled a piece of beef jerky. He hunkered down on the floor a few feet from her and ate it, paying no attention to her.

The steam from the bouillon rose and warmed her face. She stared into the cup, blinking back tears. She felt particularly vulnerable after last night's ordeal, as though not only her hands and knees had been scraped raw, but also the emotions that she had successfully kept in check for so long. If only he hadn't asked her name! It was the one question she found difficult to handle.

During the past year she had evaded questions about where she lived and what she did, how much money she made and where she had last worked. She had cheated when she had to, lied if absolutely necessary, and run away from anything that seemed too risky. She had hardened herself against life, but she could still be undone by one simple question: "What is your name?"

When she cast a cautious sidelong glance in his direction, the man was watching her. He didn't say anything, even though their eyes locked. She found that she couldn't look away. He didn't, either. She wanted to trust him; for some reason it seemed as if she could. He had been kind to her. Her sense of self-preservation made her consider his kindness from all angles. Finally she decided that he might be of more help to her if she provided answers to his questions.

"Jane Rhodes," she said quietly. "People call me that."

He studied her for a time, his eyes appraising her hair, her face, her figure wrapped in the blanket.

"But is it your name?" he said at last.

"It's the only name I have," she replied. Her throat was so swollen that she could barely talk.

He decided that she was telling the truth. "Jane, then. That's good enough." He nodded summarily and stood up. Amos bounded over to him, and he bent absently to stroke the cat's fur.

"Is the cat yours?" he asked.

"No more than I'm his. We—we travel together," she said.

"I should find him something to eat," Duncan said.

"He can have the last of the bouillon," Jane replied. "I don't think I can drink it all, anyway."

"Okay. Before long we'll be at the ranch, and I have plenty of cat food there. What's his name?"

"Amos," she said, thinking that he might laugh at this name for a cat. Cats were supposed to be named something cute. She had chosen Amos's name from a list in a name-your-baby book at a public library where she had gone to keep warm, hiding the stray cat inside her coat so that he could be warm, too. The name Amos meant "strong and courageous," and she had given him the name to remind herself that strength and courage were qualities that she must maintain in order to survive.

"Amos. I like that," Duncan said.

Then he went outside, shoving the door into place behind him. She couldn't see it, but she could imagine the deep snow outside. She couldn't recall when she'd ever seen such a fierce storm. She sipped the hot liquid, letting it ease slowly down her throat, and it both soothed the soreness there and warmed her from within. She couldn't, at the moment, recall when she had last eaten.

That truck driver! What a jerk he had turned out to be. She'd never have ridden with him if she hadn't been so cold.

If she ever got to California—no, not *if*. *When* she got to California. She would be warm all the time in California. There were palm trees there and an ocean. The sea air would banish the cough that had plagued her since October. It had been a good idea to head for California.

Anyway, it had been time to leave Chicago. She had no desire to spend another winter there. When she had first decided to leave, her choices had been California or Florida, but the ride she got at the outset of her journey was heading west, and so California it was. She'd made good progress, catching rides with anybody who would pick her up, sleeping in bus stations or shelters for homeless people along the way. Someone had stolen her coat at the shelter in Saint Louis, but a sweet-faced social worker had found her another one in a big cardboard box in her office. It didn't fit, but that didn't matter. In California she wouldn't need a coat, anyway.

"Jane?"

She swallowed her last sip of bouillon and set the cup on the floor, where Amos could lap up the dredge.

"Jane, I hear a snowmobile. It's probably Rooney, my foreman at the ranch. He'll know that I've taken shelter here at the mine and will be looking for me." Duncan gathered up the things he had taken from the saddlebag and shoved them inside.

"We can't all ride on the snowmobile," Jane said.

He glanced at her appreciatively, and she could tell that he was relieved that she was showing some reasoning power at last.

"I'll take you back to the ranch, then return for Rooney. I want to get you into the warm house. I'm still worried about you."

"I can't stay with you there, I have to leave," Jane said quickly.

"I'm not letting you leave until I know you've come through this without any damage. I don't like the sound of that cough."

"It's just a little cough, nothing serious," she said, feeling a new one rise in her throat and trying to quell it. He only spared her a sharp look and went back to the door, where he waved at someone and shouted.

She heard him talking outside, and then an older man—she guessed his age at around sixty—entered the mine and stood looking down at her with an expression of perplexity.

"Rooney, this is Jane. Jane, Rooney," Duncan said.

"Well, Duncan, this sure ain't Quixote you've found," Rooney said, stripping off his coat and handing it to Duncan.

"No, it certainly isn't. Did that old reprobate ever show up?"

"You bet he did, only minutes after you left. Say, Duncan, can you look in on Mary Kate when you get back to the ranch? I left her watching television at my house."

"I'll bring her over to my place, so Jane here won't be alone when I come back for you," Duncan said. He wrapped Jane in Rooney's coat.

"You're giving me your coat?" Jane said incredulously to Rooney, as Duncan hustled her out into the bright daylight.

"Sure," Rooney said. "I'll be fine until Duncan gets back."

"But what about my own coat?" she said, confused. She couldn't afford to lose it; what if something happened to it?

"I'm bringing it," Duncan replied. Sure enough, the old woolen coat was rolled up under his arm. Jane relaxed then, knowing that once it was dry she could have it back.

Before she knew what was happening, Duncan had bundled her and Amos onto the snowmobile in front of him. The engine roared to life, and Duncan accelerated until their speed fairly terrified her.

The snow-covered ground disappeared swiftly beneath them. The snow was blindingly white. To one side lay the mountain, and to the other a forest of dark evergreens.

Jane, closing her eyes against the dazzle, felt the trail weave and rise and twist. The wind, exaggerated at this speed, ripped into her cheeks, and she hid her face deep in the collar of Rooney's coat. Amos, secure in her arms, dug frightened claws into the fabric. Behind her, Duncan guided the snowmobile with subtle shifts of his weight. The vibration of the machine made her queasy, and the noise grated on her nerves.

She was glad when Duncan stopped the snowmobile. They were standing in front of a two-story house that could have decorated the front of a Christmas card.

If it hadn't been for the blizzard, she could have walked here last night. She wouldn't have knocked, but maybe she could have gained entrance into the nearby barn and been able to sleep there. She could have been on her way again in the morning, before these men even knew she'd been an overnight guest.

Duncan dismounted and helped her unfold her stiff arms and legs, then held onto her arm as he escorted her up the steps to the front door.

"I can manage," she murmured, but he paid no attention. The warmth inside the house felt blissful.

"Poor thing, you look frozen," he said.

"Is it all right if I put Amos on the floor?" she asked, because the cat was struggling to jump down.

"Sure," he said.

She bent to set Amos gently on the wide wooden planking underfoot, and the little cat crouched beside her feet and cautiously sniffed the air. Jane almost fell when she started to straighten to a standing position.

Duncan grabbed her and held her firmly by both arms. His grasp was strong.

"You really aren't all right, are you?" he demanded.

"I—" she began, then her knees went weak, and she slumped against him.

He swung her into his arms with little effort and stood looking down into her face. She closed her eyes against his piercing gaze, which was delivered from a pair of eyes as dark as ebony. It felt good to succumb to his strength; she had so little of her own.

He climbed a stairway and nudged open a door with his foot. She saw pale yellow walls and white woodwork. Duncan deposited her on a bed and strode to the window, where he raised a shade partway. Jane was overcome by a fit of coughing.

She tried to struggle out of Rooney's coat, and Duncan sat down on the bed beside her, helping her remove first one arm, then the other. He was so big and she was so small by comparison that she felt like a child in his presence. Feeling like a child wasn't so bad. When you were a child, you expected someone to take care of you, or at least that was the way she imagined it. You had few responsibilities. A child had all sorts of privileges that adults don't have. It would be nice to travel back in time and be a child again, if only for a little while.

"I'm going to call the doctor," Duncan said abruptly.

"Don't," she said. "It would cost money, and I don't have any."

He took her small hands in his. Her hands were cold, and this warmed them.

"I'll pay for it. I want to," he said.

"You don't even know me," she whispered, amazed that he would take care of her, even seemed to *want* to take care of her.

"No, I don't know you," he agreed.

"Then why don't you just let me go?"

He studied her for a long moment, and she was overly conscious of how his presence filled the room, dominating it and her. She had an idea that he was used to being in charge, that she was now someone he considered his responsibility—and therefore something not to be dismissed lightly.

"I doubt that you have anywhere to go," he said.

The truth of his perception staggered her. So far she had fooled herself into preserving the fiction that she was a real person with a real place to be. "I'm on my way to California," she said defensively.

"How were you planning to get there?"

"Oh," she said vaguely, "I'll get there."

"Is your car broken down on the highway? Were you trying to get help last night? Is that how you happened to flounder across the field and find yourself in the mine?"

She waited for a few moments before answering. "No, it wasn't exactly like that," she admitted finally, avoiding his eyes.

"I noticed last night that you have two terrible bruises on your shoulder and hip. Looks like you might have been in an accident," he said.

"An accident? Well, sort of," she said. He was clearly fishing for information, but she was determined not to give anything away.

"Like I said, I'm calling the doctor. He's an old friend, and I can count on him to come to the house." *And not ask a lot of questions,* were the unspoken words between them. He seemed to sense too many things about her; his perception was frightening, in a way.

He stood up and reached into a bottom dresser drawer for a blanket, which he spread over Jane where she lay. She felt so weak that she couldn't have moved if she'd wanted to.

"I'll get Rooney's granddaughter Mary Kate to come over and stay with you until Howard Walker—he's the doctor— gets here. Mary Kate is ten, and you can baby-sit each other. She won't do anything you want her to do, and she'll be an awful nurse, but at least you won't be alone."

Jane was willing to accept Mary Kate's dubious help if that was the condition to staying here where she could recover from last night's ordeal. She sighed and closed her eyes, slipping into a half sleep where all was peaceful and quiet and, most importantly, warm.

She was vaguely aware of Duncan talking on the phone somewhere in the hall. "Yes, she's conscious, but I'm worried about her, Howard. She's all skin and bones, and her color isn't good. Yeah, if you could make it right away, I'd appreciate it. Sure, and thanks. Mary Kate Rooney will be here to let you in. Yes, *that* Mary Kate. Uh-huh. I'll see you later."

Jane opened her eyes when Duncan poked his head around the open door.

"Howard is coming as soon as he can, and Mary Kate is watching television downstairs. I'm going to go to the mine and get Rooney and see to Flapjack. Don't get up. If you want something, you can call Mary Kate. She might not come, but that's another problem. You can try her, anyway."

"Okay," she said. Her throat was hurting more and more.

Duncan seemed to have second thoughts about leaving and walked over to the bed. His look was anxious and concerned, and he pressed a hand against her forehead, leaving a cool imprint when he took it away.

"You've got a fever," he said.

"I just need a little sleep to be as good as new," she managed to say.

"I hope you're right," was all he said, and then he was gone.

Somewhere a central heating unit clicked on and off, music to her ears, and she heard the faint chatter of a television set downstairs. She slept, waking up and thinking she was dreaming when she saw pretty blue and yellow-flowered draperies at the window.

This bedroom was the one she had always wanted, she mused. *Always*, she said again, reminding herself that in her case she had only wanted a room such as this one for fifteen months, the length of time that she had existed as Jane Rhodes. Before that maybe she'd slept in such a room, been part of a family, and lived in a hometown.

She slept again, and when she woke, a gap-toothed hoyden of a girl was hanging over the bed and blowing bubble gum breath into her face.

"Want to see me blow a bubble?" the girl asked, and without waiting for approval from Jane, she inflated a bubble only inches from Jane's nose. Jane watched spellbound as the bubble grew and grew, finally collapsing with a warm puff of carbon dioxide into a raggedy pink skin that covered the girl's nose, cheeks and chin.

Unconcerned, the girl peeled the burst bubble from her face and added the scraps of pink goo to the wad of gum already in her mouth.

"Want to blow one?" she asked. "It's a relaxing thing to do. You can use my gum. I just got it broken in good."

Jane shook her head, mesmerized nevertheless by the girl's bubble-blowing prowess.

"Well, if you ever want to, you have to use Yaya Yum Bubble Gum. It's the best, and it tastes good, too. Don't buy the grape flavor, get the regular flavor. The grape makes me want to throw up." She realistically pantomimed retching, leaning over the foot of the bed.

"You must be Mary Kate," Jane said.

"Yeah, Duncan told you about me, I guess. You're Jane. I like your cat. He doesn't care much for baths, does he?"

Jane pulled herself up onto her elbows in alarm. "You didn't bathe him?"

"Yep. Sure did. Or tried to. He scratched me. I think it was Duncan's pine-scented shampoo that he didn't like. Look at my scratch." Mary Kate thrust an arm bearing an angry red welt under Jane's nose.

"Where is he?" Jane asked with more than a little trepidation.

"The cat? Oh, he fell down the laundry chute. He's okay, though. He landed on a full basket of towels and things. I dried him off with a pillowcase, and he ran into Duncan's closet. I think he's sulking."

Jane swallowed painfully and hoped that Amos would have enough sense to stay in the closet until she was able to get up to defend him, although from the looks of the scratch on Mary Kate's arm, Amos didn't need defending.

"I like animals," Mary Kate went on. "Have you ever seen a llama?"

Jane tried to think. "No, I don't think I have," she said slowly.

"They're cute. I hadn't seen one either before I came to live with my grandfather. Then I got here and there was a whole ranch of them."

"You mean this is a *llama* ranch?" Jane's head whirled. All this time she'd thought that Duncan's ranch was of the cattle variety.

"Yeah. Duncan and Grandpa raise them. Then they sell them as pack animals or pets. I hate it when they sell one, but that's how they make a living. Quixote's my favorite male, but Dearling's my favorite female. They let me name Dearling myself. She's really small for a female, so she makes a good pet. I hope they never sell *her*."

They heard a knock downstairs, and Mary Kate jumped up. "That must be Dr. Walker. I'm supposed to let him in. I won't, if you don't want me to. I *hate* doctors myself. They give shots."

"You can let him in," Jane told her, and Mary Kate ran away, her straggly black hair bouncing around her shoulders.

Howard Walker turned out to be around fifty or so. He put his medical bag on a chair beside the bed and set about examining her with sure, steady hands.

When he was through, he said, "You'll have to put ice packs on those bruises. And I'm going to bandage the cuts on your hands."

She said nothing, staring into space with her mouth clamped shut. If Howard Walker thought this was odd, he made no comment. He merely wrapped her hands in bandages, took a swab of her throat to be cultured, and wrote out a prescription.

"The prescription is for an antibiotic medicine for that throat of yours," he said, peering at her over the top of his reading glasses. "I'll give it to Duncan to have filled. Treat the bruises with ice packs, but only leave them on twenty minutes at a time. Put this ointment on the scrapes on your hands three times a day. Rest in bed until you feel better, and I'll see you in two weeks."

"Two weeks! I can't stay two weeks," she objected.

He ignored this. "I want you to eat properly. Three full meals a day, no skipping. I expect to see some roses in those cheeks next time I see you." He snapped the cap back on his pen.

"But—"

He waved the prescription in the air. "I'll give this to Duncan when I talk with him. Take care of yourself," and with that he hurried out of the room.

Jane sank back onto the pillows, pressing her fists to her hot cheeks. Two weeks! She'd planned to be in California before then. How could she stay here with Duncan all that time? He'd surely want to be rid of her.

Tears stung her eyelids. She had come so far all by herself with no help from anyone. She had made it at least halfway to California, too. She couldn't give up now.

"I'll get there yet," she whispered to herself as Amos padded into the room through the open door. When he jumped onto the bed, she made room for him in the curve of her body, taking comfort once more in his company.

"SHE'S MALNOURISHED, she almost certainly has strep throat, she has a bad case of bronchitis, and those scrapes and bruises make her look as though somebody tossed her off a tall building. Who has she been hanging around with, King Kong?"

"Howard, I don't know. I found her in the old mine last night during the storm, and for a few minutes I thought she was a goner. Is she going to be all right?"

"I'd guess that she's no older than her mid-twenties, and her powers of recuperation are probably good. She'll be fine if she gets enough to eat, and if she takes her medicine. Under no circumstances should she leave here and set out on her own. Is her name really Jane Rhodes?"

Duncan shrugged. "I doubt it," he answered.

"You'll need to get those antibiotic pills, and she must take them regularly, as prescribed. If you need me, call again." Howard clapped his hat onto his head and started out the door.

"Thanks, Howard," Duncan called after him. Howard threw him a salute and crunched across the snow to his car.

When the doctor had left, Duncan called Rooney and asked him to pick up the antibiotic for Jane when he went into town to buy groceries. Then he climbed the stairs and went into the bedroom where Jane lay sleeping.

The room was in shadow, the shades drawn against the weak winter sunlight. Duncan stood beside the bed, taking in the way her blond hair, fluffier now, spread out on the light blue pillowcases. Her cheeks might have been fine porcelain, so translucent were they, and the tiny hand resting on the blanket might have been that of a doll. Lavender shadows rimmed her lower eyelids, and her eyelashes were baby-fine, but thick. She had turned her head to the side, so that he saw her in profile. Her face was like a cameo.

He sat down on the bed beside her, wondering who she was and how she happened to be traversing the wilds of Wyoming. Despite the bedraggled hair and the quality of Little Girl Lost, she looked as though she should be gracing a drawing room in eighteenth-century England, not sheltering from a killer snowstorm in an abandoned mine.

"Jane Rhodes, who are you?" he asked softly, but she didn't answer. She didn't hear him; she was sound asleep. But even if she had heard the question, he doubted that she would have answered it. Or even could have, for that matter.

Chapter Three

Jane dreamed that night of the mine, and of lying on the floor, trying to get warm. This time the floor was not so hard, and she was much more aware of Duncan's arms encircling her. She awoke suddenly and shivered, despite Amos's comforting presence against her side.

She eased onto her stomach, her favorite sleeping position, and dozed until Duncan came into the room shortly after dawn. She came awake suddenly, immediately defensive.

"Just wanted to see if you're awake," he said, disappeared, and when he returned it was with a breakfast tray heaped with food. It held half a grapefruit, steaming hot coffee, corned beef hash with a poached egg in the middle, and toast dripping with butter.

"I don't think I can eat all of this," she said, clutching the bed covers tightly to her chest.

"Eat what you can, and I'll give the rest to Amos," he told her.

"I feel like I'm imposing," she said. She slid to a more comfortable sitting position before taking a bite of the hash. It was delicious. She relaxed slightly and told herself that there was no need to be wary here. Duncan Tate meant her no harm.

Duncan leaned against the dresser and folded his arms, watching her eat. "We don't get many visitors out this way. I'm glad to have somebody here to talk to."

"You live alone?" she asked, making an effort at conversation. He seemed to expect it.

He nodded. "Rooney and Mary Kate live in a smaller house down the road. What did you think of Mary Kate, anyway?"

"She's lively," Jane said with great diplomacy.

Duncan laughed. "I guess that's one way to put it. Actually, I think she's a terror, and so does everyone else who has ever met her. She's lived with Rooney a little over two years and every day she gets worse. Last week she came over here when I was out and decided to wash all my jeans, and she used hot water. They shrank to the point that I can't wear most of them." He laughed again.

"I'm sure she meant well," ventured Jane.

"If you can stand it, I'll have Mary Kate come over again this morning. She can refill your ice packs and get you glasses of water and stuff like that. I don't like leaving you alone, but I've got some things to do in the barn."

"Doesn't she go to school?"

"The schools are having a week's holiday—something to do with the end of the semester. She'll be over in an hour or so."

"Mary Kate told me that this is a llama ranch."

"It is. The finest in the world, we like to think."

"Are the llamas here? I mean, can I see them?"

"You'll see them when you're able to get out of bed."

"Mary Kate says they're like camels."

He grinned, but seemed pleased that she was interested. "Llamas are camelids, part of the same family as camels and vicuña and alpacas. One difference between camels and llamas is that llamas don't have a hump. They've become popular in the United States in the past few years, which is how Rooney and I happened to get into the llama business. It helps that they're lovable animals."

Llamas, Jane thought to herself. Try as she might, she couldn't pull up a corresponding picture of a llama from her memory bank. It wasn't surprising; her memory worked in strange ways. Sometimes an idea about something she'd thought she knew nothing about swam unbidden to the surface, and she would spend days wondering where it came from, or what significance it had. Other times, when a memory should have been readily retrievable, it simply wasn't there.

"So you're headed for California," Duncan said.

She stiffened involuntarily. "Yes," she said.

"Just going for a visit?"

Her mind raced. What to tell him? How *much* to tell him? She had learned to mete out only enough information to get by in any given situation, and sometimes she avoided even that.

He was smiling at her in an encouraging way, and this seemed overly familiar to her. She wished he wouldn't act so friendly, because she didn't know how to react.

"I'm planning to live there," she said finally, watching carefully to see if he accepted this. He only nodded and went on to the next question.

"Is there anyone I should call? Anyone who is expecting you?"

What should she say now? If she told him the truth, that she had no one, that she'd been living on the streets due to a bizarre run of bad luck, he might not believe that she hadn't brought all of it upon herself, or that she wasn't a mental case or—well, he might think all sorts of things that would give him good reason to boot her and Amos out into the snow. She wasn't well enough to leave yet, she knew that. She had to stay here for now if she was to survive, and survive she must.

"My girlfriend—the one I'll be living with at first—is on a—a trip. To Europe. No, there's no one to call," she said, the lie rolling glibly from her lips.

If disbelief clouded his eyes, she couldn't see it; he lowered his eyelids and seemed to be thinking.

"Where does this friend of yours live?"

"In Sausalito," she said, pulling the name of the city out of thin air.

"And you have a job lined up there, I suppose?" he asked.

"Oh, of course. I'm a librarian," she said, surprising even herself with this announcement. But library work was something she knew about after spending long hours in the library sheltering from the weather. If she had to, she could probably come up with a fairly accurate description of what a librarian did all day long.

"A librarian? Then you must enjoy reading. I'll bring some books for you."

She felt a sudden sickening wave of guilt and put down her fork. Lying had become a habit out of necessity. It was a way to protect herself, and she had become an accomplished liar. But never had she disliked herself as much as she did now, after lying to Duncan.

He glanced toward her. "Is anything wrong?" he asked when he saw the expression on her face.

There was nothing to do but lie again.

"No, it's just that I can't eat any more," she said. "It was a wonderful breakfast, though," she hastened to add. This, at least, was certainly true.

He surveyed the tray. "You did all right, considering what you've been through. Amos, do you think you could eat some of this?"

Amos stretched, got up from his place on the floor near the heat register, and followed Duncan out of the room. She heard Duncan talking to him downstairs.

So. It had started again. The deceit, the falsehoods, the scrambling to cover her tracks so that no one would learn anything of importance about her or her past. Or even her future, now that she had invented a fictitious girlfriend.

She lay back on the pillows, picturing this imaginary friend, who would, if she existed, have dark hair and blue eyes that lighted up when they shared jokes. She'd drive a small yellow car, have an office job that she took seriously and a boyfriend, whom she wanted to take seriously but couldn't because he wasn't ready to settle down. Her name would be Elizabeth, a name that Jane had always loved. She would wear a gold Egyptian ankh charm on a chain around her neck.

An ankh... Why had Jane thought of that? In her mind's eye she could picture it, a cross topped with a circle on a short chain, so short that the charm rested in the hollow of a woman's throat. The woman was not the pretend friend Elizabeth, but someone real and warm and dear, some-one...*someone*. But who?

Jane squeezed her eyes shut, willing the image of a face to present itself. She saw nothing but the inside of her eyelids, a black void.

Tears forced their way between her lashes, and she beat a silent fist on the blanket. Why? *Why?* Why couldn't she remember? And where did these disconnected images come from, anyway? They intruded on her consciousness at unlikely times, empty of meaning and signifying nothing.

If only she could remember! If she could recall important things that cast light on her past, maybe she wouldn't have to start all over again. Perhaps there was someplace where she belonged, with people who would welcome her with open arms and hearts, who cared about her. Who loved her.

But of course, all of this was as much a figment of her imagination as the pretend friend named Elizabeth, or the librarian job, or any of the rest of it. The reality was that she had no one, and there was no point in avoiding it. The important thing was to get to California, and once there never to look back.

Jane sat up and swung her feet over the edge of the bed. A momentary dizziness overtook her, and she waited until it passed. In the bathroom she studied her reflection in the mirror above the sink. She looked so haggard that she scarcely recognized herself.

Everything in this bathroom was so clean and shiny. She touched an experimental fingertip to the chrome-plated faucet and quickly rubbed off the mark it left. She opened the medicine cabinet for a curious look inside and jumped when Duncan's image suddenly appeared in its mirror.

"Oh, I didn't mean to interrupt," he said.

Quickly, she closed the medicine cabinet, wishing he hadn't caught her opening it.

"I—I was wondering if you have an extra toothbrush. And a comb," she said awkwardly.

"Of course. I should have thought of that," he said. He went away for a few moments and returned with a toothbrush, a comb in a cellophane package and a hairbrush. He went away again, and Jane, waiting in the bedroom, heard him digging in a drawer in the bathroom across the hall. Soon he returned with toothpaste and other toiletries.

"There are towels on the towel rods over the tub," he told her, and then he seemed to think of something else. "Wait," he said, leaving the room. In a moment he returned bearing a pile of clothing.

"I think you might be able to find some things in here to wear," he told her. He held up a pair of jeans. "These are some of the jeans Mary Kate shrank. Maybe you can get some wear out of them. There are a couple of shirts and sweaters, all too big for you, but clean. We ought to see about getting you new clothes."

"I won't need them," Jane said with a hint of stubbornness. "I won't be here long, anyway. Only until I'm strong enough to leave."

"Dr. Walker says it will be at least two weeks," he reminded her.

Her chin shot up. "I hope to be gone before that. I can't go on being a burden to you." *And lying to you,* she thought to herself.

He rested his hands on her shoulders and looked deep into her eyes. "You're not a burden," he said quietly. "Please don't ever say that again." He removed his hands and turned quickly toward the door, as if embarrassed by his own intensity. "Enjoy your bath," he said over his shoulder, as though in afterthought.

He was so nice. Why did he treat her with such openness and trust? Perhaps he was this way with everyone, she thought, feeling a grudging admiration for him. At the same time, she felt a twinge of disdain. He wouldn't last more than a day or two on the streets.

She stopped thinking about him as soon as she stepped into the bathtub. It was a luxury to which she hadn't been accustomed. Quick washes in public rest rooms were her norm, and a cold-water shower in a crowded shelter was considered a treat. She shampooed her hair under the shower. She scrubbed her skin until it was red from the friction, and then patted herself dry with a huge white bath sheet. She had never felt so clean in her life.

When she came out of the bathroom, fresh sheets had been turned down and a note was on the pillow.

"I'll be back to see that you eat lunch," it said. It was signed, "Duncan."

There seemed no end to the man's thoughtfulness, and that only made her own deceit more unconscionable. Duncan, she thought, savoring the name. Duncan. She had never known anyone with that name before. It had a distinguished ring to it. It was different. Not like the name Jane, which was so ordinary that it was customarily used to denote anonymous people, the kind of people who didn't have a name of their own.

The simple act of bathing had exhausted her, and she fell asleep but woke up later when Mary Kate came in and jiggled the bed in a determined fashion.

"I thought you'd never wake up," was Mary Kate's impatient greeting.

"I was so tired," Jane said, pushing herself upright against the pillow.

"Duncan came in while you were sleeping. He left a sandwich for you and some soup in a thermos. Can I pour the soup into the bowl?"

"Of course," Jane said, then regretted it when Mary Kate predictably spilled soup onto the sheet. Mary Kate ran to get a damp cloth, tripping over Amos in the process. Amos scurried out of the room, clearly unwilling to tangle with her so soon after the debacles of bath and laundry chute. Jane and Mary Kate managed to mop up the soup, and Jane offered her companion half of the sandwich. Mary Kate accepted with delight.

She sat at the end of the bed, munching bologna and cheese, and firing off questions so fast that Jane's head spun. Today Mary Kate was full of questions.

"Duncan said you were in that old mine during the snowstorm. How'd you get there?"

"I walked," Jane told her.

"Far?"

"From the highway." She tried to stick to the truth; why, she didn't know. After lying to Duncan, it probably wouldn't make any difference if she fibbed to Mary Kate.

"Have you taken your antibiotic pill yet? I told Duncan I'd make sure you did."

"I took it," Jane assured her.

"Where did you come from, anyway?" Mary Kate wanted to know.

"Oh, all kinds of places," Jane said, evasively but certainly truthfully. "Say, could you hand me that glass of water?"

Mary Kate handed her the water, then settled in for more intensive interrogation.

"Where were you going? Are you planning to live there, or are you only on vacation? What kind of job do you have? Who—"

Jane thought it was long past time to interrupt this flow of questions.

"I feel really tired, Mary Kate, and my throat hurts terribly. Will you please pull down that shade? There, that's better. I think I'll sleep."

"You slept *before*," Mary Kate pointed out with a scowl, but she left the room and shut the door behind her.

Jane closed her eyes, fighting the confusion that so often enveloped her when faced with a battery of questions. There were so many questions and so few answers. It was such a helpless feeling, and you had to be careful because people's motives in asking the questions weren't always aboveboard. If you gave the wrong answers, or worse yet, if there was no answer, you could be hauled away or arrested or thrown out of wherever you were.

But Mary Kate was hardly a threat, and as for Duncan, he seemed above all to be kind and gentle. And Wyoming wasn't Chicago, where you had to be cautious about talking about yourself to strangers, or Saint Louis, where the shelter had been a nightmare, or Kansas City, where she'd had no choice but to panhandle at the bus station for money to buy food. Here the food was served regularly, and it tasted good, and no one seemed in a hurry for her to move on.

She couldn't help feeling that she didn't deserve such good fortune. And yet she had no choice but to accept it for now, at least until she regained her strength.

And then she would start her new life in California.

IN A FEW DAYS, Jane was up and about. Her bruises faded, her cough improved, and her sore throat abated. Duncan seemed happy to see her moving around the house. He would come in bearing the cold, crisp scent of the outdoors and would hang up his coat and smile at her in a way that no one had ever smiled at her before, at least within her memory. His smile brightened the days and made the cool gray and mauve shadows of winter recede into the corners of the house. For some reason that she didn't understand, it made her happy to see him smile, but she found it difficult to smile back. Usually she just looked quickly down at the floor, unsure how to respond.

Once Jane, in a fit of gratitude, tried to tell him how embarrassed she was at having to depend on him for a place to stay and for all the food that he kept pushing on her.

"Don't be silly. This is a big house, and there's plenty of room," he said easily.

When she started to feel better, Duncan invited Rooney and Mary Kate over for Sunday dinner. Duncan prepared a roast and they ate in the big dining room, where Duncan set the table with his mother's china. Jane tried to help, but she felt clumsy in the kitchen.

After they all sat down to dinner, Mary Kate entertained them with funny stories about school, and Rooney told a joke about fleas and a dog that Jane didn't understand. She laughed anyway, looking from Duncan to Mary Kate to Rooney and trying her best to fit in.

As she looked around the table at the others' smiling faces, relaxed and bright with sociability after the satisfying dinner, she knew that someday she would have friends like these in her life, people who would visit her home and relish the conversation afterward. She would figure out how to be a gracious hostess, she would learn to cook, she would—

"Jane! Jane, this is the second time I've asked you. Have you been over to see the llamas yet?" Mary Kate peered over at her, puzzled at Jane's inattentiveness.

Duncan cleared his throat. "The doctor hasn't said she could go out. It's mighty cold out there."

"I'd like to see the llamas," Jane said.

"Howard said you should stay inside for two weeks," Duncan reminded her. "It hasn't been that long yet."

She shifted uneasily in her chair. "I was thinking I could go as far as the barn. I'm feeling stronger now."

"You'd better follow Howard's instructions and wait until he gives you the go-ahead before you go traipsing around outside. Our Wyoming winters can be harsh." Thus ensued a lively discussion about the temperature, which was due to dip below zero again that night.

Jane said nothing, but since she was feeling so much better, she wondered why she couldn't leave the ranch now.

After dinner she went to her room and brushed aside the draperies to look at the llamas. She watched them with growing fascination. The llamas seemed a remarkable array of colors, sizes and shapes. They looked nothing like camels, which is what she had expected them to look like, minus the humps, of course. They sported thick woolly coats and walked with a graceful elegance.

She felt a sudden urge to get closer to them. What she could see of their gentle faces intrigued her, but since Duncan had prohibited her from going outside until the weather grew warmer, she'd have to wait. According to Rooney's weather report at the dinner table tonight, the cold spell following the blizzard seemed to have settled in to stay.

Mary Kate came into the room without knocking and stood behind Jane. "See that pale gray and white one on the far side of the herd?" she asked, hopping from one foot to the other.

"Mmm-hmm," Jane replied. She really didn't mind Mary Kate's entering without knocking; she had grown accustomed to her company over the past week. The girl seemed lonely, and so was she.

"That's Dearling, my very favorite," Mary Kate confided. "You should see her face up close. She has black rings around her eyes, so she looks just like she's wearing eyeliner."

"Why did you name her Dearling?" Jane asked.

"She's so dear, the sweetest little thing I ever saw. She follows me around better than a dog, and she never rolls in the dirt the way the other llamas do. Grandpa says that's normal llama behavior, but I think it's disgusting."

Jane had to smile at this statement, because Mary Kate wasn't exactly the cleanest person Jane had ever met, and in her travels she'd certainly come across her share of those who simply didn't care how dirty they were.

As Mary Kate babbled on, they saw Duncan step out of the barn and call to the llamas, who turned almost in unison and made their way toward him with a dignified gait.

Jane was surprised at the way the llamas craned their long necks against Duncan's body, nuzzling at his shoulder or cheek until he petted them. She hadn't expected llamas to display such affection toward humans, but she was beginning to realize that Duncan was the kind of person who naturally inspired trust.

"Duncan knows all their names," Mary Kate said. "Every one is real special to him."

As they watched, Jane marveled at the rapport Duncan had so obviously established with the animals. Trust; a sense of affinity; the exact feelings he had inspired in her.

How did he manage it? She wanted to know, because she wanted to be able to do it. How easy it would be to attract the kind of friends she longed to meet in California if such a skill were hers. She'd never actually thought of establishing a connection with another human being as a skill. But it was—and she observed Duncan carefully during the next few days in order to learn it.

She didn't want him to know that she was doing this; it would have embarrassed her to admit that she lacked such fundamental knowledge. She studied his body language, analyzed his facial expressions, did her best to commit them to memory. She realized that she was so intent on becoming an apt student that she was mimicking his movements exactly. If he sat with his legs crossed, she sat with her legs crossed. If he leaned back in his chair at the dinner table, so did she.

If he smiled, she tried to smile, although that wasn't so easy. She didn't particularly feel like smiling.

In the first few days of her stay at the ranch, whenever Duncan came in after a day's work, Jane would be downstairs watching television in the living room. She would always jump up and make herself as inconspicuous as possible, attempting to sidle upstairs to her room without drawing attention to herself. But after she started smiling in response to him, he seemed to want to comment whenever she left the room, and finally he spoke out.

"Stay down here," Duncan said one night when she got up from the living-room couch to go to her room around eight o'clock. He had just come in from Rooney's house and was settling down in his leather chair in front of the fireplace.

"I don't want to disturb you," Jane replied, but that wasn't the real reason.

He walked over to where she stood beside the staircase and cupped his hand around her chin, turning her face toward the light. She flinched at his kindly touch, and he noticed. It worried him that human contact made her so uncomfortable.

He didn't say what he had been going to say. Instead he said only, "The last thing you would do is disturb me." He released her face and she bowed her head.

"What I mean is that you have a right to your privacy," she murmured in a low tone. Having learned long ago not to draw attention to herself, privacy seemed to her like the most precious of commodities, much too scarce to squander on strangers like herself.

"Privacy!" he snorted. "I'd call it loneliness," and when she didn't move, he took her hand and tugged her back into the circle of lamplight. He sat down in a big chair, but she stood uncertainly in front of the couch until she sank onto it at last and fixed her eyes on the television screen.

They watched the program, but even though he commented frequently on the actors or the commercials, she didn't speak. She was almost comically surprised to discover that anonymity was easier to achieve in a crowded city than in a man's living room. It was something she'd simply never thought about before.

It seemed like a long evening to her. Finally, when the late news flashed across the screen and she decided she could reasonably leave, she started to climb the staircase and he spoke again.

"Don't be so afraid to make yourself at home here," he said, his eyes very dark in the shadows of the dim living room.

She paused and turned halfway around to face him. He looked so hopeful, as though it meant a lot to him for her to like it here. For some reason this made her feel wretched.

"Thank you for everything," was all she managed to say before fleeing to her room. She had wanted to tell him that all this was new to her, that she didn't know how to make herself at home anyplace.

In her room she walked to the window, where she pulled the drapery aside and stood looking out over the ranch. Tonight it was bathed in soft moonlight glimmering on the snow. The barn was outlined in stark detail, and she saw Duncan making his way toward it. He certainly seemed to set great store by those llamas of his.

Maybe it was just that he liked all animals. He seemed to delight in Amos's antics, for instance. Yesterday he had unearthed an old Ping-Pong ball for the cat and had laughed when Amos bounded and skidded around on the kitchen floor chasing it. He had mentioned that he'd like to get another dog; his faithful companion, an Old English sheepdog, had died last year.

In fact, Duncan's propensity for animals could be the reason that he seemed to have taken a liking to her. She was like a stray; in fact, for all intents and purposes she *was* a stray. A stray human. Duncan clearly saw himself as a kind of one-person humane society, feeding and sheltering her because she had nowhere else to go and because he felt sorry for her. The more she thought about this, the colder and emptier she felt. She couldn't bear pity. Clearly she needed to reassess this situation.

She was feeling increasingly restless about her role in the household. The attention she received from these people whom she barely knew was threatening to become stifling. Their interest in her was like heat in a close room—at first it felt wonderful, but as it grew warmer and warmer, she was beginning to feel as though she couldn't breathe.

Jane had become adept at blending in, like a chameleon taking on protective coloration so that people would think that she belonged. But everything still seemed strange to her. Duncan, Rooney and Mary Kate were kind and thoughtful of her needs. They were generous to a fault.

And that was another part of the problem. She was having a hard time dealing with her deceit toward these fine, decent people who considered themselves her friends.

She wouldn't have told Duncan any falsehoods if she'd thought she had any alternatives. But to tell him that he had taken a bona fide street person into his home? Someone who'd found herself lying and stealing just to stay alive? At first she hadn't doubted that he'd throw her and Amos out if he knew her true colors.

That was then. This was now.

She was well enough to continue on her journey with or without the approval of the estimable Dr. Walker. She was ready to start a new life somewhere else under her own terms.

She counted her assets. One old coat, one set of clothes, socks and shoes, and a cat.

She realized that she'd need money to get all the way to California, but she'd spent all of her meager supply before the truck driver had picked her up near Elmo. For transportation, she had no doubt that she could catch a ride on the highway, but that would only get her so far. She'd have to eat. Sometimes strangers helped out with food, but she couldn't count on that.

There was Duncan. Maybe he'd lend her the money. But no, he didn't want her to leave. He'd be furious if she suggested it, and she couldn't tell him she was planning to go immediately. She couldn't say that she had lied from the beginning and really had nowhere to go. She certainly didn't want his pity or, more to the point, didn't want to grow accustomed to it. If Duncan thought she was a pitiable creature, it wouldn't be long before she regarded herself in that light, too. Self-pity, she knew from experience, could be deadly.

Jane was aware that Duncan often left money lying around. He liked to empty his pockets as soon as he came into the house, and he had a place where he put his wallet and loose change. It was on a table right inside the front door. There was no telling how much money he kept in his wallet, and there was usually a dollar or two in change.

She heard the door slam downstairs, and she realized that Duncan had come in from the barn. Perhaps even now he was dumping the contents of his pockets onto the little tray on the table.

She heard his footsteps on the stairs. As he always did, he went into his room at the other end of the hall and closed the door.

Jane sat on the edge of her bed, staring at the lemon-yellow walls and knowing what she had to do. Unemotionally she got up and prepared her clothes for tomorrow. She would have to leave early, before it was light. She would take only the things she had brought with her.

Except, perhaps, for the money on the downstairs table.

Chapter Four

That night Duncan couldn't sleep for thinking about Jane
and her problems. She was a secretive woman, a frightened
woman, and he knew that there was more to her than she
wanted him to know. He longed for her to open up to him.
He couldn't bear the bleak expression that he so often saw
in her eyes.

There had been another woman once, his wife. He had
been too busy to pay attention to the nuances of her behavior, thinking that they would eventually pass and she would
be her old self once more. He'd been wrong about that.
Sigrid had found someone who could be more responsive to
her moods and had moved out one night a couple of years
ago.

"It's not that I didn't love you," she had told him in
parting. "It's just that I needed a man who could respond
to me. And you never could."

The sad thing about it all was that he could have, he
would have, if he'd only known how important it was to her.
It wasn't that he wasn't empathetic. If anything, when faced
with human problems, he always cared too much. But in the
macho atmosphere in which he'd grown up, it hadn't been
cool to show his feelings. With Rooney, with his father, it
had embarrassed them when he tried. He learned how to
cover up his caring, although he'd often managed to show
people how he felt by his actions.

Then when he got married, it seemed like a whole new ball game. With his wife, he hadn't known how important it was to show how he felt, which meant that he'd really bungled their relationship. As he'd told her before she left, it wasn't that easy to open up after a lifetime of suppressing the expression of his emotions.

He'd had a couple of relationships since his divorce, and he'd worked on showing that he was the kind of understanding guy a woman would want. The relationships had never been too serious, but he felt equipped to deal with women now in a way that he had never been before, and he even felt grateful to Sigrid for making him learn something important about himself before it was too late.

Sigrid was very happy now; she had married her lover, and they were living in Albuquerque. Sigrid was expecting a baby soon.

And he, Duncan, was still alone. Since Jane had come, he hadn't felt so lonely, though. It was good to have a woman around again, even a woman who hardly spoke to him.

He'd been surprised to find that, despite the impression of Little Girl Lost, he felt desire for her as he watched her moving around his house. He chose not to act on it because he didn't want to add to whatever burdens she carried, and he suspected that they were considerable. He had never, for instance, bought that cock-and-bull story about her having a place to stay with a girlfriend in California.

Tonight she'd acted so skittish. He couldn't figure her. Her moods swung from confused to grateful to disoriented to apprehensive. Most of the time she seemed to be saying, "Please, please like me." Other times, he could swear she was recoiling from his presence.

Later that night, after Jane's light went out behind her closed bedroom door, Duncan roused himself from his solitary thoughts and went out again. He walked over to Rooney's house, something he often did late at night when he couldn't sleep. Rooney claimed to need very little sleep; he usually stayed up past midnight.

The two of them had, over the years, engaged in some productive bull sessions. The topics they covered ranged from cattle breeding to llama salesmanship, from getting along with women to rearing a ten-year-old girl. It was Duncan's belief that men could only be friends with men and women could only be friends with women. His friendship with Rooney over the years seemed to bear that out. Sigrid, his ex-wife, had certainly never been his friend.

When Duncan knocked on the door, Rooney welcomed him, offering him a cup of strong coffee, which Duncan turned down, figuring that the coffee would only keep him wider awake.

"So how's Jane?" Rooney wanted to know when they were sitting at the kitchen table finishing off the cheesecake Rooney had bought in town today. Mary Kate loved cheesecake and so did Duncan.

Duncan shrugged. "I don't know. Seems like she's recovering all right in a physical way, but I don't know what she's thinking. She's a strange woman, Rooney," he said.

Rooney lifted his eyebrows. "Ain't they all?"

"Not like her. She doesn't say much and certainly never mentions anything about herself."

"What do you expect? She might have an unsavory past, after all. You don't know where she came from. You ain't even sure where she's going."

Duncan considered this and decided there was merit in it. "That makes sense, I suppose, except that she doesn't look like somebody who could do anything wrong. She's a beautiful woman, Rooney. Have you ever noticed her eyes? And her hair? She reminds me of a Dresden figurine my grandmother used to have."

Rooney shot him a keen look. "Hey, you're not starting to feel something for her, are you?"

Duncan shifted uncomfortably in his chair before answering. "I don't know, Rooney. If anything, I'm sorry for her. She's such a sad little thing. She seldom smiles."

"She looks like a lady with a secret to me, old boy. If I was you, I wouldn't want to get too close. Never know when you might regret it."

"I thought maybe she'd open up when she started to feel better, maybe tell me why she's so all-fired eager to get to California. If that's where she's headed, that is. I see things about her that don't compute. I look at that ragged coat she was wearing when I found her and I wonder, 'How the dickens did she end up with a man's beat-up old topcoat to wear?' I've nearly worn myself out trying to figure her."

Rooney got up to pour more coffee into his cup. Before he sat down again, he clapped Duncan on the shoulder.

"You always did like a mystery, son. You'd better stick to the book variety, if you ask me. That reminds me. I picked up a few more mystery books at the library when I was in town. You want to take one home with you? Might get your mind off that little gal over there."

Duncan sighed, wishing that he hadn't confided in Rooney after all. "Yeah, Rooney, show me what you've got. I wouldn't mind reading for a while before I go to sleep," he said.

Rooney produced three well-worn paperback mystery books, Duncan chose the most promising one and took it home and to bed. All the while Duncan was reading, he couldn't stop pondering the mystery in his own house.

JANE ROSE the next morning before it was light, slipping into the jeans and shirt she'd had on when she found her way to the mine. Over those she put on the old coat, grateful that it was so warm and thick. It was bound to be cold outside.

She folded the discarded shirt of Duncan's that she used for a nightgown and left it on the bed. Carefully, feeling her way in the dark and with only the night-light from the bathroom for illumination, she pulled up the blue bedspread neatly over the bed and patted it into place. She would certainly miss this bed. It had been very comfortable.

She left the comb and brush and toiletries in the bathroom. After a moment's thought, she pocketed the toothbrush. No one else would want it, and Duncan would end up throwing it away, which seemed to her to be an awful waste of a useful object.

She tiptoed over to the heat register and picked up Amos, who, barely awake, snuggled unprotestingly inside her coat. Then, carefully and silently, she made her way downstairs.

The house was quiet, the outlines of the furniture barely discernible in the dark. Swiftly she made her way through the living room, saying goodbye to everything. *Goodbye, couch,* she said to herself as she passed it. *Goodbye, television set. Goodbye, fireplace.* It seemed silly and sentimental to say goodbye to inanimate things, but at least it gave her words to occupy her mind. She was afraid that if she thought about how much she would miss all the comforts that most people took for granted, she might not be able to leave after all.

She paused at the table beside the door. She felt around for the tray where Duncan kept his money. Her fingers closed around his wallet. He was such a trusting soul, Duncan. A person shouldn't trust other people so much.

She knew she had to survive somehow but felt terribly guilty about taking his money. She picked up the wallet, anyway. She carried it into the kitchen, where she shifted her weight first from one foot to the other in indecision. Yet what else could she do?

I'll pay it back, she thought. She set Amos down on the floor, and he immediately went to his food dish and started to eat.

She knew the location of the switch to turn on the fluorescent light over the sink, and she flipped it and waited while the light flickered and blinked on. She hadn't wanted to turn on any lights, but Duncan wouldn't be able to see this particular light from upstairs even if he got up, which she figured was unlikely at this hour.

Quickly she scrawled a note on the pad beside the telephone.

Duncan,
I needed money, so I took some out of your wallet. I'll pay you back as soon as I can.
Please think well of me,

she added after a pause. That was stupid, considering that she was actually robbing the man. She didn't like the way the last sentence read but didn't want to scratch it out, either, because then the note would look sloppy, and she didn't want him to think she was the kind of person who didn't care how a note looked to the person who received it. She signed it simply, "Jane."

She checked the money in the wallet. There were sixty dollars, so after a moment's deliberation she took fifty and left him ten. She stuffed the money into her coat pocket along with a few packages of crackers that were on the counter, and started to pick up Amos.

He pulled away from her, something he did so infrequently that it took her by surprise. He continued to eat the cat chow that Duncan had left in the dish for him.

At first she thought she would let Amos finish the last of the food, because she had no idea where their next meal would come from nor how long it would be until it materialized. Then she realized that there might not be any next meal for a long time and that she was being most unfair to Amos by taking him away from a place where he was sure to be warm and well fed. In the past week, his body had filled out and he didn't look so scrawny. His fur seemed thicker and sleeker.

"Amos, I guess this is where we come to a parting of the ways," she murmured. The thought of the lonely hours without him looming ahead of her brought a catch to her throat and tears to her eyes.

"Oh, Amos," she said, gathering the cat into her arms, and she buried her face in his ginger fur one last time. Puzzled by the unexpected display of affection, he twisted in her arms and batted an experimental paw against her cheek, seeming surprised to discover that it was wet.

Blinded by her tears, she put him down and quickly let herself out of the house before she lost her resolve. Then she set out for the highway. She knew exactly how to get there. Mary Kate had told her.

"Goodbye, llamas," she said as she passed the barn, regretting that she'd never learned anything more about them, had never, in fact, seen one up close. She spared a thought for Mary Kate, wondering if the child would miss her. Then she resolutely turned her back on Placid Valley Ranch.

She reached the highway as the sun sent up feeble fingers of light from the horizon. It was cold, but her coat kept her warm enough. Her breath preceded her in wispy clouds of mist that then trailed behind her as she walked, and as she plodded along she felt herself growing weary already. She was still weak from the strep and bronchitis, she thought. She'd soon be over that, and she had brought the half-used bottle of antibiotic pills with her. They'd continue to fight the infection.

If she were lucky, somebody would stop to pick her up soon. She gazed down the road, watching as a car barreled toward her. She stuck out her thumb and it whizzed past. Perhaps she'd have better luck next time.

She traipsed stoically through chunks of dirty snow at the edge of the highway, avoiding slippery patches of ice on the pavement. The next vehicle was a flatbed truck, and the driver didn't even notice her, much less stop to pick her up.

Jane blew on her gloveless hands to warm them, then thrust them deeper into her pockets, where Duncan's money crackled against her knuckles. She closed her hand around the bills, reassured by the security of so much cash. She walked westward, but no cars came for a long time. Finally she heard one approaching in the distance.

She turned toward it and stuck out her thumb, thinking that next time she hitchhiked in cold weather, she'd make sure she wore a pair of gloves. The Jeep Cherokee roared toward her at a blistering speed. And then it squealed to a stop.

She had barely wrenched the door open when a familiar voice growled, "Get in." It stopped her flat.

"You heard what I said," Duncan told her, barely containing his fury. He reached across the front seat and grabbed her wrist, yanking her toward him. She cried out in pain but clambered inside and watched him fearfully, wondering what he would do. Certainly he must have found out that she'd taken his money.

He slammed the vehicle into reverse and backed up, completing a turn in record time. When they were heading back to the ranch, he said coldly, "That was a fool thing to do."

Jane stared ahead, unwilling to face his anger.

"The two weeks you need for recuperating aren't up yet, and I don't take kindly to thieves. Also you left your cat."

At the mention of Amos, Jane's eyes filled with tears. She let them roll forlornly down her cheeks, hating herself for stealing and for her weakness now in front of Duncan. Duncan glanced over at her as they approached the turn onto the ranch road. He tossed a Kleenex in her direction.

"Use that Kleenex," he said more calmly. "Mop up."

Obediently she wiped her eyes, then turned toward him, wanting to explain.

"I was going to pay the money back," she said.

"We'll talk about it inside," he said gruffly.

Wordlessly she followed him into the house, where Amos ran to greet them, purring and rubbing against her ankles.

"Amos missed you," said Duncan, heavy on the irony. Uncertainly Jane picked up the cat and stood stroking him, holding him up as a shield.

"What are you going to do to me? Are you going to call the sheriff?" she asked in a tremulous voice when it seemed as though they would go on standing there and staring at each other forever.

"*Do* to you?" He shook his head as if to clear it. "What do you think? That I'm going to punish you? God, you have me pegged all wrong."

"Here," she said, yanking the money out of her pocket. "Take it back."

"It's not the money," he said, running his hand through his hair and looking more disturbed than she'd ever seen him. "It's your safety. You could easily become sick again, and as for hitchhiking, it's a dangerous thing to do!"

Something broke inside her. This man who lived such a safe and secure life—what did he know about survival? Had he ever had to live on the streets, wondering where his next meal was coming from? Had he ever tried to get a job and discovered that no one would hire him because there was no proof on paper that he existed?

"Don't tell me how to live!" she said. At her outburst Amos jumped down and ran away, and she didn't blame him.

Duncan's surprised look only spurred her on.

"I've been living from hand to mouth, scared to death because people try to hustle me and hurt me and—well, you can't possibly know about the real dangers I've faced! Hitchhiking seems tame by comparison."

"Jane, I only meant—"

"Try getting through the winter with no warm clothes! Try to find a job when you don't have a social security number! Try to find a little warmth and human kindness where none exists, and if that fails—if that fails—oh, God, why am I trying to tell you?" The money slipped unnoticed from her hand and fluttered to the floor, where it lay between them.

For a long time Duncan was quiet. The only sounds were those of her breathing and, once, a cough.

Duncan thought of Sigrid. If he had listened to her instead of brushing her off when she tried to speak to him of the matters closest to her heart, things might have been different.

"Why *are* you trying to tell me?" he inquired at last, repeating Jane's question, and his tone was so soft and gentle that she turned around, incredulous that he wasn't still angry.

He walked to her and put an arm around her shoulders. It was such a touching gesture that she felt her reserve starting to crumble. She wanted to reach out to him, to make him hold her in his arms and comfort her. He was so strong and solid; he was so nice.

"You're trying to tell me because you want to tell someone," he said, steering her to the couch and easing her down beside him. His eyes radiated goodness and goodwill, and she wasn't afraid of him. She wondered how he was able to find forgiveness in his heart after she had abused his hospitality, and she felt pained on his behalf because he had misplaced his trust in her.

"Tell me," he said, and when she looked at him she saw such sympathy and understanding that all the barriers fell away. After that, there was nothing else to do but begin her story at the beginning.

Chapter Five

Her life began—her present life, that is—one frosty November morning on the outskirts of an Illinois cornfield almost fifteen months ago.

The first thing to penetrate her consciousness was an inadvertent blow on the right leg, delivered by a muddy boot.

The first words she heard were, "What's this?"

The first object in her line of vision was a scared young boy breathing open-mouthed into her face.

"She's dead, Pop, ain't she?"

A warm hand touched her cheek, and she moaned.

"No, she's not dead. Run call an ambulance, Ollie! Quick!"

The boy's panicked footsteps crashed away through the nearby woods, and Jane became aware of tentative fingers checking her legs and arms for broken bones. When the man noticed that she was looking at him, he said, "There, now. I've sent for an ambulance. Just lie quiet, and it'll be here in a few minutes."

She was cold, so cold. And her head ached with the worst pain imaginable. The only reply she was able to make was another groan.

The ambulance took her to the Tyree Township Hospital, a small rural facility with only fifty-seven beds, and as soon as she reached the emergency room, someone asked for her identification.

"She doesn't have any," the farmer in whose field she had been found told the admitting clerk. The clerk followed the gurney right into the emergency room cubicle and stood clucking over her as the nurses swabbed the cut on the back of her head.

"Next of kin?" the clerk asked briskly, her pencil poised over the proper line on the form.

"I don't know," her rescuer said, stepping in to help when he realized that Jane wasn't able to speak.

"Honey, what's your name?" the clerk asked her, when she saw that Jane's eyes had opened.

It was a question that drew a complete blank.

"Well?"

She tried very hard to form words. "My n-name?" she managed to say.

"Yes, honey. I've got to have a name."

"Can't think," Jane mumbled. She felt as though she were wrapped in an invisible cocoon, sealed off from everyone and everything. Everything, that is, but the pain in her head.

"Well, that's okay. You just rest, and I'll be back in a few minutes," the clerk said as the punch bell on the admitting desk began to ring wildly, signifying that someone was looking for her. She disappeared through the twin swinging doors, and Jane felt a sense of relief at no longer being badgered for information that she couldn't give.

A doctor came in. "I'm Dr. Bergstrom," he said. He peered into one eye, then the other. He shook his head over her bruised cheekbone, her swollen eyelid, and then sewed up the cut on the back of her head.

"How'd all this happen, anyway?" he asked as he was stripping off his surgical gloves.

"I don't know," she answered in a small voice.

The farmer, who told her hesitantly that his name was Carlton Jones, explained to Dr. Bergstrom that he had stumbled upon her lying not far from the highway in a ditch on the edge of one of his fields, when he and his son were out looking for a lost hunting dog.

"There she was, lying there like she was dead," he said. "I thought she *was* dead. At first I figured she might have had an accident on the highway, but there was no car anywhere around."

"Do you remember anything?" Dr. Bergstrom asked her.

"No," Jane whispered. The sharp pain in her head had subsided to a dull, pounding ache. She didn't know these people or this place or about any accident. As far as she was concerned, this experience was the first thing that had ever happened to her. She didn't know who she was or where she was supposed to be, although she understood that she was expected to know these things and that these people were beginning to be annoyed that she did not.

Mr. Jones apparently knew the doctor, and the two men engaged in an intense discussion out in the hall, during which Jane heard Mr. Jones say, "But Doc, I don't know anything about her. I *sure* can't pay any hospital bill."

The doctor said wearily, "We'll go ahead and admit her to the hospital, but I have to call the police."

After that, the doctor, forcing a stiff smile, hurried back into the cubicle, and Jane was wheeled into a dingy little room with beige walls, cracked plaster on the ceiling, and nineteen-fifties-vintage venetian blinds with one slat missing. Finally, thankfully, she slept.

When she awoke, a man she'd never seen before was lounging beside her bed.

"I'm Detective Sid Reedy of the Tyree County Sheriff's Department," he said in an impersonal tone.

She blinked.

"I'm trying to find out a few things about your accident," he said.

"I don't remember," she murmured, but he hadn't heard her.

"What's that?"

"I don't remember," she said in a louder tone.

"I have to fill out a report," he said, slapping a clipboard against his knee. "Why don't you just tell me what happened?"

"All I know is I woke up and a boy was looking at me."

"Right. You were lying in a ditch between Jones's field and the highway. What I need to know is how you got there."

"I don't remember," she repeated, sounding even to her own ears like a broken record.

"Look, lady, it's late, and I'd like to get home in time for dinner just this once. So if your boyfriend pushed you out of a car or something, don't be embarrassed. I've seen and heard everything, believe me. Just let me fill out my report and I'll leave you alone." He was frowning at her now.

She squeezed her eyes tightly shut, trying to figure out if that was what had happened. But if she had a boyfriend, she couldn't picture his face; if she had been riding in a car, she couldn't recall anything about it. She forced herself to narrow her range of thoughts down to a single pinpoint somewhere inside her brain, trying to remember, to remember....

"Well?"

The sudden question interrupted her effort. A crushing feeling of helplessness descended on her. If only she could satisfy these people—the admitting clerk, the doctor, this insensitive policeman. They all demanded something that she couldn't give, and she felt so sad that it wasn't within her power to help them.

"I'm sorry," she said, on the verge of tears. "I'm really sorry."

He slapped the clipboard against his leg again, and the noise startled her.

"Okay, okay," he muttered, and he strode out of the room, slamming the door behind him.

Tears were etching shiny trails down Jane's cheeks and falling unheeded onto the pillow by the time a nurse arrived. The nurse's name tag identified her as R. Sanchez.

"Oh, did he upset you? Can I get you anything?" asked the little nurse, who appeared to be very young.

A name, she thought, staring at the nurse's name tag with longing. *Get me a name.* But she didn't say it.

Dr. Bergstrom didn't return to her room until late that night. He wore an expression of concern.

"Having any luck with your memory?" he asked.

She shook her head.

He sat down beside the bed. "Try to remember what you were doing the day of your accident. Who you might have been with, where you went," he urged quietly.

Jane tried, but there was nothing. No associations, no fragments of conversation, no faces.

"It's just—blank," she said unhappily.

"I've had the police run a missing persons check. There's no one who matches your description. No accidents have been reported along that particular stretch of highway, either. You seem to have appeared out of nowhere."

She swallowed and stared at him. "What's going to happen to me?" she ventured.

He stood up and shook his head. "I hope you're going to remember something," he said grimly before he left.

But she didn't remember anything. As far as she was concerned, she was nobody.

It was extremely frustrating not to be able to identify anything about her past life. At night when she was alone she would stare up at the stained ceiling above her hospital bed and wonder, *Who am I?* The more she tried to figure it out, the more defeated she felt. There seemed to be no clues.

Her clothing was ordinary, the kind that could have been bought in any J. C. Penney store anywhere in the United States. When a search was conducted in the area where she had been found, someone turned up a purse that might have been hers. It was handmade of a coarsely woven wool fabric, but there was nothing in it to prove that it belonged to her—no money, no personal effects, and most importantly, no identification. Someone put it in the closet along with the salvageable clothing she was wearing when Carlton Jones and his son found her. She would take it with her when she left, she supposed.

Dr. Bergstrom brought her a United States atlas, and she sat for hours poring over it, hoping that one of the town names or river names or highways might seem familiar. Because Chicago was the nearest big city, the sympathetic little nurse, whose name was Rosemary Sanchez, brought photos of some of the places there—O'Hare Airport, Lincoln Park, the Magnificent Mile, a five-story Picasso sculpture. None of them jogged her memory.

She watched television, hoping that she would see clues to her background on the local news. She didn't.

After a feature story about her plight in the local newspaper, Rosemary began to call her Jane Doe, first as a kind of joke, then more seriously. By the time she left the hospital two weeks later, it was the only name she knew. The hospital staff had grown so fond of her that they took up a collection to pay her bill, because as far as anyone knew, she had no insurance, and she certainly had no money.

A welter of good wishes accompanied her discharge. Rosemary tied helium balloons to the wheelchair that they insisted she ride to the door, and an aide settled a bouquet of flowers in her arms. Besides the handwoven purse, she carried a small donated suitcase that was too big for the meager change of clothes someone had given her.

Dr. Bergstrom had, with great difficulty, found a place for her to stay in the nearby medium-sized town of Apollonia, Illinois, where the department of social services had agreed to help her find a job. But her assigned social worker, a Miss Bird, whose task it was to pick her up at the hospital and install her at the shelter for battered women where she was to stay, turned out to be a malcontent who was miffed because she would have rather been out shopping for her trousseau.

When they got to the big converted house in Apollonia, Miss Bird all but pushed Jane out of the car and would have driven away before Jane retrieved her suitcase from the back seat if Jane had not yelped in protest. There wasn't time to grab the bouquet of flowers or Rosemary's balloons. Jane was abandoned at the curbside and left to introduce herself to the shelter's administrator, who stated with some irritation that Jane didn't really fall into the category of women that the shelter was supposed to help but would be allowed to stay anyway, since they had an opening.

Jane felt abandoned, exhausted, worried and confused. She was subject to incapacitating headaches that did not abate even with the strong pain medicine that Dr. Bergstrom had prescribed.

For two weeks Jane lived at the shelter, helping the other women care for their children when she could. The women were grateful but wary for reasons of their own. Jane made no friends.

When Jane went to the social services office for her first appointment with Miss Bird, who was supposed to help her find a job, she was curtly informed that the woman had been fired.

"Is there another social worker I should see?" Jane asked anxiously as she stood at the counter.

A harried clerk looked up from her filing.

"What?"

"Have I been assigned to another social worker?"

"I'll look it up in a minute," the woman said with a sigh.

After a short time, the clerk disappeared into a back room for fifteen minutes. When she came back, she stared at Jane as though she'd never seen her before.

"Can I help you?"

"I was waiting to see if I was assigned to another social worker," Jane reminded her.

"Oh, sure." The woman leafed through a pile of folders. "You're supposed to talk to Mrs. Engel, but she's got appointments scheduled all afternoon. You'll have to come back tomorrow."

Jane did return the next day, only to be informed that Mrs. Engel was out sick. And that day she was asked to leave the women's shelter.

"It's not that we want you to leave," the administrator of the shelter told her apologetically. "It's just that we need your room for a woman with two children, whose safety could be jeopardized if she doesn't get out of her home. Surely you understand."

"Of course," Jane said, and quietly packed her suitcase.

When she left, she had no idea where to go. She headed for the local McDonald's and sat there for four hours, nursing a blinding headache and trying to summon up the nerve to ask for a job. When she did, the manager told her that he was sorry, but he had no openings. She was terrified when she walked out. Where was she to go? What was she to do?

Thus ensued several days and nights when Jane, her head pounding, wandered the street by day and slept in the bus station by night. Finally the night manager at the bus station told her that she wasn't welcome there anymore. She would have to find somewhere else to sleep.

But where? She had no money, and she had no car. She had no identification. She didn't even have a name.

She forced herself to think optimistically and managed to land a job in a small restaurant called the Buttercup Café, slinging hamburgers behind the counter. An advance on her salary made it possible for her to rent a room in a run-down house. Jane, whose spirits had lifted, didn't mind, though. At least it was a place to sleep.

Then, perhaps because of the poor nutrition, she caught a particularly bad cold and lost her job when she couldn't work for a week. And when she didn't have enough money to pay her rent, she was politely asked to leave the boarding house.

At her wit's end, she called Mrs. Engel, the new social worker, from a pay phone and asked for an appointment.

"I can't see you until Monday," Mrs. Engel told her.

"But I'm really desperate," Jane said. By this time she was talking in a monotone. She had no energy to put into her voice. Her head had been aching steadily for several days, and the pain showed no sign of abating.

"I'm so sorry, but I have a full schedule. What time can you come on Monday?"

"I need help now," Jane said, her spirits sinking even further. This was Thursday. Monday was four days away. How would she survive until then?

"Ten o'clock Monday is the best I can do," said Mrs. Engel.

"All right," Jane replied. After she hung up the phone, she felt around in the coin return pocket in case her quarter had fallen into it, but it hadn't.

She couldn't think of anyone else who might help her. The people in the hospital in Tyree seemed far away; after all they'd already done for her, she couldn't expect more help from them. Even the nurse—the helpful one, Rosemary—wouldn't want to hear from her now. Jane was all alone.

That night Jane lingered outside a bar beneath a lamppost decorated with a Styrofoam candy cane in honor of the winter holiday season. Finally, summoning all her nerve, Jane stopped one of the patrons when he was on his way out. He bought her suitcase and the clothes in it for five dollars, squinting curiously at her in the dim light. Jane spent two dollars and sixty-nine cents on a skimpy hamburger, French fries, and a glass of milk at an all-night diner.

By the time the first angry streak of pink sunrise appeared in the eastern sky, Jane was walking along the highway outside town, hoping desperately that someone—anyone—would offer her a ride.

Finally an elderly couple with a small dog pulled over to the side of the road and beckoned her to get into their Buick. Jane didn't hesitate; she climbed right in.

"You look like you need a ride," the woman said, peering at Jane over the top of the front seat. "You going far?"

"Chicago," Jane said.

"So are we," the man told her. "Then we'll be traveling on to Milwaukee."

"We're going to visit our son in Chicago for Christmas and to our daughter's house in Milwaukee for New Year's," the woman supplied. "Are you going visiting, too?"

"No, I'm looking for a job," Jane said.

"Seems like if we're going to be riding all the way to Chicago together, we ought to be better acquainted. We're the Fosters—Betty and Herman. Our dog is Trixie. What's your name?" the woman asked.

"Jane," Jane said reluctantly. She didn't want to give her last name as "Doe." They wouldn't believe her, and her head hurt so much that she wasn't up to elaborate explanations.

"Jane what?" the woman asked.

A moving van hurtled past in the other lane, and on the side of it was emblazoned Rhodes Moving and Storage.

"Rhodes," Jane said. "Jane Rhodes."

"Well, Jane Rhodes, would you like a doughnut?" The woman reached over the top of the seat and waved a box of freshly baked doughnuts under Jane's nose.

"Thank you," Jane said gratefully and took two when the woman insisted. Trixie clambered into the back seat and licked one of the doughnuts, so Jane ended up sharing it with the dog, and afterward Trixie curled up with her head on Jane's lap, which was somehow comforting.

When they arrived in Chicago, the Fosters exchanged puzzled looks when Jane wasn't sure where she wanted to be dropped off, and finally they let her out of the car on Sheridan Road near an elevated station around the corner from where their son lived.

"Are you sure you don't want us to take you somewhere else?" Betty Foster called out the open car window, looking askance at the papers blowing around in the gutter and a few questionable characters hanging out in front of a store where all the signs in the window were printed in a foreign language.

"No, this is fine," Jane said, thanking them with a confident smile.

After the Fosters' car pulled away from the curb, Jane looked hopefully around her at the tall buildings, the traffic-clogged street and the people streaming in and out of the el station. A Salvation Army Santa stood on the pavement, energetically clanging his bell. From somewhere floated the tinny strains of a Christmas carol. Across the street were two restaurants, and the structure on the corner looked like an office building.

This was clearly a city where lots of things were going on. There were many places to work, and one of those jobs could be hers. Maybe, just maybe, she'd find the luck that had eluded her so far.

She lifted her chin and headed directly into the wind, not minding that the bite of it nearly took her breath away. She had made it to Chicago, tomorrow she would find a job, and soon everything would be all right. It was, after all, a season of hope. This New Year would be a new beginning in her new life.

THERE WAS MORE to her story, but Jane had to pause for a moment to catch her breath. The only sounds were the steady tick-tock of the clock on the mantel and the throaty rumble of Amos's purr.

"I think I'll put on the coffeepot," Duncan said. "Would you like a cup?"

She nodded, and he studied her for a moment before he stood and went into the kitchen. Amos stretched, got up, and followed Duncan.

What was Duncan thinking? she wondered. Did he believe her story, or did he think she was making it all up? It did, now that she thought of it, sound pretty fantastic. But it was true, all of it, every detail. She wished with all her heart that it wasn't.

She sighed and wiggled her right foot, which had gone to sleep. When the feeling returned, she went into the kitchen, where Duncan was refilling the sugar bowl.

"I thought I'd fix sandwiches," he said. "Neither of us has eaten, I suspect."

"I'll do it," she said.

He pressed his lips together. "All right," he said. "I guess you know where everything is."

Jane found sliced roast beef in the meat drawer of the refrigerator and piled it high on rye bread, the way she knew Duncan liked it. It was funny how many things she knew about him after living here during the past week. How he liked his coffee strong, for instance, and that he saved the daily newspaper to read at lunchtime. He also knew many things about her, as evidenced by the way he ran a bit of cold water from the faucet into her coffee, because she didn't like it either too strong or too hot.

"Aren't you going to eat?" he demanded when he saw that she had made only one sandwich.

"I'm not hungry," she murmured, setting the plate with the sandwich on it on the kitchen table at the place where he usually sat.

"Don't be silly," he said. He took another plate out of the cupboard and deposited half of his sandwich on it.

"Sit down and eat it," he directed. When she saw the stern expression on his face, she sat. She still wasn't sure that he wouldn't turn her over to the local sheriff for stealing his money.

He didn't speak before he took the first few bites of his sandwich, but after that he set the sandwich on the plate and leaned back in his chair.

"I take it things didn't work out for you when you got to Chicago," he said abruptly.

Her mouth was full of food, and she shook her head. That was an understatement.

"So you're going where?" His eyes pierced her.

Jane swallowed. The food sat like a lump somewhere in her chest, but she decided to continue the fiction she had started when she first arrived.

"California," she said. "I told you that I'm going to California. I want to start over there."

He stared out the window, apparently lost in thought. Though his face remained still and expressionless, his eyes were dark and gleamed with—what? She was reminded of a fire, damped and believed quenched, but with a glowing coal at its heart.

"What's your girlfriend's name?" he asked, shooting the question at her abruptly.

"Elizabeth," she said, lifting her chin and daring him to dispute this.

"Elizabeth *what*?"

"Elizabeth...um, Elizabeth *Maxwell*," she said, glimpsing the coffee container on the counter.

"Maxwell? Are you sure about that?" he asked, sounding dangerously skeptical.

"Well, she just got married," Jane improvised, worried that he might try to trace an Elizabeth Maxwell and not sure how common that name was. "Her name is Smith now."

"Right. Elizabeth Smith. You've already told me how you made up your own name. Do you expect me to believe this— this *bull* about an Elizabeth Maxwell Smith?"

To his amazement, she burst into tears.

He hadn't had any idea that this was imminent. Since this morning, when he'd first realized that she'd fled into the frigid Wyoming winter, he had drastically revised his assessment of her. She was deceptively frail looking, he had decided, a delicate beauty who, underneath that soft, fragile exterior resembled nothing so much as a steely trap. He hadn't expected tears.

While he was still trying to figure out how to respond, she dried her eyes on her sleeve and glared at him in defiance.

"All right," she said. "I lied. I have no girlfriend in California, no place to stay when I get there. I don't have a job and I'm not a librarian. I'm going to California, though. That much is true."

He appeared to be thinking things over, and she didn't speak again. *He's going to throw me out,* she thought in growing panic as time passed and he said nothing. *He's trying to figure out whether to have me arrested.*

"Look," she said. "I'm sorry I took the money. I knew when I did it that I shouldn't have. Just let me go now, and I won't bother you anymore."

"Go?" he said. "Are you joking?"

She swallowed the lump in her throat.

"Just let me out of here, let me go," she repeated, becoming distraught. She rushed out of the kitchen and yanked her coat from the closet near the front door, knocking over a kitchen chair in her haste.

"Keep Amos, please," she said as she struggled into her coat. "I can't give him a good home, and you can. If you'll just keep him for me, I'll send for him when I get to California, or maybe I'll send money for his food, if that's what you want—"

"Jane," he said, gripping her shoulders hard and shaking her so that the hair fell back from her face.

"Let me *go*," she said, tugging away from him so that she could place a well-aimed kick, if necessary.

"I want to help you," he said forcefully.

"I told you I want out of here," she said, grating the words, through clenched teeth.

"Didn't you hear me, you little fool? I'll help you," he repeated, and finally the words sank in.

She all but went limp. "You will?" she said unbelievingly.

He retained his grip on her. "I'll buy you a plane ticket to California," he said.

"Why?" she asked warily.

"Because you've had some bad breaks," he said, clipping the words off sharply.

"No one else ever cared enough—I mean, no one else ever wanted to help." She wrenched her shoulders out of his grasp.

"Well, I do. I'll lend you money, help you get some identification, whatever you need to start this new life you seem to want so desperately. But it'll have to be on my terms."

Jane stared at him. She might have guessed that there would be a catch. Of course he would have conditions, and she could well guess what they might be. As an attractive woman wandering the streets and traveling the highways, she had been subjected to the most disgusting and brutal suggestions. There were many ways that she could have made money, but she'd never gone in for that sort of thing. Never had the heart for it. Now Duncan was going to be like all the rest of the men who had tried to hustle her. She had been wrong to think that he was different.

"Aren't you interested in what those terms are?"

When she didn't answer, he said, "All right, then. I'll tell you. I want you to stay here until you're well. Until the weather is warmer. Until spring."

She waited, figuring that there was more to it. Finally she lifted her eyelids and saw that he was looking at her with an expression of compassion, which somehow was not what she had expected.

"And?" she said boldly. She might as well get this over with; there was bound to be more. She wanted him to come right out and say whatever else he expected.

"And?" he repeated.

"And what kind of payment do you expect for this kindness?" she said.

"Pay—" Dawning enlightenment spread across his face. To her amazement, a dark flush started at his collar and spread upward. He began to pace the floor.

"I want nothing from you, Jane. Nothing except your promise to stay here until you're well again. After that I will see you off on a plane and you'll never have to see me again.

That's all, everything. I require no—*favors*," he said, underlining the word with scorn.

She stared at him. To her utter amazement, she believed him. True, he was a normal red-blooded American male. True, he had been deprived of steady female companionship ever since his wife had left. But he was apparently not looking for the kind of relationship that she had supposed.

Jane was overcome with a feeling of shame. It was only natural for her to think what she had thought; that this was a man who saw the opportunity to claim some sort of benefit from the fact that she was indebted to him. And yet she should have known—she *did* know—that Duncan Tate was a trustworthy sort and that he would do nothing to harm her.

"I'm so embarrassed," she said, dropping her face to her hands. That way she wouldn't have to look at him.

He uttered a long sigh and touched a hand to her arm.

"Don't be," he said. "I can see why you might have thought that I—that I—oh, hell, what am I trying to say?"

He waited a moment and continued. "Look—um, Jane. My intentions are honorable. It so happens that I have plenty of room here, as well as the financial resources to help you get a fresh start. It's irrelevant at the moment that you happen to be a very beautiful woman. Anyone in your circumstances would warrant my help. So what about it? Will you take me up on it, or are you so all-fired stubborn that you'll try to sneak away again?"

She lifted her head. He was, miracle of miracles, smiling at her. His good humor in the face of all she had done humbled her.

Maybe this was the chance she had prayed for, the lucky break that she had dreamed about. Was she too stupid to recognize good fortune when it stared her in the face?

There was an old-fashioned settle beside the door, and she sank onto it.

"I can't believe you mean it," she said, her eyes searching his for reassurance.

"Of course I mean it," he said. "I don't say things that I don't mean."

"I wish I hadn't taken your money. I can hardly bear to look at you when I think of it."

He stood before her, his hands linked through the loops of his jeans. "We'll never mention the money again. Okay?"

She pressed her fingers to her eyelids, fighting tears. "Okay," she said, overwhelmed by his generosity. "But I want to repay you for your kindness. I'll stay, and I'll work around the house or cook or look after Mary Kate—"

He started to laugh. "Looking after Mary Kate! Now that's a fitting punishment, if ever I heard one."

Jane lifted her hand and stared at him, wondering how he could joke. "What I'm trying to say is that I'm grateful. Maybe this is the best chance I'll ever have to get back on track. To make it."

"So you'll stay? Until spring?" He looked anxious and unsure; she didn't want him to change his mind.

"Until spring," she agreed quickly.

"Let's shake hands on it," Duncan said.

She stood up, and they shook hands solemnly, then Duncan helped her remove her coat and hung it in the closet.

"I'm overdue for an appointment in town, so I've got to leave," Duncan said. He ran upstairs, where she heard him rattling around, and he hurried out with a quick goodbye. In a minute or two she heard the roar of the Cherokee's engine, as it disappeared up the drive toward the road.

And then she saw that Duncan had left the money she'd stolen on the table near the door.

She couldn't believe that after what she'd done, he would go away on the very same day and leave her alone with not only the money she'd taken from his wallet but with all his possessions. If she'd had a mind to run, she could have stolen him blind.

Jane had no desire to run anymore. Now all she wanted was to prove herself worthy of Duncan Tate's help. She felt a sudden rush of warmth and gratitude toward him. She had lost her faith in people, but he had shown her that goodness and mercy still existed in this world.

Her guilt about what she had done to him was tremendous. But she'd have plenty of time to make it up to him. Because she was going to keep her promise.

She would stay until spring.

Chapter Six

Jane didn't know how to behave around him, and so in her confusion she turned away entirely and, for solace, withdrew into herself. She crept silently around the house when he was there; she didn't eat meals with him, but took a tray to her room. At night she heard the chatter of the television set and the hollow echoes of Duncan's boot heels as he moved about downstairs, and only came out of her room for a late snack if she was sure he wasn't in the house.

These avoidance tactics proved successful for the next few days, until finally he called her on it.

She thought he'd left the house for his office in the barn. Duncan usually came in at lunchtime, ate while he read the daily newspaper, and sometimes watched the television set, and immediately afterward she'd heard the front door slam, but he must only have opened the door for Amos, she realized later.

She was coming out of her bedroom when his solid bulk blocked the hall, so she dodged him, only to have him move right along with her.

"What's this all about?" he demanded.

"What do you mean?" she answered, her heart stepping up its beat. She was sure of his essential goodness, but no matter how much she liked him, she couldn't help being fearful of people; she had been conditioned to it on the streets.

"I mean I want to know why you're avoiding me," he said, wrinkling his forehead at her. He had a way of cocking his head to one side and waiting for her replies, and he did this now. He didn't seem angry, only perplexed, but there was something forceful in his manner too, and that alarmed her.

In her limited experience, most people who were prepared to be forceful were also inclined to be mean, and although this didn't square with what she knew of Duncan's character, her body went into its flight-for-survival mode. Her shoulders tensed, her stomach knotted, and her eyes widened.

"Come on, Jane, you know you've been staying out of my way," he said. "Ever since the day you tried to walk out of here, you've crept about trying not to run into me, and you've managed to be pretty successful at it, too."

He waited to see what she would say, and she wished that she were anywhere but here, facing Duncan Tate, having to explain her actions. Before she came here she hadn't had to answer to anyone, or if she had, it had only been under duress and to people who were uncommonly nosy about things that were none of their business, such as, "Where do you live?" or "Who was your last employer?" Her favorite defense had always been to hightail it out of there, but that wouldn't work in this instance. Duncan was too big and fast and too smart to outrun; he'd already proven it, when she'd set out on her little jaunt up the highway.

"I didn't think you'd want to see me," she murmured, focusing on the top of his right shoulder, which was on the level of her eyes. She wouldn't look at his face. His expression would only make her feel guiltier than she already felt.

"If I didn't want to see you, I wouldn't let you stay here. I'd send you over to Rooney's, or put you up in the tack room in the barn," he pointed out in a gentler tone.

"After what I did—" Jane whispered, looking stricken.

"Eaten up by guilt, are you?" he said. "Well, maybe that's all to the good. If you feel guilty about certain things, I guess you'll keep your part of our bargain."

She noticed that, true to his word, he was being careful not to mention the money she'd stolen. But her eyes involuntarily glanced up at the suggestion that she didn't intend to stay until spring.

"I'm going to do exactly what I said I would," she said defensively. "I'm not going to run away again."

He relaxed visibly and smiled. "I'm glad to hear that, but I think we need to talk about how we're going to run this household while you're here. There's got to be a better way than the way we've been doing it."

"Just tell me what to do, and I'll do it." She felt cornered; she had no desire to sit down with Duncan and discuss anything.

"I *am* telling you what to do," he said smoothly, taking her hand and pulling her along the hall, down the stairs and through the house until they stood in the kitchen.

"Where to have this discussion, that's the question," he mused out loud, finally dragging her along to the seldom-used dining room, with its eight-armed chandelier and his mother's rose-patterned china arrayed along the top of the buffet.

"This will do," he said, looking around with satisfaction. "I don't use the dining room much, but the table is a good place to sit and face each other with our concerns. Sit down, Jane. Well, don't just stand there! Sit down!"

Embarrassed, she pulled out one of the heavy chairs and sat.

"Now, the thing about this meeting is that it probably won't be the last one we have. Anytime something concerns one of us, we have the right to discuss it. Okay?" His dark eyes sparkled at her.

She seemed to have no choice but to go along with him. Certainly she had no idea what it took to live in harmony with other people in a real household, and her assumption that the best way to go about it was to stay out of everyone's way was apparently wrong, at least in Duncan's eyes.

"The thing that bothers me most is that you're here, but I never see you. You used to come down to the kitchen, help with the dishes—"

"Haven't I been helping out enough?"

Duncan sighed and looked frustrated. "Look, this isn't about helping around the house, although I appreciate the things you've done. It's about why we never see each other anymore." His eyes were direct and honest.

"Under the circumstances, I didn't want to see you," she said in a small voice, deciding that if he was going to be upfront about the way he felt, she could be forthright, too.

He studied her for a moment. "I thought you understood that all is forgiven," he said.

She looked down at the table, wishing she could crawl under it. "I guess I didn't really believe it," she said. It was the truth.

For a long time neither of them spoke, and again she didn't dare look at him.

Finally he stood up and walked around the table until he stood in front of the window, staring out. Outside the rugged landscape rose into shadowy white peaks in the distance; pines stood green-black against the mountain slopes.

"I said I didn't want anything from you, but I was wrong," he said in a low tone. He heaved a great sigh and turned around. Her eyes widened as she waited to see what he would say next.

"Don't worry," he said hastily, "it's not what you think." He walked over to her chair and stood in front of her. "What I want from you is companionship," he said quietly.

"I don't understand," Jane said, at a loss for words. She'd never suspected this side of Duncan before. She'd been so caught up in her own problems, her own attitudes, that she'd never considered him as a real person with real wants and needs.

"I don't like living alone," he said in a purely conversational tone as he sat down again.

"But Rooney—Mary Kate—" Jane stammered, at a loss to think how he could feel alone with them living right next door.

"They have their own lives," he said calmly. "Rooney is a good friend, but he's wrapped up in making his granddaughter toe the line, and rightly so, I suppose. As for Mary Kate as a companion—well, she's only a child. In my limited experience, ten-year-olds don't make especially good friends for anyone except other ten-year-olds."

"I thought you'd like your privacy," she said, regaining her composure.

"I told you one time that to me, privacy is the same as loneliness. I meant it," he said.

She sensed his emotion; it was there in his eyes for her to see. She wanted to look away, because it embarrassed her, but maybe this was the way people were supposed to make contact with each other. She managed to hold his gaze until he smiled, and this almost, but not quite, broke the tension.

"So no more hiding when I come into the house. I enjoy your company around here at night, even if it's only watching television together. And meals—why can't we eat at the same table?"

"We could," she said, feeling out of her element. Didn't he realize that she knew nothing about carrying on a one-on-one relationship with another person? She hadn't grown close to anyone since they'd found her in that ditch.

"Would it be so hard for you? Am I so difficult to be around?" He smiled at her again, this time more engagingly, and she felt the considerable pull of his magnetism.

"You're not, Duncan. I wish I could explain. You see, I don't think you understand. It's just—just—"

He watched her struggle for words and realized that she wasn't making excuses not to interact with him but was struggling to express a thought that she couldn't get a han-

dle on. He waited patiently while she tried to articulate it
and wished there was something he could do to wipe that
pinched look from her face and the confusion from her eyes.

"I'm not trying to avoid talking to you right now, at this
moment," Jane finally explained, her face flushing. "It's
just that sometimes it's like that for me—I can't get the
words out. It might have something to do with that blow on
the head."

"Take your time," he told her, wishing that he knew more
about amnesia and how it worked.

"Anyway, what I was trying to say is that I'm not so much
afraid of you as I am about being around other people. I've
learned that you're to be trusted, and Mary Kate and Rooney too, but once I get past that point I don't know how to
act. I always had to be careful of other people getting too
close so they wouldn't steal what money I had, or of people
who had less than honorable intentions, or—well, I'm sure
you get the idea. And now..." Her voice trailed off.

"It's okay, Jane, you don't have to talk about it if it up-
sets you," he said.

"I want to. Before I didn't, but now I do." She drew a
deep breath, for some reason feeling free to be straight with
him as she never had with any other person within her
memory. Maybe it was because he had been so open with
her, but for whatever reason, it was as if all her emotions,
pent up for so long, burst forth.

"Don't you see that I haven't had a background of being
close to anyone?" she said in a rush. "I don't remember any
family. And I never made friends when I was trying to survive out on the streets. The plain truth is that I don't know
how to act around you, Duncan. And it's not just you. It's
everyone else, too." When she finished speaking, her eyes
searched his face for understanding.

He didn't know what to say. It was, he thought, perfectly
natural to assume that the people we deal with every day
have the same frame of reference that we do. And yet, as in
Jane's case, it wasn't always true. Often when dealing with

other people we assume too much. We should make an effort to think the way they think. If he had, he might have approached her in a more gentle way.

He raked his fingers through his hair in frustration. "I'm sorry," he said. "It never crossed my mind that just being here with me might take a great effort on your part."

"How were you to know?" she said, calmer now.

He closed his eyes for a minute, and when he opened them, he saw that hers were brimming with tears.

"Is something wrong?" he asked.

She shook her head and wiped the tears away before they could spill down her cheeks.

"No. It's a relief to talk to someone. I've never been that honest before. With anyone. I've had to lie and cheat and—"

"Shh," he said comfortingly, reaching over and stilling her lips with two fingers. The bodily contact startled her, and he took his fingers away, but not before he noted that she had very soft lips.

"I'm not going to lie anymore," she said with great determination. "Ever."

He glimpsed the steel behind those blue eyes, the same toughness that had helped her to survive so many hardships. He cleared his throat. "You don't have to promise me anything else," he said uncomfortably. "You've already promised me the one thing that I wanted—for you to stay until you're well."

She shook her head. "Saying that I'm through lying wasn't a promise to *you*," she said. "I'm making a vow to myself. It's a bad habit, Duncan, and I can't build my new life, the one I'm going to have, on a foundation of untruths. One lie begets another and another. After a while you're making things up all the time, and then you hate yourself for it, and soon other people start hating you, too. There's no point in waiting to start over in California when I can begin here."

"It's really important to you, isn't it? This California business, I mean?" he asked.

"I want it more than anything. I had to have some kind of goal, otherwise I'd have stayed in the same rut forever. I couldn't live that way anymore. Amos and I deserve a better life than that. We'll make it."

"Yes, Jane, I believe you will." He stretched and stood up, looking down at her. She was beautiful but unsmiling, and tension still hardened the lines of her face. *I'd like to see her happy* was the thought that leaped into his head, but he shook it away. Happiness wasn't something he could bestow; it was something she'd have to find herself. Life and a ruined marriage had taught him that. All he could provide was a safe place where she could pull herself together, and maybe a few amenities.

"How about a bowl of ice cream? There's enough for Amos if he wants it," he suggested lightly.

"Are we through talking?" she asked.

"I hope not," he said, and then he laughed. "Was it so awful?" he asked.

"No, it made me feel better," she admitted.

For a moment Jane thought he was going to slide his arm around her shoulders, but perhaps he thought better of it, because he let her go through the door first and followed her into the kitchen.

She watched as he took the ice cream out of the freezer and began to spoon it into cut glass bowls. She felt a surge of gratitude toward him, not only for his forgiveness and for the kind manner in which he treated her, but also for the emotional release he had provided for her when she needed it.

There was more to breaking free from her past life than she had suspected, she knew now. The surface accoutrements of a new life, like an apartment and a job, were important. But she also needed to do some work on herself. Before, she hadn't known who she was or how she was supposed to act.

Now she still didn't know her identity—she might never know it.

But she knew that if there was anyone in the world after whom she wanted to model her behavior, it was Duncan.

THE NEXT DAY Duncan came in and tossed a couple of mail-order catalogs onto the couch.

"Here," he said. "You need to order some things to wear."

"I can't," she told him, shifting Amos, who was purring in her lap, to one side. "I don't have any money."

"I don't mind charging them to my accounts. You can pay me back."

"Duncan, I—"

"Only order what you absolutely need, then. You can't go on wearing my old blue jeans that don't even fit you, and you'd probably like to have a few shirts in your own size. Shoes, too. The ones you wear are pretty ragged. And you should own a decent pair of boots."

She flipped through the pages of the catalogs. A few basics wouldn't cost much, but how did she know when she'd be able to repay him?

He leaned over the couch, resting one hand on the back. "I have faith in you," he said quietly. "By letting you borrow the money, I'm saying, 'You're going to make it, kid.'"

She felt flustered, but Duncan seemed to want to take care of her; it pleased him. She decided to be gracious.

"All right," she said. "I'll order some things. Only what I need, though."

"Good," he said and went away whistling.

She ordered three blouses, a pair of gray wool slacks, sturdy outdoor boots, and, something she couldn't resist, a long warm flannel nightgown printed with tiny bluebells.

Jane spent her days looking after the house, taking long naps with Amos curled up beside her on the couch, and reading Duncan's paperback mysteries, of which he had several hundred. She was intrigued by the way the heroes and heroines of these books always triumphed. They seemed to run into none of the insurmountable problems that were posed by mysteries in real life; for instance, in her case, the puzzle of who she was. At present, she was content not to worry about that. It was enough to appreciate living in this house and to spend much of her day dreaming about her future. Her past seemed less important now that she was no longer living it.

After a couple of weeks, Jane realized with a start that she hadn't had one of her crushing headaches since she arrived on the ranch. There were even definable periods every day when she felt an emotion that she cautiously identified as happiness.

It first manifested itself as a lightness of being, which then transformed itself into joy in being alive. At first she was wary of this feeling that was so unfamiliar. She thought it was a fluke. As the days went on and it didn't go away, she learned to believe in it, much as she was learning to trust that there would always be enough food to eat and a warm place to sleep.

There are people, she thought, who have always had a place to sleep and plenty of food. Probably they've never contemplated what life would be like without these things that are so necessary. And likewise there are people who have always known this contentment, this—and she was still almost too superstitious to think the word—*happiness.* Duncan Tate was almost certainly one.

Although perhaps she was wrong about the happiness. He was unfailingly cheerful, more so every day, she thought. But was he happy? Sometimes a shadow of sadness slipped over his features when he thought she wasn't paying attention, and she wondered about it. She thought that maybe it had something to do with his former marriage. Jane had been told about that by Mary Kate, who had fallen into the habit of dropping by to visit with Jane every afternoon after the school bus dropped her off.

"I didn't know Duncan's wife very well," Mary Kate said one day as they were sitting together in Duncan's living room, cutting pictures out of magazines for one of her school projects. "But Sigrid was pretty. When she went away, Duncan left to go find her, and after he came back, he never talked about her again."

"Never said anything at all?" Jane asked curiously. She had found a gift set of bath powder and cologne in the bathroom; it must have belonged to Duncan's ex-wife. It seemed odd to think of Duncan married.

"Nope, he never mentioned Sigrid again. What food group is chocolate cake in, Jane? Do you know?"

"I'm afraid not," Jane admitted.

"Well, anyhow, Sigrid didn't come back after she left even to get the things she didn't take with her. Duncan gave me her scarves and I play dress-up with them. Do you want to play dress-up sometime?"

"Sure," Jane said, pasting a picture of a stick of butter on a notebook page.

"Sigrid was a rotten cook," Mary Kate told her. "And she didn't love the llamas like the rest of us do. So I'm glad she left, mostly. Especially because you came. You know, cutting out pictures of all this food makes me hungry. Let's make some banana pudding, Jane. Duncan loves it."

So they made banana pudding, and Duncan did love it, and that was all Jane found out about the long-departed Sigrid.

She couldn't imagine a woman lucky enough to have Duncan for a husband leaving for any reason whatsoever. And if Sigrid had stayed, chances were that Jane wouldn't be here at all. She didn't think that Sigrid, or any woman for that matter, would have allowed Duncan to take her into his home the way he had.

Sigrid's loss. Jane's gain.

IT WASN'T LONG before Jane discovered soap operas.

At first the stories seemed incomprehensible, because she

didn't know the plot lines, but as she began to feel better, she didn't nap in the afternoon anymore and began to watch TV after lunch. Soon it became clear to her that daytime serials were an educational vehicle that she couldn't ignore.

Man to woman, woman to woman, man to man—all relationships were covered in detail. Table manners and other points of etiquette were demonstrated. Relationships were discussed. She was fascinated because she knew so little about such things.

To sleep with a man on the first date or the third? This was a week-long issue on *Luck of the Irish*. Skulduggery in business? An endless discussion of that very thing went on in *Thunder's Echo*. Love offered, love denied? It was the stuff of *Restless Hearts*.

Most people learned about such things over the period of a lifetime, but many of Jane's values had flown away with her real life. She had to laugh at the absurd melodrama of some of the plots on these TV shows, but nevertheless, they provided her with a way to set up a new system of values. They also allowed her to provoke interesting conversations with Duncan.

"What do I think about children moving back with their parents after they've grown?" he repeated in puzzlement, when she hit him with that question one night at dinner, after watching a segment of *Luck of the Irish* where this dilemma was featured.

"A lot of kids do that," she answered.

"I'm not one to comment since I've always lived here at Placid Valley Ranch. I'm one who never left home," he said, and then he proceeded to tell her how he had taken over the operation of the ranch after his father was thrown by a bucking horse and subsequently died.

Another time she brought up the subject of a May-December marriage, currently being considered by two characters of widely divergent ages in *Restless Hearts*. This opened a spirited discussion in which Jane came out for and

Duncan remained vehemently against, saying that his father had been much older than his mother and that it hadn't always worked for the best.

It was a way to get to know each other, Jane reflected, and when Duncan, curious, asked her at lunch one day where and how, considering her loss of memory, she'd formed such strong opinions, she innocently told him that she'd been watching soap operas.

He threw back his head and laughed. "Honest? No fooling?" he said when he stopped.

She was embarrassed, but nodded.

He sobered instantly. "I'm not laughing at you," he said. "I'm pleased that you've found a way to learn about things you need to know." He knew how isolated they were out here on the ranch, but hadn't realized that Jane needed more human interaction. He supposed that he, Rooney and Mary Kate didn't contribute much to her development as a person.

He had been thinking about Jane a lot lately. After their serious talk, Duncan had figured that the pact between Jane and himself was an even exchange.

He protected her from the world; she protected him from loneliness and introspection.

Loneliness hadn't become a habit, but introspection certainly had. It was one that he would like to break, one that was as counterproductive as—well, as the lying that Jane had confessed afflicted her.

But how could he have stopped looking within himself when there wasn't any other place to look? He hadn't known the answer to that question until Jane came.

Now, instead of endlessly inspecting his own feelings, he had a distraction, and a pleasant one. Day by day she slowly lost the guarded air that made her seem slightly removed from him and took on a glow that might be the beginning of a more favorable outlook. Sometimes she hummed or sang around the house, which pleased him. His mother used to do that; he'd always considered that her low lilting voice, rising and falling with tunes she'd picked up from the radio, had made this house a home when he was a kid. After she died, there was no more music; his father had mourned her until the day he died. But now there was Jane to sing, and hearing her took him back to a happier time.

It would have been fun, he thought, to do everything for her. To give her everything. Or to shoulder her burdens for her so that she had nothing to do but lean against him. He didn't, because he knew it wouldn't work, and she would only end up resenting it.

When she went away he would surely miss her, but at the moment that didn't bear thinking about.

For now he would enjoy.

Chapter Seven

The next day Jane met the animals that Duncan prized so highly.

An unexpected warming trend sent temperatures soaring, and the sky was so blue and the sun so bright that Jane, who was feeling stronger every day, didn't want to stay indoors. She was pleased when Duncan called her on the telephone from his separate line in the barn and asked her to pay him a visit.

When Mary Kate stopped by the house on her way home from school, Jane suggested that she walk to the barn with her.

Mary Kate, acting her usual loquacious self as she skipped along, expressed delight that Jane was finally going to get a close-up look at the llamas.

"Before the snow came this winter, the female breeding llamas had their whole yard next to the barn to walk around in. Then it snowed and there were these huge drifts, but not so many on the east side of the yard, because Grandpa and Duncan built the barn so that it shelters the llamas from the weather when they're out in their pen. They shovel the snow out of the pen pretty often, so it's clear.

"Then there's the male llamas over in the stable in back of the barn. Llamas are used to cold weather, you know that? They come from some mountains called the Andes and it gets real cold there, Grandpa says. Oh, Jane, you'll finally get to meet Dearling. Aren't you excited? You should be. She's wonderful." Mary Kate gave a happy little hop so that her long ponytails bounced.

As they approached, the llamas inside the pen ambled over to the fence. One or two of them walked nervously forward, which made them look as though they were eager for this contact with humans.

"What's that noise they're making?" Jane asked, as soon as she realized that the strange sounds she was hearing came from the llamas.

"They hum. Listen, they're saying, 'Who's that lady with Mary Kate?' " She laughed and ran ahead to open the gate.

Mary Kate tugged at the gate until it opened and went inside, carelessly leaving it ajar. Once she herself was inside the pen, Jane struggled with the lock, which was so stiff that the bolt almost wouldn't slide home. When at last it was secure, she turned her attention to the llamas.

The first thing that struck her was that they all looked so different from one another. There seemed to be no one particular mold. This llama had a long neck and was tall enough to look her in the eye. That one was small, about the size of a large German shepherd. Some had ears that perked up, others' ears were slightly rounded. But all were graceful in a strangely elegant way. Jane was entranced with their looks.

Mary Kate's arms encircled the neck of the smallest llama in the pen. She rubbed her face against the curve of its neck, and the llama nuzzled her shoulder.

"This is my Dearling," she said proudly. "Isn't she beautiful?"

"She certainly is," Jane said warmly, moving cautiously closer as she spoke. Dearling didn't move, only looked slightly more alert. She seemed very tame.

"You can pet her," Mary Kate told her. "She won't bite or spit."

"Spit?" Jane asked, a little unnerved.

"Llamas spit, but hardly ever at us. They spit at each other, usually when they're having an argument over food, or over who is going to stand where or something dumb like that."

"Oh," said Jane, nevertheless preparing herself to dodge llama spittle. But Dearling was standing quietly, blinking her expressive long-lashed eyes and chewing her cud. Jane reached out and tentatively stroked the silky wool. Dearling leaned toward her at her touch, and Jane became bolder. In a few seconds, Dearling was sniffing at her clothes, and when Jane bent closer, the llama lifted her head and blew gently into Jane's face.

"Is she getting ready to spit?" Jane blurted after jumping away.

Mary Kate giggled. "No, that's what she does when she wants you to know that she likes you," she said.

Jane moved closer to Dearling and, acting out of instinct, blew gently into the llama's face.

Mary Kate laughed delightedly. "You're friends now," the girl said with great certainty.

Jane left Mary Kate with Dearling and walked around the muddy enclosure examining the other llamas. This was a pen for breeding females and their young; several young llamas huddled close to their mothers. Some of the females were roundly pregnant. All seemed boundlessly curious about her, and none were oblivious of her presence.

Duncan came out of the barn and stood watching her, a smile playing across his features. She returned his smile. Today he looked so proud of the llamas, and his stance was one of lord and master. A couple of llamas ambled toward him as if going to pay their respects.

When they reached Duncan, they nosed against his sleeve and rubbed their heads on his shoulder.

"Easy, there, Pumpkin, and stop it, Stardust," he told them affectionately. To Jane he said, "I walked out here with a corn muffin in my hand this morning, and they would have gladly relieved me of it. I guess they're looking for more goodies."

"They're beautiful," Jane said, "but I wasn't prepared for them all to look so different from one another."

"Come into my office in the barn," he said, holding the door open for her. "I'll show you some photos of llamas that we've raised."

Once inside, he opened a photo album on his desk. Jane sat on the edge of the desk and thumbed through it.

"This one has such pointed ears. And some of their necks seem shorter than others," she observed as she turned the pages.

"There are a lot of individual differences. I suppose there's no real standard of llama beauty. A pretty llama is whatever you think it is. Some people like them to be a solid color, and others prefer spots. Some think small llamas are wonderful, others like big ones."

"I didn't expect them to be so tame."

"These in the pen are females, which tend to be more affectionate than males, although sometimes I have to remind visitors that these aren't cuddly stuffed animals. They aren't really meant to be fussed over or coddled, though I have to admit that I do my share of it."

"So does Mary Kate," Jane said. She gazed out of the window at the child, who was talking to Dearling as the llama followed her around the yard.

"Ah, Mary Kate," Duncan said with a sigh of exasperation.

Jane shot him an inquiring look. "Has she done something wrong?"

"Well, not lately. Rooney and I are holding our breath, waiting until the next time. There will be a next time, I can guarantee it."

"Oh, Mary Kate's not so bad," Jane murmured in the child's defense.

"You weren't here when she let Quixote, my prize stud, out of his stall. And you weren't here when she set fire to Rooney's house. Or when she—"

"Never mind, I get the idea," Jane said wryly. She didn't need to be told about Mary Kate's affinity for trouble.

"Although I do think that the kid is behaving better since you've been around," Duncan said, eyeing her intently.

"I've tried to keep her company. She's an active little girl who seems to need a lot of attention."

"I guess you're right, and Rooney and I don't have time to give it. She's a plucky kid, and I'm fond of her, but I can't help thinking how smoothly things ran around this ranch before she came here."

"She said she's lived here for two years."

Duncan sat down on his swivel chair and toyed with a carved wooden llama paperweight.

"Mary Kate came here after her parents died in an accident. Rooney wanted her to come live with him, and she's been here ever since."

"How sad," Jane said, and meant it. She knew what it was like to be cut loose in the world with no place to go and no one to care.

"That's what Rooney thought," Duncan said. "He's always adored Mary Kate, and she was his flesh and blood, so he didn't want strangers bringing her up. I guess it's safe to say, though, that her presence here has changed his life."

"And yours," Jane said.

"And mine," Duncan agreed. "Maybe it needed changing." This he said thoughtfully, and his eyes seemed to reflect other more complicated thoughts that he didn't choose to express. Jane thought of Sigrid and wondered if Duncan still loved her.

He stood up. "You haven't met our stud males yet. Come on, they have their own stable behind the barn," he said.

They walked to an outbuilding, to which Jane had paid scant attention before because it was barely visible from the house. In front of it stood fenced pens, each separate from the others, and at the sound of Duncan's voice several llamas ambled out.

"This is Thor," he said, gesturing at a chocolate-brown llama with short-tipped ears and a heavy wool coat. "That's Paco hanging his head over the door. And this—this is Quixote."

Quixote was a majestic llama, taller than the other males, with banana ears and substantial bone structure. His coat was a golden reddish brown, and his wool was coarse with longer guard hairs.

"Is he your favorite?" Jane asked.

Duncan appeared reluctant to favor one llama over another. "He's our prize breeding stud. He came from very good stock, so he's quite valuable. And yes, maybe I am partial to him." He reached up and scratched Quixote behind the ear.

At that moment Mary Kate came around the corner of the barn.

"Jane!" she called, tramping along with Dearling following close behind.

"I guess I'd better go keep an eye on Mary Kate," Jane said.

"That's probably an excellent idea," Duncan told her. She waited for him to return to the barn with her, but he waved her away with a grin. "You go on," he said. "I have work to do in the stable."

Back in the barn, Mary Kate led Jane into the tack room. Here harnesses and saddles hung on wooden pegs on the walls, and panniers for the llamas were draped across a couple of sawhorses in the corner.

"I'm going to put a halter on Dearling," Mary Kate said as she stood on tiptoe to lift one of the halters off a high peg.

"Does Duncan let you do that?" Jane was skeptical.

"Sure," Mary Kate said. "He likes me to do it. I trained Dearling almost all by myself." She held the halter in front of the llama, and Dearling nosed into it. Mary Kate fastened the buckle on the left side before leading Dearling out of the barn. Jane tagged along behind, and the three of them headed toward the house.

"Hey," Duncan called from over near the stable. "Mary Kate, how about walking up to the road to get the mail?"

"Okay," Mary Kate said. "Will you come, Jane? It'll be fun."

"How far is it?"

"Grandpa says it's exactly a half mile from here to the mailbox," she said.

"Oh, I'd love to go for a walk," Jane said, feeling her spirits lift. It was such a beautiful day, the finest they'd seen since she'd arrived. She could clearly see the tops of the surrounding mountains. Alongside the driveway, fence posts stood in stark geometric purity against the snow of the pasture. Mary Kate led Dearling, who daintily picked her way around the remnants of snow in the rutted tracks. Once Mary Kate stopped briefly to adjust Dearling's halter, then they resumed their walk.

"Tell me about training Dearling," Jane said as they rounded a bend.

"I started last summer. Dearling's not much more than a baby, you know, and I begged Duncan to let me work with her. At first Duncan didn't want me to, but my grandpa said, 'Oh, Duncan, what could it hurt?'"

Jane smiled at this cannily accurate mimicking of Rooney's deep voice.

"Duncan said to get Dearling used to me by touching her and playing with her, but I was already doing that, so it wasn't such a big deal. She likes me, she really does!" Mary Kate looked over at Dearling and smiled.

"She's very fond of you. I can see that," Jane said.

Mary Kate beamed. "Duncan said that training a llama to like wearing the halter means adapting to the llama so it will trust you. Then, because it trusts you, the llama is ready to develop a habit, for instance, putting on a halter. So after I was sure she trusted me, I stood on the same side of Dearling every time I took out the halter, and I held it up to her face very, very patiently while I talked softly in her ear. Pretty soon Dearling got so she wasn't scared, and finally one day I just slipped the halter over her nose."

Jane wondered if training a child could be accomplished in the same way—by adapting to the child to establish trust and then encouraging the child to develop the habit of good behavior. While she was pondering this, Mary Kate dropped back to walk beside Dearling and to whisper into the llama's ear. When she returned to Jane's side she took her hand.

"Actually," Mary Kate confided, "after I got the halter on her, it wasn't all that easy to lead Dearling. It was because at first I left the halter too loose, and she didn't like it. And then she wouldn't walk—she'd sit down! That was funny, but I didn't think so then."

"What did you do?" Jane asked with an amused glance at Dearling, who seemed to sense that they were talking about her.

"Oh, I'd get behind her and push at her backside, trying to get her up on her feet, and she'd just chew her cud and look at me like I was crazy. Duncan laughed at us, but then he came into the pen and showed me how to tighten the halter so it wouldn't flap against her head. After a while Dearling was walking right alongside me. This summer I'm going to teach her to pull a cart. Then she can take us for rides. You'll like that, won't you, Jane?"

"Well, I—" she began, but suddenly stopped. She wished that she could think of an easy way to tell Mary Kate that she didn't plan to stay at Placid Valley Ranch that long. While she was casting about in her mind for something to say, Mary Kate thrust Dearling's lead into Jane's hand and ran ahead to the mailbox.

When Mary Kate came back, she resumed leading the llama and handed Jane the packet that she'd removed from the ranch mailbox.

Jane leafed through the mail and found several business-size envelopes with windows, a journal from a llama-breeding association, and a small pink envelope postmarked Albuquerque, which could easily slip out of the packet if she weren't careful. Realizing that she'd fallen behind Mary Kate and Dearling, she slid the pink envelope into the pocket of her coat and tucked the rest of the mail under her arm as she hurried to catch up.

From where she walked, she could barely see the house within its shelter of evergreen trees, but something softened inside her when she remembered that she lived in that picture-perfect house now, if only temporarily, and had her own warm bed to which she returned every night. She also had food to eat whenever she was hungry, Amos had a little plastic cat dish that Duncan had surprised them by bringing home one day, and she drank from her own favorite coffee mug on which Duncan had written her name in Magic Marker. And Duncan. She had Duncan.

Duncan to talk with, Duncan to joke with, Duncan to watch television with, and Duncan to eat meals with. At first she had felt constrained in his presence, it was true, but their relationship had become easy, even comfortable. If Jane had had a brother, she would have liked him to be just like Duncan Tate.

"This summer, maybe you can help me train Dearling to pull the cart," Mary Kate said, picking up the threads of their conversation again.

Jane decided that there was no avoiding this; she might as well confront the matter head-on. She wasn't about to participate in promoting any kind of falsehood, especially one as misleading as the one that tempted her now.

"What's wrong? Don't you want to work with me and Dearling?" Mary Kate peered upward, suddenly anxious.

"It's just that I won't be here this summer," Jane said quietly.

"Not *be* here! Why, you *have* to be here!" Mary Kate exclaimed in real dismay.

"Duncan and I agreed that I would stay at the ranch until spring," Jane told her as gently as she could.

Two red patches appeared on Mary Kate's face, one on each round cheek. Her chin jutted in defiance.

"I don't want you to leave," Mary Kate said from between tight lips.

"I never meant to stay here," Jane pointed out. "I only stayed because I was sick and couldn't leave."

"Well, I was talking to Duncan just the other day, and we talked about this summer and the llama cart and everything, and I said you could help maybe, and Duncan said he'd try to talk you into staying longer than spring. So there."

Jane didn't know how to reply to this. She knew that she had made it clear to Duncan that she would leave for California in the spring. Did he really think that she might stay longer?

Mary Kate appeared tense and fretful when they parted, but Jane waited until after dinner with Duncan that night to broach the subject of her staying until summer. True, she could have let it ride, but she had become sensitive to Mary Kate's emotional makeup, and she didn't think it was wise to raise the child's hopes. Better, she thought, for Mary Kate to know from the outset that Jane was not going to become a permanent fixture at Placid Valley Ranch.

She chose a quiet moment after dinner, when Duncan had finished watching the evening news on TV. He listened carefully while she told him all the reasons why he shouldn't lead Mary Kate to think that she, Jane, was planning to stay at Placid Valley Ranch beyond the time that they had agreed upon.

Duncan, who was sitting in his big leather chair near the fireplace, stared at the floor in front of the hearth for a long time after Jane finished talking.

"I suppose I was wrong," he said slowly. "I didn't realize that Mary Kate would take it for granted that you really would stay through the summer. Maybe I encouraged her to think that there was a possibility, but I thought she knew that it was just conjecture."

"She takes everything literally, and she doesn't understand conjecture," Jane told him. "Mary Kate is a child who has experienced enough rejection in her life. I wouldn't want her to think that I'm rejecting her, too."

Duncan smiled at her. "You've become attached to her, haven't you?"

"Well—"

"I watched you walking up the drive today with Mary Kate holding your hand. You looked as though you belonged together."

Jane jumped up, suddenly feeling agitated. She stood staring into the fire, trying to sort out her feelings. She *had* tried to build a relationship with the girl, mostly because she felt sorry for her.

But to be more honest about it, perhaps the reason that she had grown close to Mary Kate in the short time that she'd been here was that she herself craved closeness. She had Amos, but he wasn't a human being. He couldn't talk to her. But Mary Kate did, and Mary Kate had made her feel welcome here, even needed. She had never identified within herself that desire to feel important to someone before; it came as a surprise to her that the urge existed at all.

"Mary Kate needs the gentleness of a woman," Duncan said. "It's good that you're here for her."

Jane whirled and looked at him, and then found that she couldn't look at him because his gaze was so penetrating. She turned away again and opened the glass door over the face of the mantel clock. The key lay beside it, and for the next few seconds she wound the clock. It was just busy-work, but something to do with her hands seemed important at this point.

When she had closed the glass cover again, Duncan said, "You're welcome to stay at Placid Valley Ranch as long as you like, Jane. I thought you knew that."

Because she didn't know what else to do, Jane sat down on the edge of the raised hearth, the fire warming her back.

Across the room, Amos lay curled up on the couch, the tip of his tail trailing across his nose.

"I'm only planning to stay until spring," she said.

"I know that was our original agreement," Duncan said. "But if you want to change it, we can always renegotiate."

"No," she said. "You're so kind to me. But I want to be free to set out on a life of my own. To have a home of my own. To make friends. I want meaningful work that will allow me to be independent. I'm not ungrateful, but now I'm at the point where I can see an end to my quest, and I want to get on with it."

"You really know what you want, don't you?" he said. His eyes were somber now.

She nodded.

"The last time I saw such determination was when my wife left," he said reflectively.

"You haven't ever spoken of her before," Jane said. She wouldn't have known about Duncan's former marriage if Mary Kate hadn't told her.

"She found someone else, and she left me a couple of years ago. By the time she'd made up her mind to go, there wasn't anything I could do or say to make her change her mind."

"Do you ever see her anymore?"

"No, she lives in Albuquerque with her new husband. We keep in touch, but—" He shrugged.

The mention of Albuquerque reminded Jane of the pink envelope that had arrived in today's mail. She jumped up and went to the closet, where she rummaged in her coat pocket and produced the envelope. Silently she handed it to Duncan.

He slit the envelope with a brass letter opener and read the contents quickly. When he had finished, he tossed the pink paper onto a nearby table.

"Well, what do you know," he said heavily. "It's from Sigrid. She's had a baby girl."

He looked so sad that Jane sat down on the ottoman in front of his chair. She regarded him with a frown.

"Duncan, is everything all right? With you, I mean."

He lifted his shoulders and let them fall. "I thought it was. I figured I had handled the situation with my wife—I mean my ex-wife—pretty well. I was over it. But now I get this birth announcement from her and I feel like going and burying my head in the sand. Explain *that*." His face, usually so handsome, suddenly seemed to have developed lines where none were before.

Jane felt at a loss for words. Behind her the fire crackled and spat glowing sparks up the chimney, and outside the wind had picked up. She felt as though she'd like to melt into a small invisible blur rather than talk about this. She had had so little experience with events that normally occurred in people's lives that she had no store of wisdom from which to draw at the moment. Yet she suspected that she was the only person in Duncan's life with whom he could discuss the things closest to his heart.

"I can't explain why you feel the way you do, Duncan," Jane said after she had groped within herself to find the right words. "I can only tell you that it seems to me that you're fortunate to have been married once. It must be wonderful to find someone you want to spend the rest of your life with, and even if it doesn't work out, at least you have something. For a while."

"You're right, Jane. It was a good marriage, a strong marriage, for a time. And when it failed..."

"When it failed, it couldn't have been entirely your fault," she pointed out.

He focused his eyes on her. "Once I thought it was. I've tempered that judgment, because I see now that we both were at fault. I wasn't sensitive enough to her emotions, or at least I could find no way to let her know that I was, and she was wrong, because she didn't try hard enough to make me understand how important it was for her to know that I cared. And I cared, Jane. I really did."

"I know you did, Duncan," she said softly.

"This birth announcement underlines the truth that Sigrid and I can't do it over again. It's too late for that."

Jane rested her hand on top of his. "Sigrid thinks enough of you to share her news about the baby. You should both congratulate yourselves on managing to split up without hard feelings."

"In a way I wish she hadn't sent the announcement. It makes me see that she's been going forward with her life while mine has stood still. She has a husband and child, and I have—well, I have a herd of llamas and a ranch foreman. Oh, and don't forget Mary Kate." He gave a snort, which was probably meant to be a laugh but fell short of the mark.

Jane was relieved that Duncan was trying to make light of his situation.

"You've forgotten Amos and me. We're here," she said before she thought.

His eyes suddenly went bleak. "But only until spring," he said.

Duncan continued to look at her, and all at once the room seemed too hot, the fire too bright, his expression too needy.

Overhead the mantel clock's tinny gong struck the hour, and Amos stirred.

Elaborately casual, Jane stood up. "I guess I'll turn in," she said.

"It's early," Duncan pointed out.

Jane faked a yawn. "That walk to the mailbox must have tired me out," she said. It was a lame excuse, but at this point anything would be. Duncan looked as though he was ready to pour out his soul to her, and she wanted to avoid that at any cost. Suddenly she knew that any kind of intimacy was more than she could handle.

He said nothing, only watched her as she fled; never had the staircase seemed as long as it did on this night. When she reached her room, she discovered that her heart was pounding out of all proportion to the physical effort involved in running up one flight of stairs.

Almost immediately she heard his footsteps mounting the stairs, and she went to her door and listened for the sound of his door latch. She didn't hear it, and presently he walked past her room on his way out of the house. That wasn't so unusual; he often went over to Rooney's place in the evening.

It took all her willpower not to open her bedroom door and speak to him as he passed, although she realized with a start after she heard the front door slam that she had no idea what she would have said.

Chapter Eight

The next day Duncan woke up, looked at himself in the mirror, and said to his reflection, "You fool." After that he cut himself shaving and had to look all over for his styptic pencil, which he never found.

He was a fool for pouring his feelings out to Jane last night, when it obviously made her so uncomfortable. And he was twice a fool because he'd been entertaining the thought that Jane would stay past spring. That particular season, which he had long considered a time for beginnings and renewal, would this year be a time of ending. He found that he didn't relish the idea of her leaving.

He had grown accustomed to Jane at breakfast, to Jane humming as she dusted the furniture, to Jane folding the clothes fresh from the dryer and looking over her shoulder to greet him when he came in during the day. He had grown accustomed to *Jane*. Or whoever she was. That her name wasn't really Jane did not matter to him. What mattered was that he had grown to care about her. Her story touched him; he couldn't imagine not having a past.

His past was with him constantly. He had grown up here on the ranch, helping his father and Rooney with what was essentially a cattle operation in those days. His mother had been a delicate, gentle woman not unlike Jane. They sometimes visited his maternal grandparents in Moscow, Idaho, where his grandfather was a professor at the University of

Idaho. His grandparents and his mother always seemed slightly startled that she had married a rancher who was many years her senior and that she now lived on an isolated ranch in Wyoming.

Duncan was an only child, and there was never any doubt that he was going to take over the ranch when he grew up. His mother, fragile until the end, had died of complications from the flu when he was thirteen. Duncan had vivid memories of the events leading to her death, which was why he was so insistent that Jane take care of herself.

Then ten years ago, when he was only twenty-two, his father had died. From then on, Duncan had relied on Rooney's help and advice in running the ranch, and when Duncan decided after much thought and study to convert from cattle to a llama-breeding operation, Rooney had encouraged him to ease into this new livestock management program. They both needed a challenge, and llamas could provide it.

Their venturesome endeavor proved worthwhile. No longer regarded as novelties for zoos and animal parks, llamas had recently come into their own in the United States as pack animals and wool producers. Last year he and Rooney had sold their best breeding female at auction for $80,000. The sale was a triumph for Placid Valley Ranch, and it validated Duncan's decision to become a llama breeder.

He couldn't imagine what it was like for Jane, who faced the monumental task of recreating herself after losing her memory. What would it be like to have no memory of your heritage and no guidance from the past? How would you know who you were, much less what you wanted to do with your life?

It was good, he supposed, that Jane had set goals for herself. But why California? Why so far away? Why couldn't she stay here?

Silly questions. After all, there was no work for her here. There were no apartments such as the one Jane would like to have, and as for friends, well, he and Rooney and Mary Kate were just about it. In town she might meet people, but Durkee, Wyoming, was thirty miles away and consisted of little more than a post office, a gas station and a convenience store where, in a shed out back, the owner sold junk as a sideline. Duncan hardly thought that the town of Durkee was enough to keep Jane here.

After giving up the search for the styptic pencil, he went downstairs, surprised at how late it was. Jane sat at the kitchen table leafing through his mother's cookbook. She had been trying to learn to cook, with mixed results.

"Good morning," she said brightly. Her hair held the color of the sunlight streaming through the kitchen window; the fine strands shimmered like gold.

"Good morning," he returned. The place where he had cut himself shaving still smarted.

They heard footsteps on the back stairs that were followed by Mary Kate's sharp knock. "Duncan," she called. "I've brought the Sunday paper."

This was a Sunday morning ritual in which Duncan had long participated with Mary Kate; she walked to the road and retrieved the Sunday newspaper from the box beside the mailbox, and in return, Duncan read her the comics. This ritual persisted, even though at the age of ten Mary Kate was able to read the funnies to herself. Now she peered through one of the windowpanes in the back door, and he hastened to let her in.

"Are you ready for me to read the comics to you, Mary Kate?" Duncan asked.

"As soon as I pet Amos," Mary Kate said, dropping her coat onto the kitchen floor and darting into the living room in pursuit of the cat.

"Come back and pick up this coat," Duncan ordered. "And hang it in the closet."

Mary Kate, having caught Amos, walked slowly back to the kitchen, scratching him under the chin. The cat closed his eyes in obvious bliss.

"Amos likes me," Mary Kate bragged. "The other day he let me rub his stomach and didn't even move. He didn't used to let me do that." She set him down gently on the floor and picked up her coat without complaint.

"Mary Kate, why don't you stay and have French toast with Duncan and me?" suggested Jane. "I'll make it while Duncan reads you the comics."

"You're making French toast?" asked Duncan.

"I found this recipe for Orange Blossom French Toast, and we have all the ingredients. I think I'd like to try it."

"Oh, good," Mary Kate said, grinning from ear to ear.

"We'll be in the living room," Duncan said, leaving Jane to her recipe.

It all seemed so domestic to Duncan, with Mary Kate sitting close on the couch as he read, Amos purring on the rug at their feet, and delicious aromas floating in from the kitchen.

He tried to recall ever having this cozy feeling on a Sunday morning when Sigrid was here, but all he remembered from those days was Sigrid's discontent at being cooped up here on the ranch with only Rooney and himself for company, Mary Kate having arrived shortly before Sigrid departed. And when Sigrid had cooked, it had been done grudgingly. Unfortunately, his ex-wife had never taken to life at Placid Valley Ranch.

He read to Mary Kate with one ear cocked toward the kitchen, where Jane hummed as she went about her tasks; he loved the way she hummed as she worked. Duncan looked up between comic strips, catching a glimpse of an ankle as she temporarily moved out of view, appreciating the way her hair curled against her cheek, and was rewarded for his vigilance by her glance in his direction and a fleeting half smile before she turned toward the stove again.

"The French toast is ready," Jane called finally, and he and Mary Kate sat down with Jane at the kitchen table to eat hot French toast made from a recipe that Duncan recalled from when his mother was still alive. It almost seemed like the old days to Duncan, like the time when he lived here with both parents, to be pouring steaming orange syrup out of the gravy boat with the spout that he had chipped when he was about Mary Kate's age, to be joking and teasing and laughing with Mary Kate and with Jane, who kept urging French toast on him until he asked her if she expected to feed the whole French army. Jane laughed at this, her cheeks slightly flushed with happiness, and Duncan thought, *Why, Jane likes this kind of atmosphere, too.*

After Mary Kate went home, Duncan lighted a fire in the fireplace, then he and Jane spread out the sections of the newspaper on the floor and took turns reading them, passing the most interesting items back and forth with a comment or two. Jane brought the coffeepot into the living room, and Duncan remarked that she made wonderful coffee. Jane replied offhandedly that it was one thing she had learned to do at her short-lived job in the restaurant in Apollonia.

Finally, when the newspaper was neatly piled to one side of the couch, Duncan poked at the fire and, because he was curious, said, "You never talk about your life before you came here. You've never told me how you managed to get along in Chicago."

Jane, sitting on the floor, leaned back against the couch and clasped her hands around one knee. "It doesn't seem like entertaining conversation," she said.

"I suppose you would like to forget about that period of your life," he suggested.

She stared into the fire. "No, not forget, exactly. I'm still trying to come to grips with what happened to me. Maybe talking about it would help. I keep having flashbacks to the hard times, especially to the period when I was in Chicago. It didn't turn out the way I expected, that's for sure." Briefly she looked unsure of herself, like the Little Girl Lost she'd been when he found her.

"What do you mean?" he asked.

"When I arrived in Chicago, I tried to get a job right away, but it's hard to get a job when you have no past," she said.

"What happened?"

"Well, when I went to fill out the job applications, they asked for a social security number. I didn't have one, which posed a problem."

"Didn't you tell your prospective employers about your situation?"

"I was always afraid that if I told anyone I was an amnesia victim, they'd think I wasn't a good risk, so usually I left the space for the social security number blank. If an employer asked me about it, I'd say I'd left my social security card at home and didn't remember the number. Usually that would work for a few weeks or months."

"You could have applied for a social security card," Duncan pointed out.

"I did. The people at the Social Security Administration told me I had to have a birth certificate in order to get a social security number, but of course I didn't have a birth certificate. At that time I was still having severe headaches, and I couldn't pull myself together enough to decide what to do next."

"Poor Jane," Duncan said sympathetically.

"Poor *somebody*," Jane agreed. "I know I have a name as well as a birth certificate somewhere, and probably I have a social security number, too. But there seems to be no way to find out who I am."

"There must be people who knew you before your accident, who were your neighbors, co-workers, something. They must be worried sick about you."

"As far as I know, no one ever came forward to say I was missing. You'd think someone would, wouldn't you?" she said wistfully. Her eyes seemed large and dark, mirroring her sadness. Duncan's heart went out to her.

"Someone like you, someone so beautiful—yes, it does seem as though someone would have cared about you and looked for you," he replied softly.

"Do you really think I'm beautiful?" she asked unexpectedly.

The question took him by surprise, but he didn't have to hesitate. "Yes, I do, Jane. Very beautiful," he said.

She seemed satisfied with his answer. "Beauty isn't a quality that I identify with myself," she explained. "I was so busy trying to survive that I didn't care what I looked like, as long as I was neat and clean. Oh, that reminds me of something I've been meaning to mention. I found a portable sewing machine in my closet, Duncan. Would you mind if I used it to make myself some clothes? Somehow I think I can figure out how to sew."

"Of course," he said.

"There's material, too. I wonder if—"

"Take anything you need," he said. "The machine was Sigrid's, and the fabric was hers, too. She didn't want to take it when she left."

"If you want to ask her again if she wants her sewing machine, I won't mind," Jane said. She hadn't known it was his former wife's; she'd surmised that it had belonged to his mother.

"Nonsense. Sigrid hardly used it, and she won't want it now."

"Thanks. Duncan. I think I'll go upstairs and look through the patterns. She must have been about my size."

"No. Sigrid was heavier," Duncan said; somehow he felt uncomfortable comparing the two women.

"Well, anyway, I guess I'll go upstairs."

"Please don't," Duncan said.

"What?"

"I said, please don't go. This is my only day off. If you go, I'll have to spend another Sunday alone. I enjoy your company." There was a cajoling tone to his voice; he'd never used it before.

Jane, who had risen to her feet, sat down on the couch. "Duncan, I think we should talk about this," she said slowly.

"Is it worth calling one of our meetings?" he asked with a grin.

"Meetings— Oh, I'm not sure. Maybe." She looked confused.

"Well, what's bothering you?" he asked.

"You know what I mean. You're getting too attached—I mean, I'm getting too attached—oh, I don't know." She bit her lip in chagrin.

"You think it will be harder when you leave if we become close now," Duncan supplied.

"Yes, I suppose that's it," she said unhappily.

In the fireplace, flames crawled upward until they consumed another log. The heat made Jane's face glow, and Duncan wished that he'd initiated this discussion sooner. In it he saw a replay of her insistence that Mary Kate not get any ideas about Jane's staying past spring. He stared at her, at a loss as to how to impress upon her how much he wanted her to reconsider.

Jane had blossomed, losing that wan, debilitated look that she'd had at first, and the ample food had filled out that slight frame of hers. The delicate shadows under her cheekbones had disappeared. When she had asked him if he thought she was beautiful, he had felt like shouting out his answer, because not only was she beautiful, but she had imbued this house with that beauty, and for that he was grateful. He had never realized how drab and dull his life had been before she arrived.

He liked everything about her; the way she cared for that little cat of hers, her interest in the llamas, her responsible shepherding of Mary Kate, her thoughtful ways. She didn't deserve the buffeting that life had meted out to her, and he wanted to make it up to her.

He wanted—but what difference did it make what he wanted? At night he often thought of her lying alone in her bed. In his fantasies she came to him, looking soft and ethereal, and he imagined reaching up to her and pulling her down to him, imagined being absorbed into her.

"I suppose we could become too attached to each other," he said with all due gravity, but his thoughts refused to run in this groove and instead leaped around inside his head bearing images that he had only dared to dream. Jane in his bed, Jane stepping naked from the shower and reaching for a towel, her shape outlined by the light from his bedroom, Jane everywhere.

The real Jane wrinkled her forehead, unaware of the way he had pictured her. *What a pity that she will never know*, he thought, and before he knew it, moving as if in a dream, he had taken her chin in his hand, turned her face toward his, and kissed her on the lips.

"Duncan!" she said when he released her. Her eyes widened and darkened; he sensed how much he had shocked her.

"I couldn't help it," he said truthfully.

She looked rattled. "It's just—just—"

"Just what?"

"That I've never thought of you in that way. Never."

"How do you think of me?"

She ran a hand through her hair and looked off into space somewhere over his left shoulder.

"As—as someone who has been more than kind to me. As someone who is easy to be around. Easy to respect. Oh, Duncan, I don't know," she said in obvious dismay.

Quickly he masked the disappointment in his eyes. She didn't reciprocate his feelings. She had no inkling of how he felt. He found her innocence very moving, although at the same time he was annoyed by it.

"Forgive me, Jane," he said, knowing how abject he sounded. That was genuine, too, as real as his feelings for her.

"This changes things," she said with certainty. She looked perturbed in a way that he had never seen her.

Duncan, you idiot, now you're three times a fool, he told himself. Aloud he said, "It needn't change anything. It was a whim, a mark of affection, and no more than that."

"I'm reading too much into a simple kiss. Is that what you're trying to say?" Her troubled eyes rested on him, seeking reassurance.

"Yes, perhaps. It was a mistake, and it won't happen again." He sounded stiff and formal even to himself. No telling what she thought.

She sighed heavily and leaned back on the couch, massaging her elbows through an old sweater of his that was a favorite of hers. She closed her eyes and seemed to be deep in thought.

He was angry with himself. He'd muddled their relationship, that was for sure. In the past few weeks he had allayed her basic mistrust with both words and actions, and then, with one misguided kiss, he had destroyed what they had. He couldn't allow himself to show his bitter disappointment that she didn't reciprocate his feelings; he made himself adopt an air of icy detachment.

"I think it's time I went to my office in the barn," he said. He got up and took his coat out of the closet.

Jane was up immediately.

"Duncan, I'm not angry. Only confused," she said. She looked so lovely standing there with the winter sunlight from the window slanting across her face.

"Confused," he repeated.

"I've had a lot to deal with where men were concerned," she told him. "All of them weren't as nice as you."

He paused in the act of shoving his Stetson onto his head.

"Which means what?" he asked, the ice starting to melt.

"That as far as I know, I've never had the chance to develop a normal relationship with a man. That I've never even wanted to."

"And do you want to now?" he demanded.

Her eyes searched his.

"Maybe," she said, her voice a mere whisper.

He shook his head. All this was almost too much to fathom. He was accustomed to being straightforward and up-front with his relationships. He didn't know about all this hemming and hawing and trying to figure out the meaning of the many nuances that could be felt when a man and a woman were getting to know each other.

But he wanted to learn, and most of all he didn't care to repeat past mistakes.

"Like I said, I'm going to the barn. I'll be back in time for dinner."

"Shall I roast the chicken as we planned?"

"Sure," he said, able to give her an easy smile.

She handed him his muffler because he had forgotten it in his haste, and he felt her eyes on his back as he made tracks toward the barn. Whatever had happened back there, it was a surprise to him that he felt pretty good about it, when all was said and done. Except that he didn't know what his next step should be, or if there would even be a next step.

AFTER DUNCAN LEFT, Jane went upstairs and sorted in a desultory way through the fabric that Sigrid had not taken with her. It was hard to think about sewing now that the situation with Duncan had taken this new and disturbing twist, although he had reassured her about it. *A simple mark of affection,* that was what he had called his kiss. She decided that she could accept this explanation. After all, he had asked for nothing more.

She sat with neatly folded packets of fabric in her lap, reviewing her experiences with men, or at least all the experiences she could recall.

There'd been a lecherous fry cook in one of the restaurants where she'd waitressed for three weeks; he'd been more than twice her age and claimed to have arthritis, but he was certainly agile enough when it came to pinning her up against the shelves in the pantry. Fortunately, she'd been fired before things went too far. Then there was the calculating owner of a laundromat where she'd been employed to make change and sell detergent powder. He was married and the father of two little girls, but that didn't stop him from asking her out.

A man who worked at an employment agency had promised her a pleasant office job if she'd move in with him, and a teenage newspaper vendor had once blurted that he had a crush on her. And a wino in a shelter had forced his attentions on her, until she was rescued by a minister who was there to provide chaplaincy services.

She might say that her experiences with men had been less than satisfying; or, being honest with herself, that they'd mostly been terrifying. It wasn't easy to trust men after what she'd been through.

She reminded herself of a few standouts: the concerned and kindly Dr. Bergstrom, who had treated her after she was found in the ditch, a thoughtful shelter attendant who had let her stay in the building to use his phone to look for work during the day, when homeless people were expected to vacate the premises, and, of course, Duncan.

Duncan. She liked him so much. If she were ever to fall in love with someone, she'd like it to be with someone like him.

In a sense, Jane was curious. She knew her experience with men had been mostly limited to the deadbeats, the down-and-outers, the immoral and the lechers. This was not a fair cross section of American men. It was reassuring that someone of Duncan's caliber thought she was beautiful, liked her, and was physically attracted to her.

Duncan had always made it clear that he recognized her as a real person, someone unique. When he kissed her, he was reaffirming that sense of herself that she had long hoped to develop. Also, and this surprised her, she had liked kissing him. She hadn't pulled away. But she knew that what she felt wasn't love.

Though she had had little experience as far as she knew, she understood what went on in a physical relationship between men and women. She had heard plenty of talk about it; there were all those affairs on the daytime dramas, and when she'd lived on the streets, she had even seen frantic, shadowed real-life couplings. That kind of thing seemed ugly and shameful. She had never had any doubt that love was the ingredient that made sex worthwhile.

But to make love—ah, that was an experience that she had begun to anticipate with pleasure. To lie in a man's arms, to be cherished and adored so much that he wanted to be that close to you and you to him; it seemed like a wondrous way to express affection.

When she thought about it, she couldn't imagine the act of intercourse taking place without love. It was a value left over from her past life, her other life, the one she'd had before she became Jane Rhodes. That and other values kept popping up out of nowhere, often confounding her. How did she know that love made what went on between men and women special? If she had experienced it in her past life, it was one of the things that she longed to remember.

Her attitude toward love caused her to wonder if she had ever been in love, just as her knowledge of fabrics and sewing inspired the question, *Did I lead a very domestic sort of life? The kind where I often sewed, say, for my children?* Had there been a man to love, children for whom she sewed little overalls and pajamas, dancing costumes and dresses?

Duncan's kiss had shown her that she was ready to learn more about herself, including satisfying her curiosity about a real relationship with a man, present as well as past. She'd meant it when she'd told him that she thought he was lucky to have been married once.

She stood up, tossed the fabric onto the floor, and went to the window where she could see the barn. She half wanted to march over there and confide her feelings to Duncan, because he was the only person she had to talk to.

Only this was something she couldn't discuss with Duncan.

She sighed and picked up a large piece of blue wool. She loved the way it felt between her fingers, and she idly inspected the warp and woof of the fabric. Warp and woof? How did she know those terms? The warp was the thread that ran lengthwise in the loom, and the woof was the name for the threads that crossed the warp.

She sank onto the edge of the bed, overcome by this glimpse of knowledge. She hadn't known that she knew anything about fabric or how it was made; the information had merely arrived unbidden out of that vast black store hidden somewhere within her brain.

What else did she know that she couldn't call to mind? Would she ever remember all of it, or even most? In the future, what important snippets of her past would drift into her consciousness from time to time, perplexing and confusing her? How would she deal with them when they did?

And what if she developed a relationship with a man, and then one day the memory of a husband and children surfaced? What on earth would she do then? Who would come first—her old family or her new relationship?

How would she deal with something like that?

Chapter Nine

Any concerns about getting too close to Duncan were squelched by the distance he effectively put between them during the ensuing week. He spent long hours in the barn, barely talked to her at meals, and either rode into Durkee or went over to Rooney's every night. She watched television and waited for his tread on the back porch in the evenings. Most of the time she was already asleep when he came home.

She missed the easy rapport that had developed between them, but at least she had Mary Kate for company. Mary Kate continued to drop by every day after school.

One day Mary Kate arrived at her usual time, and Jane hurried to let her in.

"Hi, Jane," Mary Kate said breezily as she dumped her book bag on the couch. "Let's go over and talk to the llamas today."

Without too much regret, Jane turned off the TV set.

"Okay," she said, slipping on her coat. "Maybe you can explain more about their ear movements to me." This was something that they had only briefly touched upon on their other visits to the llamas, and Mary Kate was pleased to oblige Jane's request.

"Grandpa says that the Indians in Peru called the llamas their silent brothers," Mary Kate said importantly as they shoved their hands deep into their pockets for warmth and headed toward the barn. "That's silly, I think, because everyone knows that llamas hum, and that isn't what I call silent. Anyway, they communicate in other ways. Duncan calls it body language."

"Give me an example of llama body language," Jane suggested as they reached the pen and Mary Kate unlatched the gate. Jane went through and left Mary Kate to put the latch back on. Dearling knew Jane now, and she was always friendly to her.

"Well, see how Crystal's ears are laid back? That means she feels unhappy or maybe threatened. And see how Dearling's ears are perked forward? She's interested in you. Sometimes when I want to get the llamas to do something, I just put my hands up to my ears like this, and I move them the way a llama would in order to say something." Mary Kate put her hands up into the sides of her head and wiggled them at Dearling in llama fashion. Dearling pointed her ears even farther forward. Jane could have sworn that the llama was smiling.

"I don't know what you said in llama ear language, Mary Kate, but Dearling must like it," Jane told her as she stroked Dearling's silky head.

Mary Kate giggled. She hugged Dearling around the neck. "Come on into the barn, Jane. Let's say hello to Flapjack and the other horses."

Dearling followed them as they left the pen, and once again Jane let Mary Kate fasten the latch after them. It was only by chance that she glanced back to observe that the gate was swinging free.

"Mary Kate," she said. "You've left the latch undone."

"Oh, will you fasten it, Jane?" Mary Kate said carelessly.

About this, Jane was prepared to be firm. "*You* do it," she said. "You know that Duncan and your grandfather think gates and latches are very important." She, as well as Mary Kate, knew the results of her irresponsibility on past occasions.

Reluctantly Mary Kate turned and went to the gate, latching it carefully this time, so that the llamas were secure in their pen. Jane double-checked the bolt to make sure that Mary Kate had done the job right this time. She could well imagine Duncan's fury if his breeding females were somehow to escape.

In the barn, the horses were in their stalls. Flapjack swung his head around with interest when they approached him.

"Good old Flapjack," Mary Kate said. She went to a sack hanging from a nail on the wall and produced a carrot. "Here," she said to Jane, "you can feed this to him."

Jane held the carrot on the flat of her palm and Flapjack gobbled it down. He was a beautiful animal. His coat was shiny and black, and he had a white star on his forehead. She stroked his nose; it was like rubbing warm velvet.

Mary Kate led her from stall to stall, reeling off the names of the horses.

"Here's Rabbit, my grandfather's horse. And this is Nellie Mae. Grandpa rides her sometimes. Here's Diggory; Sigrid used to ride him. This is Jericho, my pony, but I'm getting too big for him. Grandpa says he'll have to get me a bigger horse this summer."

"Why don't you just ride Nellie Mae? Or Diggory?"

"Well, I tried to ride Nellie Mae one time and she tried to scrape me off on a fence post. And Diggory's getting kind of old. I want a pretty little mare, maybe a roan. Do you like roans?"

"I don't know much about horses," Jane admitted.

"Well, this summer when I get my mare, you and me can ride together. You could start out on Diggory. He's real gentle."

Jane stopped stroking Diggory's smooth flank and turned toward Mary Kate. "But I told you I wasn't going to be here this summer," she said patiently.

Much to her surprise, Mary Kate's face flushed red, except for a white line around her mouth. "I won't let you leave," she said in quiet fury. "I won't."

The child was suffering, Jane could see that. And yet Jane wouldn't, couldn't change her mind.

"Mary Kate, please try to understand. I—''

Mary Kate's blue eyes flashed and she stomped her foot. "You're not leaving here, Jane, you're not!''

"But—''

"You're staying! Forever and ever! I'll hate you if you go away!'' And with that Mary Kate wheeled and ran out of the barn, slamming the door behind her so hard that the rafters shook and Nellie Mae let out a startled whinny.

The tantrum had happened so quickly and so fast that it momentarily stunned Jane. She waited for a moment, thinking that a repentant Mary Kate might return as quickly as the angry Mary Kate had slammed out. But the young girl didn't come back, and after a minute or so, Jane looked around and saw Dearling calmly chewing her cud in a corner.

Jane sighed. "Come along, Dearling,'' she said, putting her arm around the little llama's neck, and an acquiescent Dearling followed Jane as though she was used to doing this every day of her life. When they reached the females' pen, Jane unlatched the gate and shooed Dearling inside, taking care to make sure it was securely fastened when she closed it.

She looked around in vain for Mary Kate. Well, she had probably run home and was sulking. In any case, Jane didn't feel like discussing her departure again. The child refused to understand that it was inevitable.

Jane felt heavyhearted and sad, wishing she could do something to help Mary Kate, but the more she thought about it after she got back to Duncan's house, the more sensible it seemed to leave well enough alone. Dispiritedly Jane pushed aside Mary Kate's book bag, which lay forgotten on the couch, and resumed hemming a skirt she had made for herself.

After a while, she heard Rooney's pickup truck start up over by the barn and hoped, for the child's sake, that he had decided to take her to town with him; she knew he was going because he had stopped by earlier to ask if she and Duncan needed anything from the grocery store.

Jane tied off her thread and went into the kitchen to check on the pot roast. In a few minutes, she saw Rooney walking purposefully up the freshly shoveled path to the back door.

She met him there. "I thought you went to town," she said with some surprise.

Rooney's eyebrows were knitted in the middle of his forehead. "I was going to," he said. "Then I heard Duncan take my truck. Do you know where he went?"

"Duncan? I don't think he went anywhere, because he told me he was going to be looking over the account books in the barn until supper."

"But I heard it start up and thought he must have decided to run an errand."

"I don't think so," Jane said.

"Well, tell Mary Kate she can ride into town with me when Duncan gets back with my truck," Rooney said.

"Mary Kate's not here," Jane replied, her heart turning over.

"Not here? She always stops by after school." He looked rattled.

"She did, but when we were over in the barn, we had a— a slight disagreement, and I assumed she went home," Jane told him. Her forehead wrinkled in a frown. Where could Mary Kate be?

"She's not at the house," Rooney said flatly.

The thought occurred to them at the same time.

"The truck!" both exclaimed.

"She couldn't drive your pickup truck," Jane said, shaking her head in denial.

"The keys were in it—maybe she could. I'm going over to the barn to see if Duncan is there," Rooney said, sprinting away.

"I'm coming, too!" Jane called after him and followed, pulling on her coat as she ran.

Duncan was bent over paperwork in his office, and glanced up in surprise as Rooney and Jane burst through the door.

"Mary Kate's gone, and so is the truck!" Rooney shouted.

The three of them ran outside and stood for a moment scanning the ranch. Llamas in their pen looked up in interest. The darkness of a lowering sky hinted at snow in the offing, and there was no sign of Mary Kate. The pickup truck was nowhere in sight.

"Where could she go?" Jane wondered aloud as they all clambered into Duncan's Cherokee.

"To the highway," Rooney said grimly as a few flakes of snow began to waft out of the sky.

"She wouldn't," Jane said with certainty.

"You don't know Mary Kate the way we do," Duncan said in an ominous tone.

Duncan drove as fast as he could in the frozen rutted tracks of the driveway. It wasn't easy driving, and Jane doubted that a child could handle a truck under these conditions. Jane realized that none of them knew what to expect. What had ever possessed her to take Rooney's truck?

Jane recalled the anger Mary Kate had shown when she was acting out her frustration at Jane's certain departure; maybe the youngster had deliberately decided to misbehave in a really big way in order to get everyone's attention.

"There! That's the truck," Rooney said, sitting forward in his seat and squinting ahead through the downy swirls of snow.

Jane saw that the pickup truck had pitched headlong into a high snowdrift, denting the snow with its bumper. Clouds of vapor unfurled from the exhaust pipe, and the engine was still running. Loud country music blared from the truck's radio.

Duncan leaped from the Cherokee and wrenched open the door on the driver's side in an instant. Out tumbled Mary Kate.

"Grandpa!" exclaimed Mary Kate, throwing herself into her grandfather's arms.

Duncan reached inside the pickup and turned off the ignition key, silencing both engine and radio. It was suddenly very quiet.

"You scared us," Jane said, shattering the stillness with her shaking voice.

Mary Kate blinked at her. "I didn't mean to. I only wanted to drive the truck."

"We'll talk about it when we get home," her grandfather said, and they could tell from the tone of his voice that he was furious. The air was filled with frosty clouds of vapor from their breath.

"Is the truck okay? I didn't mean to hurt it, but it slid off the road," Mary Kate said, once they were in the Cherokee.

"It looks like there's no great harm done. You were lucky, young lady. Exactly where did you think you were going?" Duncan inquired, glancing briefly over his shoulder as he backed and turned.

"To the mailbox. I thought that if it was a half mile to the mailbox and back and I drove at one mile an hour, it should take me an hour to get home. I drove real, real slow."

"Well, 'real, real slow' or not, it was a stupid thing to do, and I'm going to reckon with you when we get back to the house," Rooney said.

Mary Kate looked momentarily chastened, then said, "I had to scrunch the seat way forward to reach the pedals, and I sure wish I knew how to get the emergency brake off."

"You mean you drove all the way up here with the emergency brake on?" Duncan asked in disbelief.

"I guess so," Mary Kate said with a shrug.

"Where'd you learn to drive, anyway?" Duncan asked.

"By watching you and Grandpa."

"Well, next time watch how we release the emergency brake before we shift into gear. Just in case you decide to go for any more little outings around the neighborhood."

"She ain't going on any more little outings," Rooney grunted. "I can promise you that."

Duncan let out Mary Kate and Rooney in front of their house and parked the Cherokee at the barn. When he and Jane had returned to the house, Duncan said, "I thought Mary Kate spent her afternoons with you these days."

Jane heaved a giant sigh. "She usually does, but today we had a disagreement. In a way, I suppose that it's my fault that she took the truck."

"Don't be silly. Mary Kate's always doing something she shouldn't do. You know that."

"I think she does these things when she wants more attention and isn't getting it. Like this afternoon." Quickly Jane related how Mary Kate had insisted that Jane mustn't leave the ranch, and how she had firmly told her young friend that her departure was inevitable.

"Rooney tries to cope the best way he can," Duncan said. "It's hard being mother, father, sister and brother all rolled up into one. Mary Kate will certainly miss you when you're gone. She models herself after you, and, as a matter of fact, ever since you arrived here, her behavior has improved."

"I can't take credit for that," Jane objected.

"Of course you can. You're good with her, you know. She listens to you."

"I'm company for her," Jane said.

"No, it's more than that."

Jane thought about it. He was right. She discovered that she felt good about making a difference in Mary Kate's life, even for so short a time. She was pleased that Duncan had noticed it.

"Mary Kate is a sweet child. All she needs is love and attention," Jane said.

"So do we all," Duncan said reflectively. Then, as though he realized he had said too much, he stood up and went to the door, giving her one long last look before going out and closing the door softly behind him.

She stared at the door, wishing he had stayed. They had just shared more of themselves than they had in days. She heard the rumble of the Cherokee's motor as Duncan left, and went up to bed before he came home.

While she was lying there in the dark, she realized that their conversation had not been about Mary Kate as much as it had been about themselves.

MARY KATE'S PUNISHMENT for driving her grandfather's pickup truck turned out to be a restriction to their house every afternoon for a week and a strict prohibition on any contact with Dearling. This hit her harder than any of them anticipated.

Jane, who stopped by the Rooneys' the next day to drop off some cookies that she had baked, happened to arrive when Mary Kate was throwing a tantrum.

"But Dearling won't know what happened to me if she doesn't see me for a whole week," Mary Kate was raging when Jane stepped inside the door.

"I didn't know what happened to you, either, when you disappeared with my truck," Rooney pointed out.

"It's not fair, it's not fair," the young girl sobbed as she ran off to her room.

"Thanks, Jane, for the cookies. I'm sorry Mary Kate's in such a state," Rooney said apologetically.

Jane had to speak loudly to be heard over Mary Kate's crying. "You're welcome, and tell Mary Kate I said hello," she told Rooney, but Jane found the child's sobs heart-wrenching. She knew that Rooney felt that he had to punish Mary Kate for such a serious offense, but she wished he had chosen some way other than prohibiting his granddaughter from seeing Dearling. The llama seemed to be a stabilizing influence on Mary Kate, and she knew that to the child herself, this must be the cruelest punishment that Rooney had ever devised.

Jane went to the barn every day to get Dearling and to talk to her the way Mary Kate did, but knew that as far as the llama was concerned, she wasn't a good substitute. She always had the feeling that Dearling was looking over her shoulder, expecting to see Mary Kate come bouncing around the corner of the barn any minute.

It was a slow week, and when Mary Kate was finally released from her restriction, Jane didn't have the heart to say no when Mary Kate, showing her old exuberance, appeared on the back doorstep, begging her to come over to the barn for a reunion with Dearling.

Dearling seemed thrilled to see Mary Kate again, butting her in a playful fashion and blowing gently into her face. Mary Kate laughed delightedly.

"She didn't forget me, did she, Jane?" she said, her arms locked around Dearling's neck.

"No, Mary Kate, it would be pretty hard to forget someone like you," Jane said with a smile.

When clouds blocked out the sun and it became too cold to stay outdoors, Mary Kate, in a lively mood, insisted that they go into the barn, but not just to see the horses.

"Does Duncan let you play in there?" Jane asked doubtfully.

"Sure. Let's play hide-and-seek."

"Well..."

"Come on, Jane, don't be a stick-in-the-mud. I'll be It and you hide." Mary Kate turned her back, hid her eyes against the side of the barn, and began to count loudly by fives.

"Wait a minute," said Jane. "What am I supposed to do?" She wanted to honor Mary Kate's request; it seemed the least she could do after Mary Kate's long confinement, and the child was obviously lonely for playmates.

Mary Kate stopped counting and wheeled around. "Haven't you played hide-and-seek before?" she asked incredulously.

"I don't think so," Jane said. All this made her feel exceedingly incompetent.

"I'm It. I count all the way to one hundred by fives, and when I'm through counting, you're supposed to be hidden. Then I try to find you." Mary Kate crooked an arm over her eyes and started counting again.

Jane looked around her frantically, trying to figure out where to hide. Duncan's horse hung his head over the door to his stall and whinnied. A couple of barn cats, half tame, jumped down from a barrel and ran into the shadows.

Jane, still not completely comfortable around the horses, decided to avoid their quarters as hiding places. Mary Kate had already counted all the way to seventy before Jane finally let herself quietly into the tack room and concealed herself behind the sawhorses where the llamas' panniers were stored.

"Ready or not, here I come," Mary Kate cried, and Jane could hear her slamming doors and growing progressively closer in her search.

When she found her, Mary Kate pounced. "There you are! Now it's your turn to be It!"

So Jane hid her eyes and counted, and afterward she found Mary Kate behind some old clothes hanging in a cubbyhole beside Duncan's office door. The game went on for almost half an hour, much to the interest of Flapjack and the other horses.

They were both tiring of hide-and-seek when Jane found Mary Kate in what appeared to be a storage closet that was seldom used; the door was behind a heap of tractor parts. When Jane opened the door unawares, suddenly Mary Kate reached out, caught her by the wrist, and pulled Jane down into a pile of something soft and warm.

Jane sputtered and pulled herself to a sitting position. Whatever it was, the stuff was full of dust, and she began to sneeze.

"What *is* this, anyway?" Jane asked when she had her sneezing under control. She picked up a handful of it and rubbed it between her fingers.

"It's llama wool," Mary Kate replied, taking a clump of it and lobbing it at Jane. Jane tossed a fistful back, and soon they were exchanging volleys of it, until Jane began to sneeze again.

Finally they pulled themselves to their feet, and Jane brushed the wool off her clothes. It was feathery light to the touch; she held it up so that she could see it better. The fibers were long and ranged in color from white to every imaginable shade of brown and gray.

"It's beautiful," Jane said, reaching down for another handful. Something about the fibers seemed to awaken a tactile sense that she'd never known she had. Suddenly she longed to feel the pull of it between her fingers as she twisted and drew it out into yarn.

Confused by this thought, she stood there staring down at the wool. A tiny blip of memory sparked her consciousness. It reminded her of the time when she had been sorting Sigrid's fabric and had realized that she knew the meaning of the terms warp and woof.

"Jane? Jane! Come on over to our house, I want to make some hot chocolate. Grandpa said it was okay as long as I use hot water from the tap and instant cocoa. Jane? Don't you want some hot chocolate? You can bring a bag of that wool, if you want. Duncan wouldn't mind."

Jane followed, her mind cluttered with newfound information that seemed to unwind from a dark place inside her head. In order to spin wool, she would need a spinning wheel. She had used one before. She knew it. And as for the wool from the llamas, it seemed softer than sheep's wool. She had no idea how she came by this information; she just *knew*, that was all.

Wool, spinning wheels, warp and woof. What did they all mean? What relation did they have to her past life? All she knew was that she wanted to encourage more such knowledge to unfold from her subconscious. Maybe it was the key to the person she had once been.

That night she asked Duncan about the wool in the closet.

"Oh, we've been collecting llama wool as long as we've had llamas, which means that there's many years' accumulation of it. Most of it is in bags, but Mary Kate got in there one day and opened several of them, leaving the wool strewn about. You're welcome to all of it, if you like."

"I need a spinning wheel, Duncan," she said.

"A spinning wheel?" he said with some surprise.

"So I can spin the wool into yarn. Don't ask me how I know how to do it. I just do."

Duncan regarded her with a smile and more interest than he'd shown in a week. "A spinning wheel, huh? Well, what do you know."

"Do you have any idea where I can get one? Are there any catalogs around where I might be able to order it?"

"I'll see about it," was all Duncan would say, but she noticed that when he came back from the barn later that night, he walked around suppressing a sly smile.

Duncan left the ranch before she woke up the next morning and didn't leave a note to let her know when he'd be back. She ate a solitary breakfast, but by the time she was loading her dishes into the dishwasher, she heard the Cherokee coming down the driveway.

She stood at the door and watched wide-eyed as Duncan opened the back doors of the Cherokee and unloaded a very old spinning wheel.

"Where did you get it?" Jane asked, wearing a big smile as he brought it in and set it down in front of the fireplace.

"Friend of mine in Durkee has a little junk shop. I recalled seeing this in there one day and wondering who in the world used spinning wheels anymore. Now I know." There was laughter in his eyes.

Jane tentatively approached the spinning wheel. It was dusty, but the drive cord was taut and no parts were missing.

"Are you sure you know what to do with this thing?" Duncan asked skeptically.

"Yes, oh yes," she said happily. "I just don't know how to thank you."

"I guess none of those characters on the soap operas you've watched have ever been given a spinning wheel, right?" He was laughing at her now, and in a new spirit of fun, she chased him out of the house, returning to gaze at the spinning wheel for a long moment before she went to get the llama wool that she had spent last night laboriously picking and cleaning in preparation for the day when she would spin it into yarn.

It felt strange but familiar to sit at the old wheel and begin the rhythm of twisting and drawing out the wool as she pedaled with her foot. She worked tentatively at first; then, as yarn coiled on the bobbin, she became more confident. By the time Duncan appeared for dinner, she had spun a skein of lovely brown yarn.

After that she spun every day, feeling more at ease with the spinning process as time went on. *I wish I had a skein winder,* she thought to herself, then wondered, *How do I even know what a skein winder is?* But she *did* know that a skein winder could be attached to the spinning wheel for the purpose of skeining up the wool she was spinning. It was just another example of random memory, and it frustrated her with its hint of her unknown past.

Later that week as she sat spinning, Duncan, who had started staying home in the evening hours, said, "You look so contented when you work at that."

She smiled at him. "I feel good when I'm spinning. I don't know how it figures into the life I once lived, but I'm sure it was a skill that was important to me. Here, Duncan, hold your hands up. I want to wind this yarn around them."

Duncan complied, his eyes never leaving her face as she swayed from side to side, wrapping the wool around his outstretched hands.

"You know," she said, "I don't think that going to California is going to be enough. I think I want something more, something else."

"Such as what?" Duncan asked in surprise.

She divested his hands of the wool and wrapped the skein carefully in tissue paper. She took her time in answering. "I don't think I can start a new life until I know who I was. Who I *am*."

"You said that no one could find out anything about you after they found you in the ditch," he reminded her. "They checked police reports, missing person reports, newspaper accounts, everything. Didn't they?"

"Yes, but at the time I had to leave the search up to others, because I was too ill to work on it myself. Now that I'm feeling stronger, I'd like to attempt to figure out where I came from, where I lived, what I did for a living." Her face became dreamy. "I try to see myself in a house somewhere, sitting at a desk balancing a checkbook, perhaps, or walking my dog. Do you suppose I had a dog? And if I did, where would he be now? I've got to find out my true identity, Duncan." She wrapped her arms around her knees and rested her chin on top of them.

"Why is this so important all of a sudden?"

"I keep learning things about myself, suddenly realizing that I know how to use a spinning wheel, for instance. I've come to hope that eventually I might remember who I am, but what if that happens when I'm in the middle of a new life? What if I were suddenly to regain my memory and realize that I've got a husband and a couple of kids someplace? Wouldn't I have to go back to them?"

"I don't know," Duncan said, as though this was a new thought.

"You've always understood before," Jane said urgently. "Don't you see why I need to know?"

For the first time since she'd known him, Duncan seemed unnerved.

"Well?" she prodded gently, wanting his blessing and needing his help.

"I suppose you're right," he said, but his features had become strained and taut, and a muscle in his eyelid twitched.

"Help me," she said in a pleading voice. "You will, won't you?"

He turned to her, and for a brief moment bewilderment flickered in his eyes. He overcame it quickly. "If that's what you really want," he said slowly.

"I think it is," Jane said. "I know it is."

"Then that's what we'll do," Duncan said, but he looked less than enthusiastic.

"What's wrong? Don't you like the idea?"

"In some ways," he said.

"What does that mean?"

He shrugged, and his eyes burned into hers. "You might not like what you find," he said.

She stared at him, then managed a smile. "I'll have to take my chances, I guess."

"Why not leave well enough alone, Jane?"

She thought about it and said, "I'm more afraid of not knowing who I am than of knowing."

"They say that what you don't know can't hurt you," Duncan offered.

"What you don't know certainly can hurt you, especially if it rears its ugly head at an inopportune time," Jane retorted. She softened her tone when he drew his lips into a tight line, and continued, "Anyway, I'd love to find out that I have a family—mother, father, brothers and sisters. I feel so—so alone in the world," she said with an embarrassed half laugh.

"You have us," he said, encompassing the ranch with a gesture. "You have me, Mary Kate and Rooney."

She was glad he considered her part of their close-knit little group, and her heart warmed to him. "Mary Kate and Rooney—I don't know them as well as I know you," she said slowly. "But you—you've been wonderful to me, Duncan. My own brother couldn't have been more decent."

"On that, I think I'll call it quits for the evening. Good night, Jane," he said gruffly. He stood up, put on his coat and headed toward Rooney's.

She had said something wrong. But what? That she wanted to find out who she really was? Or was it her comment that he had been as kind to her as a brother would have been? She had meant it only as a compliment.

Anyway, why wouldn't he be pleased that she thought of him as a brother? They were both really alone in the world. She had no known relatives, and he had none living. Was it only that he had trouble thinking of her as a sister? Did he think that she was being overly familiar in even suggesting that they had a brother-sister kind of relationship? Or was it only that he had never considered how comforting it would be to have siblings that he could depend on when he needed someone?

Okay, so she wouldn't say anything like that again. She felt that she had overstepped her bounds, or failed him in some indefinable way, or—oh, what was the use?

Feeling vaguely troubled and unsure of her ground, she gathered her skeins of yarn and went upstairs to bed.

Chapter Ten

A brother. She thought of him as a brother, for Pete's sake. It was not an auspicious sign.

What would it take to show her that he cared for her in a way that was anything but brotherly? How could he get that point across without scaring her half to death?

Her emotions were still raw; she admitted that she was wary of men. Still, he thought she had learned to trust him. No, he *knew* it. So it must be something else that made her hold back.

He studied himself in the mirror the next morning while shaving. Was he physically attractive enough to appeal to her? He'd never had any complaints in that department before, but his face was more weathered now than it had been when he was in his twenties, and there were deep lines around his eyes. He had all his own teeth, and his hair wasn't receding yet. No beer belly; the work around the ranch kept him in shape.

He tried parting his hair on the other side, but he didn't think the change made any appreciable difference in his looks, so he parted it again the way he always had. He swished mouthwash around his mouth, just in case. No sense in taking chances.

When he went downstairs, she smiled at him while she was taking eggs out of the carton, and, acting as normally as he could, he found a package of bacon in the refrigerator and stuck it into the microwave so that the slices would separate more easily.

"Good morning, Duncan," Jane said serenely.

"Morning," he replied as he laid the bacon slices in a pan and shoved it back into the microwave oven to cook.

They sat down at the table when the eggs were ready, and Jane asked, "How am I doing on the eggs?"

"Just the way I like them," he told her, and it was true, too. "How am I doing on the bacon?"

She munched on a piece, holding it daintily between thumb and forefinger. "Exactly crisp enough," she said.

They went on eating, and Duncan wondered if this spirit of cooperation between them was the problem. Was it possible to be too compatible? It might be better if they didn't get along so well. Still, he couldn't imagine having a squabble with Jane. They always talked everything out, which was the way it was supposed to be—but it certainly hadn't been that way with Sigrid.

"I've been thinking," Jane said carefully before they got up from the breakfast table, "about going back to Illinois. To talk to the people who found me." She watched him, waiting for his reaction.

This was mainly one of dismay, although he didn't want her to know that. "Have you been thinking about this long?" he asked.

"The idea seemed to be in my head when I woke up this morning," she admitted with a little laugh. "It's become a possibility since I've found out that I might be able to sell my llama yarn."

"How did you find that out?"

"I was looking through one of those magazines you get from the llama breeding association, and I found an article about llama owners who sell and use the wool for knitting, crocheting and weaving. In the classifieds there was an ad placed by a woman who wants to buy yarn, so I phoned her. She wants to see samples. I'll have my own income if she buys some." Jane's eyes were shining.

"You mean you'd use the money you make to pay for a trip back to Illinois?"

"Yes," Jane said. "I'll pay you back what I owe you, don't worry. I can travel cheaply and—"

"Forget about the money. What about our bargain? You promised you'd stay until the cold weather's over," he said gruffly.

"I'm well now, and I'd only be gone a week or two. I'll come back, Duncan. I promised you I'd stay."

He couldn't share her pleasure in this idea; he didn't want her to go. He was still concerned about her health, and for reasons that he recognized as purely selfish, he didn't want her to leave the ranch. Such a journey would remove her from his sphere of influence.

"Duncan?"

He hurriedly drank the last of his coffee. "You can do whatever you want, I suppose," he said and fled the house, feeling her reproachful gaze on his back.

He was ashamed of himself for being unfeeling, but he needed time to get used to the idea of her leaving, even briefly. And he didn't want to talk about it with her. Thinking about it was hard enough.

Then he came up with the idea that Jane might be able to find out the things she needed to know about her past without ever leaving the ranch. He didn't mention this to her. In fact, he spoke to her very little during the next few days. He was aware that she was waiting for him to mention her proposed trip, but he didn't. If she was making plans to go, he didn't want to know.

Behind the scenes, calling from the barn where she couldn't hear, he spent the next few days telephoning. He called the sheriff's department that had handled the investigation of Jane's case in Tyree County, Illinois, and was told that the investigating officer was long departed from the department. A new man answered the phone, and to Duncan's surprise, the fellow told him that he had stumbled upon this unsolved case during his first week there and had been curious about it ever since.

"It's like this," said the detective, a guy named Bill Schmidt. "A woman appears in a ditch near one of the locals' cornfields, and nobody knows where she came from. Afterward, nobody knows where she went, either. I mean, I can't figure it, you know what I'm saying?"

"I know," Duncan assured him. "As it happens, she's here with me. What we still don't know is where she came from. Are there any leads?"

"Leads? You got to be kidding. The case isn't closed, but it might as well be. We're overworked and underpaid around this place, you know? We don't have time to work on old cases."

"What if I brought her to Tyree, so she could see the records of her case?"

"There's not much to see, although she's welcome to go through our file. The guy who investigated told some of the fellows around here that he figured that her boyfriend got mad at her and dumped her out of the car. Or something like that."

"Something like that," Duncan repeated. Various scenarios flashed through his mind, and inwardly he shuddered.

"You could talk to Jones, the farmer who found her. He has a kid who was with him that day. Practically fell over her where she was lying in the ditch, I hear. It's not something you'd forget easily, you know what I mean?"

Duncan hung up, wondering if he had made any progress. He decided that he had at least made a contact with someone who was chatty enough to convey whatever information he knew, and at least this Schmidt fellow sounded interested and energetic. That was something.

He placed his next call to the administrator of Tyree Hospital, who was polite but could not provide any information at all.

"No, Mr. Tate, as far as we know there were no identifying labels in her clothing. She had no identification whatsoever. I'm sorry we can't help you," she said.

Discouraged by this dead end, Duncan hung up the phone when the conversation was over, shrugged into his coat, left his warm office and trudged toward the house, which was lighted from within by the lamps Jane always turned on in the evening. He recalled all too well what it was like to come home to an empty house. He had done that every evening since Sigrid left, until Jane came.

A chill wind nipped at his cheeks. The night was clear, and in the pen beside the barn, the llamas shuffled and hummed to one another. The pungent scent of wood smoke drifted toward him, and he realized that Jane had lighted a fire in the fireplace. It was good to be going home to Jane.

Under the shelter of the porch, welcoming light beamed from the windows, casting a mellow glow over the snow. As he drew closer he could see Jane's blond head bent over her spinning wheel, and he smiled to himself. She had taken to that thing and made it her own, and he was pleased that she had shown this new interest. New interest? It must be an old interest, otherwise she wouldn't know how to do it. He wished he understood more about how her memory worked. Or didn't work.

And if her memory did improve, where would that leave him? Especially if there were, as she had pointed out, a husband and children somewhere, anxiously awaiting the return of a wife and mother. The thought of Jane as someone else's wife was like a wound to the heart.

He had fallen for her, and she thought of him as a brother. Someday she would pick herself up and move away, and that would signal the end of warm welcomes in his house, the end of companionable evenings sitting beside her as she spun, the end of the connectedness that he had begun to feel for another human being.

He supposed Jane never thought of that. She was too all-fired eager to start a new life in California, of all places.

Well, let her go if she wanted. He wouldn't stop her. He would even help her, if that was what it took to keep her happy; he had given his word about that when he was persuading her to stay until spring.

It hadn't been hard to be kind to her when she needed kindness, nor had he had a hard time forgiving her for stealing from him, and he hadn't found it difficult to bear with her in those early days, when she still didn't trust him. No, with Jane everything was easy, including falling head over heels in love with her.

The hard part was going to be saying goodbye.

HE THOUGHT ABOUT IT for a long time before he reluctantly told her about calling the Tyree County sheriff's department and the Tyree hospital. The main reason that he wanted to tell her was that she seemed determined to find out about her past, and he didn't want her to discover later that he had been there first, without telling her.

The opportunity to divulge this information came at dinner one night when she told him with quiet pride that she had sold her entire store of llama yarn to a hand knitter in Vermont.

"I didn't make a lot of money, but it's a start," she said. "As soon as I can afford it, I'm going back to Illinois and try to retrace the path that led to that ditch in Carlton Jones's field."

Duncan felt his mouth go dry, but could no longer keep from telling her what he knew. "Jane, I have news," he said.

She stopped chewing and swallowed. She gave him a questioning look.

"I called the Tyree sheriff's department the other day. I talked to the detective on the case, Bill Schmidt was his name. He's not the officer you talked with after they found you. He's a new guy who took over after the other one left. Anyway, he says he'll let you look at the records if you want to."

"Look at the records?"

"The report of the detective who came to your hospital room."

"Detective Sid Reedy," Jane said slowly. "I remember that day."

"If you'd like to talk to this Schmidt, why don't you call him up? Maybe he could send you a copy of their records. And you could phone Carlton Jones tonight, if you'd like."

"I want to go there, Duncan. To see if standing in that ditch outside Tyree brings back memories of anything that happened to me. To ride along the highway and try to figure out why I was there and where I was going." Her gaze was steady.

"Are you sure, Jane, that this is what you want to do?"

"Absolutely sure."

Duncan decided from the set of her chin that Jane was going to go on the trip whether he liked the idea or not. He heaved a big sigh. "Well, if you're so set on going, I'll lend you the money," he said. "It'll take a while to make enough money from selling your wool, and you should probably go as soon as possible, so your tracks won't get any colder than they already are." He surprised himself by offering this; he still didn't want her to leave.

"I've already imposed on you too much," she said.

"You'll pay me back," he pointed out. "How do you plan to get there, anyway?"

"By bus, I guess. It's probably the least expensive way to go. There must be a Greyhound leaving from Rock Springs."

"I think you should fly. A bus trip would be so tiring, and you're still recuperating," he said, watching her closely. She had suddenly gone thoughtful.

"Is anything wrong?" he asked.

"I'm scared, Duncan," she said. She turned wide eyes upon him, and he saw the panic in them.

"You said you wanted to go!"

"You have to admit that taking off by myself on a search like this is pretty intimidating," she said.

He considered this. True, she had seemingly come into her own here at Placid Valley Ranch, but then again, this was a place where she felt comfortable. The world had not treated her well the last time she'd been out in it on her own, and the things that had happened to her were hard for her to forget.

"I could go with you, I suppose," he said after a while. He hardly dared to hope that she would agree to this. But he was rewarded by a leap of interest.

"You could? Really?" She seemed dazed by his offer.

"If you want me to," he said.

"It's another imposition," she said slowly.

He regarded it as an opportunity, but he didn't say that. "I'd rather fly than take the bus. Will you call the airlines and make the reservations, or shall I?" he asked, expecting an argument or at least a long discussion, but she surprised him.

"I will," she said, smiling the brilliant smile that always made his heart turn over, and went to do it right away.

"YOU AND JANE are going to do *what*?" Rooney asked, when Duncan told him that they would be leaving.

"Search for her past," Duncan said.

Rooney scratched his head. "What for?" he inquired.

"She's afraid she left some loose ends that might need tying up," Duncan told him.

Rooney considered this. "Well, she might have. You never can tell," he agreed after a while.

"So we're going to fly to Chicago, rent a car and head for southern Illinois."

"One question for you, Duncan," Rooney said. "Why the hell do you care?"

"Hey, you know I like to read mysteries. Why not try to solve one?" Duncan managed a crooked grin, but he was well aware that he couldn't admit how much he cared for Jane even to Rooney, who was his closest friend.

"I sure hope you won't be gone long. Jane either. Mary Kate is going to miss her like crazy."

"You and Mary Kate will have to hold down the fort around here, Rooney. You think you two can manage it without Mary Kate demolishing the whole place?"

"Jeez, Duncan, I don't know. Just to make sure, why don't you take Mary Kate with you?"

Duncan laughed. "I don't have anything against southern Illinois, that's why. Anyway, she's been behaving herself pretty well since she drove your pickup into that snowbank, hasn't she?"

"Yeah, but the truck ain't never going to be the same. She burned up the emergency brake, you know."

"It could have been a lot worse."

"A lot of things could be worse. Which brings us back to our original subject. Why don't Jane leave well enough alone?"

"Because she can't, Rooney. And if she can't, I can't, either." With that, Duncan jammed his hat on top of his head and walked out of Rooney's house into the cold night air. Let Rooney make anything he wanted out of that statement. Being in love with a woman who had no intention of staying with him was hard enough; not talking about it was even harder. Maybe Rooney would get the hint and understand how it was between them.

"BUT I THOUGHT you were staying until spring!" Mary Kate cried accusingly.

"I am, Mary Kate. In fact, I should be back before then," Jane said.

Mary Kate tossed the wool she had been carding for Jane onto the floor and jumped up from her seat at the kitchen table. "I want to go with you," she said.

"That's impossible, you know. You have to go to school."

"I hate school. I hate everything," Mary Kate said.

"That's not true—you love Dearling," Jane reminded her.

Mary Kate stuck out her bottom lip. "Uh-huh, I love Dearling," she agreed. Her expression darkened. "You said you were going to teach me to spin."

"I can show you how to spin with a simple drop spindle before I go," Jane said soothingly. "And I'm hoping you'll take care of Amos for me while I'm gone."

Mary Kate considered this. "He does like me," she conceded. Then she frowned again. "Do you have to go, Jane? Absolutely have to?"

"Yes, Mary Kate, I do. It's really important to me to find out my real name and where I came from. I've decided that I can't go on with my life until I know."

"Why?"

"Because I keep remembering fragments of it, and I'm curious about them."

"Why?"

"You would be, too, wouldn't you? Think how you would feel if you didn't know where you came from or where you belonged."

"Why?"

Jane was growing impatient. "Stop playing this silly 'Why?' game with me, Mary Kate. I'm trying to talk to you the way I'd talk to another adult."

This seemed to sober Mary Kate. "You are?"

"Sure. You're my friend. I'll miss you when I'm in Illinois, you know."

"You'll miss me? Really?"

"Really. And I'll bring you a present."

"A present!"

"What would you like?"

Mary Kate considered this. "A frilly dress. With ruffles and petticoats and sleeves that you can see through."

"A frilly dress?" Jane was stunned. Mary Kate wasn't the type for party dresses.

"Yeah. A pink one."

"Well, okay," Jane said dubiously.

"Something nice, Jane. Really nice," urged Mary Kate.

Jane smiled. A soft shade of pink would brighten Mary Kate's sallow complexion.

She bent to hug Mary Kate. "I'll buy you the nicest, pinkest, frilliest dress I can find," Jane promised.

DUNCAN AND JANE left the ranch a week later and flew into Chicago in early afternoon. They rented a car and left the city, Jane staring with conflicting emotions at the buildings looming against the city's skyline. Behind them jets soared up and out of O'Hare Airport, and Jane couldn't help but recall all the times she used to wish she was on one of them and headed for California.

"You're awfully quiet. Is everything okay?" Duncan asked anxiously.

"Not really," Jane was able to tell him.

"You look tired," he said.

Jane pulled down the car's visor and checked her reflection in the mirror. Her face was pale, and there were deep circles under her eyes. She had hardly slept at all last night. She shoved the visor up again and tried to smile through her fear that somehow the city might swallow her up again, if she wasn't careful.

"Seeing Chicago again makes me feel like I've been socked in the stomach," she said.

"Was living here that bad?"

"I couldn't keep a job, I was constantly trying to find a place to keep warm, and I mostly lived in shelters for the homeless. One time some men came in a police wagon and started rounding up people on the streets, and we heard later that they'd been taken to a mental hospital. I thought they'd get me next, and I hid in the basement of an abandoned building with some other street people until I was sure the threat had passed. Yes, it was that bad." She hunched herself into the corner of the seat.

"Didn't you go to the authorities and explain what had happened to you? That somebody was supposed to help you get on your feet and find a job?" he asked incredulously.

"Sure, but no one seemed especially interested. I don't think anybody believed me. The prevailing attitude was that I was a lot better off than a welfare mother with children, so I was left to fend for myself. I was still having headaches when I lived here, and it made holding a job difficult."

"You don't seem to be having headaches now," Duncan observed.

"It's really odd, but I don't think I've had a headache since I fell and hit my head in the snowstorm the night you found me in the mine," she said. They were on an interstate now, driving past neat subdivisions. Traffic moved faster, and she sat up and looked around. Now that they were away from oppressive tall buildings and ugly warehouses, she felt better.

"And your cough is almost gone, too," Duncan said, trying to cheer her.

"The antibiotic medicine did wonders. I thought I'd need a warm climate to shake it," she told him.

"Is that why you decided to go to California?" he asked. He was curious as to why she had chosen that particular state for her new start.

"There was another reason, too. All the time I spent in the library trying to keep warm, I used to read a lot. One of the magazines I read outlined a training program they have there. I thought I could learn to use a computer, so I could get a good job someplace."

He sent her a sharp look. "Is that what you still want?"

"Maybe. Oh, I don't know. It all depends on what we find out on this trip. Perhaps I have marketable skills and I just don't know it." She stared out the window at a passing blue van. It was a Ford Econoline, and it somehow seemed familiar. She shook the feeling off because there was nothing she could tie it into; there was no van like it at the ranch.

The flat land stretched out white and frozen on both sides of the road. They were in the country now, and the roads were straight with few intersections between the towns. Duncan held their speed at a steady fifty-five miles per hour, and the dotted line in the middle of the road hypnotized her so that all she wanted to do was let her head loll back against the seat. They played the radio to break the monotony, but soon it became part of it, droning on and on about commodity prices or community happenings that had nothing to do with them. They were travelers in a strange land, part of the landscape but curiously detached.

It was growing dark when they reached the outskirts of Springfield. Duncan pulled the car off the interstate and into the parking lot of a large chain motel. Jane waited while he went inside and registered them in two different rooms.

When he came out, he seemed to be thinking about something else, and she had to ask him their room numbers twice. The rooms were on an inside hall, and Jane trailed behind him, lugging the suitcase she had borrowed. He offered to carry it for her, but she refused. Duncan shook his head, as if to say that it was her own business if she didn't want his help, which made her feel as though she had fallen short of some mark that she hadn't even known was there.

He unlocked the door of her room for her and handed her the key.

"Let's eat dinner later at the restaurant across the street," he suggested. "Say, at seven o'clock?" His eyes in the light from the lamp on the wall seemed overly anxious.

She smiled and he seemed to relax. "I don't have a watch," she reminded him. "I won't know when it's time."

"I'll call you on the phone," he promised. He shifted awkwardly back and forth; Jane thought about asking him if the unfamiliar shoes he wore hurt his feet. At home he always wore boots. Suddenly feeling shy with him, she didn't ask him about the shoes.

"I'll see you later," she said instead, and went inside. She heard his room door open and close next door.

Jane set her suitcase on the luggage stand and looked around. The window faced the parking lot, where she could see their rental car. She closed the sheer draperies, but not the heavy light-blocking ones, and moved restlessly around the motel room, examining it. She opened a door, thinking it was a closet, and found its twin shut and latched. The second door must open on Duncan's room. She closed the door on her side very carefully so that he wouldn't hear.

After that, an inspection of the dresser drawers turned up a folder full of stationery; she hated the dresser with its plastic top, but the little plastic glasses in their wrappings of cellophane on the tray there amused her. She tested the double bed, which after the comfortable one at Duncan's ranch seemed hard, and the rust-colored carpet was ugly.

She'd grown accustomed to the welcome of a lived-in room full of lemon-polished furniture and scented with the fragrance of wholesome food cooking in the kitchen. *You've gotten awfully particular,* she chided herself. A few months ago she would have counted herself lucky to be in a room such as this for only a few hours. Here there was all the heat she could want, there were clean sheets, and no one was around to tell her to move on.

But she had changed since she arrived at Placid Valley Ranch. What had once seemed like enough—a warm place to live, plenty of food—was not adequate for her needs now. She had to have more. She had to know who she was.

She lay down on the bed to rest, and before she knew it she was asleep. She didn't wake up until Duncan called her on the phone.

"Hi, beautiful," he said. "Are you ready to go to dinner?"

"I fell asleep," she admitted, thinking that "Hi, beautiful" didn't sound like the kind of thing Duncan would say.

He laughed, and she didn't let him in on her puzzlement.

"I'll be knocking on your door in ten minutes or so," he told her.

When she hung up the phone, it was a few seconds before she could move. All at once Duncan was acting differently. Had he been this way on the ranch? She didn't think so.

There he had always been helpful and forthright; she could usually tell what he was thinking. As soon as they'd checked into the motel, he'd changed. It was as though he was trying to figure out how to act in these circumstances, as though he were trying to impress her.

But why?

She was used to his habits, used to the way he acted around her, used to *Duncan*. She didn't want anything between them to change.

What was she thinking? That Duncan was interested in her in a way that she couldn't accept?

No, that was ridiculous. They'd already covered that ground the time that he'd kissed her.

If anything was wrong, it must be her imagination.

Chapter Eleven

She and Duncan had never been anywhere together except on the plane today, and she realized that she was as nervous about it as a girl on her first date. Which was an unfortunate comparison, she told herself. This wasn't a date. This was just Duncan.

When he rapped twice, she opened the door to her room. He'd had his hair cut before they left Wyoming, and while it usually grew slightly down over his ears, now it didn't. His ears looked pink and shiny, as though he'd scrubbed thoroughly for this outing, and she wanted to smile at the idea. Instead she only stepped into the hallway to join him.

When he took off his coat in the restaurant, she saw that he had put on a suit. She'd never seen him wearing a suit before, but he looked wonderful in it. She couldn't recall ever thinking that Duncan was handsome, but now she realized with a start that there was no man in the restaurant who was better looking.

The waiter came to take their order. Duncan ordered a steak, and when Jane hesitated and said that she didn't know what she wanted, he ordered the same thing for her. She was glad, because she found that she couldn't think about the choices on the menu with him sitting across from her, looking as though he was hanging on her every word. This was another difference from the way things were at the ranch.

What to talk to him about? She cast about for something, anything. She didn't understand why it should be so hard to think of a topic; talk had always seemed to flow easily between them.

She knew that Duncan was having an equally hard time trying to start a conversation. But this was small solace when her tongue seemed to have turned to lead, and her brain was too mushy to think. She had an idea that they were both thankful when the waiter brought their salads.

Every word Duncan said seemed pulled from him; it was unnatural, unreal. Jane wished that she had made this journey alone, and then was glad she hadn't. She was grateful for his presence and most of all for his help. His help... Maybe they could talk about tomorrow.

"Do you think I should bother to go to the hospital when we get to Tyree?" she asked.

He latched onto her question as though it were a lifeline. "I think the first stop should be the sheriff's department. Then you can decide if it's worthwhile to go see this Carlton Jones and his son, or whether you want to drop by the hospital."

A shadow passed across her face. "I know all the nurses and doctors at the hospital would be glad to see me. I was a favorite. Yet I'm reluctant to go there." She finished the last of her salad and sat back.

"Why?" Duncan wanted to know.

She shook her head. "Why should I deserve any more of their attention?"

"They'll be happy to see that you survived," Duncan said. "There's a lot to be said for that. It wasn't easy."

"No, it wasn't," Jane said, recalling all the times she'd been evicted and the close call when she might have been shipped off to the mental hospital; when you were on the streets, if anyone suspected you of acting irrationally, they'd get suspicious. Sometimes it was hard not to act irrationally when your head had been aching for a solid week and you'd gone without a decent meal for that long, too.

"It's not easy for you to think about those days, is it?" Duncan observed with a sharp look after the main course arrived.

"I suppose not," Jane responded. "After all, I don't feel that far removed from that time in my life."

Duncan stopped eating and held her gaze with his own. He reached over and covered her hand where it rested in her lap. "Those days are over," he said firmly. "Believe it."

Embarrassed by the steadiness of his gaze, she lowered her eyelids. They finished eating in silence.

After dinner, Duncan surprised her. "Let's go into the lounge," he said.

Through an archway framed by wrought iron scrollwork Jane saw a bar where people were sitting and drinking, and from farther inside came the sounds of a live band.

"I don't know," she said doubtfully, but Duncan overcame her objections when he took her hand and led her inside.

In the small cocktail lounge they were seated at a table about the size of one of the big dinner plates at the ranch, and Jane commented on this. Duncan laughed. She hadn't thought that what she said was all that funny but was pleased that Duncan thought so. Maybe she'd think of something else to make him laugh. She couldn't stand the way either of them was acting tonight.

They ordered drinks, but Jane didn't know what to order and took Duncan's word for it that she would like a whiskey sour on the rocks. When it arrived at their table, she sipped it and made a face.

"It tastes like rotten lemonade," she said, and he smiled but didn't laugh.

"Why don't we dance?" he suggested. He started to get up, but her hand on his arm stopped him.

"I'm not sure I know how," she said, eyeing other couples on the dance floor. One man was whirling his partner around and around in wide circles; as Jane watched, he dipped her so that her long hair touched the floor.

"All you have to do is follow me," Duncan said as though that settled everything, and before she knew it they were standing on edge of the dance floor facing each other. Jane's knees felt a bit unsteady, but she thought it was because of the alcohol in her drink. She put her left hand on his shoulder, the way the other women on the floor did with their partners, and discovered to her consternation when he took her right hand in his that her palm was sweaty. If he noticed, he didn't react.

The beat was slow and rhythmic, and the tune was not something that she recognized. It was good music for dancing, however, and as she loosened up, she found that she was stepping on Duncan's toes less and less. He wasn't a spectacular dancer, like the man who was showing off on the opposite side of the floor, but after a while their feet began to move in predictable patterns.

He looked down at her. "See, I told you it would be easy," he said, his eyes glinting with pleasure. He pulled her slightly closer, and she stiffened again, but when she learned that it was easier to follow him when he held her like that, she relaxed.

He smelled of fresh pine scent, and she remembered that Mary Kate had told her that he used a pine-scented shampoo. She smiled at the memory. That had been on the first day that she'd arrived at the ranch, when Mary Kate had given Amos a bath with that shampoo.

Duncan chose that moment to lean away from her. His expression was puzzled. "Something funny?" he asked.

"Just remembering something Mary Kate said," she told him, and he replied, "Let's not worry about Mary Kate while we're on this trip." After that he pulled her so close that his chin rested against the top of her head and her body was pressed against the length of his.

The colored lights over the bandstand glowed bewitchingly. She and Duncan let the other dancers flow around them and moved their feet only slightly, and Duncan held her closer and closer until she was full of the scent and the feel of him in her arms. For that was where he was, in her arms, and the sensation was so new and so overwhelming that she chose not to say anything until she could get a handle on the way she felt about it.

On the occasions when the music stopped playing, they didn't sit down but waited for it to start up again. Before they'd got up to dance, while she was watching the other couples on the dance floor, Jane hadn't realized that dancing was anything more than a refined type of exercise. She hadn't been prepared for the way the music made her feel, or for her reaction to being so close to Duncan.

It was confusing. She had already decided—in fact, she thought that they had decided together—that their feelings for each other weren't sexual. And yet this was definitely a sexual stirring. Sexual electricity, even.

When she'd lived in Chicago, there had been buildings that she passed every day; she had gotten used to the look of them. And then for some reason, maybe when she was riding a bus or walking down a street she seldom used, she'd look up at a building that had seemed so familiar before and wouldn't recognize it from the new angle. Away from the ranch she was seeing, feeling, experiencing Duncan from a different perspective.

They had forgotten about their unfinished drinks on the table, and when the band took a break, they came back to find that the ice had melted. Duncan took one taste of his whiskey and soda and made a face.

"I'll order more drinks," he said.

Suddenly she didn't want to dance anymore, didn't want to sit across from him at this tiny table and make small talk. Fill-in words weren't enough, *she* wasn't enough. She wasn't up to any further posing or posturing for his sake or hers.

"I—I think I'm ready to go back to my room," she said quickly. "It's been a long day." She could think of no other way to put an end to whatever was going on between them.

For a moment he looked as though he was going to object, but then Duncan apparently decided to play along and to ask no questions. He paid the check without comment, although she knew that he was watching her. She turned away, unwilling to explain herself.

Duncan had driven the car across the highway to the restaurant in case it started to snow, and neither of them spoke as they drove back to the motel. She turned slightly to look at him, admiring his strong profile. He didn't speak; maybe he felt as constrained as she did.

At the door to her room, Jane turned to face him and forced herself to smile.

"Thanks, Duncan. It was a lovely dinner," she said. She had to restrain herself from the impulse to reach out and touch his cheek with her fingertips.

He smiled, too, but the smile didn't reach his eyes.

"I'll see you in the morning," he said. "We'd better get an early start."

"Right," she said. Her heart started to pound, and she knew that if she didn't go inside her room right away, he would bend his head and kiss her.

"Good night," she murmured quickly, and closed the door, leaving him standing there.

At that moment she was sure that Duncan recognized the highly charged emotional tension that was developing between them, and that in some way he was even responsible for making it happen.

She slept fitfully between the chill sheets of her bed, jolted awake several times during the night by unfamiliar noises. People talking in the corridor, doors opening and closing, the moan of the plumbing pipes—all of this made her uneasy. She felt so alone in her sterile motel room. She knew that it would be unseemly for Duncan to sleep in the same room with her, but all the same she missed the familiar sounds that accompanied him. At the ranch she could hear him running the water in the morning as he shaved, knew the familiar *thwump!* that his closet door made when he closed it just before coming downstairs in the morning.

She was lonely, she realized. Lonely for Duncan. Lying on her stomach, clutching the stiff motel pillow, she finally slept.

BREAKFAST THE NEXT DAY was hurried because they wanted to get on the road. Fresh snow had fallen in the night, and ice had left hoary patterns on the car's windshield. Duncan scraped the ice and snow away, and soon they were headed south toward Tyree.

Sometimes they didn't see a car for miles on the rural roads; the only things that accompanied them on their journey were wires swinging from pole to pole in front of fields white with snow. Duncan seemed worried, withdrawn. Jane tried to engage him in conversation several times, but after she realized that he wasn't responding in anything but monosyllables, she gave up. She wished he would be his old self again. If anyone had the right to be anxious and upset this morning, she did. After all, she was facing the prospect of finding out who she really was, and she could only imagine the impact that the discovery would have on her goals and her dreams.

Jane kept consulting the map on the seat between them. Forty miles to Tyree, then thirty, then twenty.

As they approached the town, Jane's throat went dry and she tried to remember the passing scenery. That billboard—did she recall seeing it on the day of her accident? That house in the middle of that field—was the yellow brick familiar? But nothing seemed like anything she'd seen before.

Once they were there, Duncan drove directly to the sheriff's department and they went inside to meet Detective Schmidt, the man who had replaced the other detective on Jane's case.

Schmidt, a wiry fellow with a good-natured grin, ushered them into the boxy room that served as his office and invited them to sit down.

"So you came back to find out if anybody knows who you are, is that right?" he asked.

"I'm hoping that someone will remember something that will help me find my identity," Jane said.

"Everybody familiar with this case seems to think that you were pushed out of a car onto the highway that runs past Carlton Jones's farm. You had a head injury. I tend to think that you were driven to Tyree and dumped by somebody passing through. Do you remember anything at all about the events preceding your appearance in that ditch?" asked Schmidt.

Jane shook her head helplessly. "No," she said quietly. "Nothing."

Schmidt studied her intently for a moment. "Well, that makes it tough, you know what I mean? Now, as far as Tyree goes, this was kind of a big case. The papers around here published your picture and told the story of how you were found. Seems like someone from these parts would have come forward at the time if they knew you."

"There was no one," Jane said. "No one."

Schmidt shoved a folder across the desk. "This is what you came to see," he said. "Everything we have on 'Jane Doe' is in there. Do you go by any other name?"

"I use the name Jane Rhodes, but I know it's not my real name," Jane said. She leafed through the information in her file. It seemed sparse, and she tried to cover her feelings of disappointment. She had been hoping for more.

"You said you've never closed the investigation," Duncan said.

"That's right. 'Course, we didn't get very far. No clues. Mighty strange, you know what I mean?"

"Where do you think we should start looking for clues?" Jane asked.

"Talk to Carlton Jones and his teenage son, see if they remember anything. We asked them the usual—you know, like did they recall any strangers in the area that day, that sort of thing. They didn't have a clue. I hear that the kid was

pretty upset, he thought you were dead when they found
you. He might be glad to see that you're very much alive.''

"Do you think she's in any danger?'' Duncan asked,
looking up from Jane's file. "It says here that they thought
at the time that her head wound might have been caused by
a blunt instrument. Is there any chance that somebody
might come after her now, if she starts asking around?''

Schmidt considered this. "I can't say,'' he said after a
while. "Maybe, maybe not. Seems like if somebody wanted
to hurt her, they would have done it before. She was a patient in the local hospital, she worked in Apollonia, she was
there for anybody to find.'' He eyed Jane. "Anyone ever
make any threats? Bother you in any way?''

Jane thought about the men who had tried to abuse her,
the person who had stolen her coat in Saint Louis. Those
weren't deliberately calculated actions, though; they had
happened on the spur of the moment.

"No,'' she said.

"All I can say is, report anything that worries you, but we
think you're safe,'' Schmidt told them.

They stood up to leave, and Schmidt said, "Good luck
with your search. We'll be in touch with your number at the
ranch in Wyoming if we find out anything more, but
frankly, we don't have the manpower to do the kind of
painstaking work you're going to be doing.''

"Can you suggest a place to stay around here?'' Duncan
asked as they were about to walk out the door.

Schmidt chuckled. "There are only two, but I'd recom-
mend the Prairie Rose Motel. Turn right at the light and go
two blocks. And good luck with your search.''

They checked into the last two rooms available at the
small Prairie Rose and went out again to a nearby Western
Steer steak house for a quick dinner. In the foyer of the restaurant Jane used the phone to call Carlton Jones. He
seemed pleased to hear from her, to know that she was in
good health, and he readily invited them to the farm after
dinner.

Jane sat forward in her seat as they drove to the farm, peering out at the dark fields on either side of the car.

"Do you recognize any of this?" Duncan asked.

She shook her head. "It's so dark," she said. She strained to see something, anything that would give her her bearings. "Slow down, Duncan, I think that's the sign Mr. Jones told me to look for," she said at last.

The sign said Jonesdale Farms, and the road led to a brown-shingled house surrounded by trees. The path to the door was shoveled clear of snow, and when they knocked, Carlton Jones welcomed them with an expansive smile.

"Come in, come in," he said, rubbing his hands together.

Jane stood awkwardly on the mat before the front door.

"Let me take your coats," he said. He spirited their coats into an adjoining room and hurried back. They sat in his living room and Carl, as he asked them to call him, wanted to be told Jane's history since she left Tyree. She obliged, skipping over the worst parts.

"The reason we're here, Carl, is that I'm hoping you might know something more about how I happened to be in that ditch," she told him earnestly.

"I wish I did," he said with a doleful shake of his head. "But I told the sheriff's men everything I knew. First thing I knew was when I found you there."

"You don't recall a car, or perhaps an odd noise, or anything at all the night before?" Duncan asked.

Carl thought for a moment, then shook his head again. "I looked for tire tracks or something at the side of the road, but I didn't see any. I wish I could help you, but, well, I don't know anything more."

Duncan stood up. "Then I guess we won't waste any more of your time," he said.

"Please don't go," Carl said. "I've made coffee, and Ollie and I baked a cake. Imagine that," he said with a chortle, "I baked a cake! My wife died a few years back, and I've had to learn to take care of Ollie and me almost from scratch, but I'd never thought I'd be baking cakes.''

Thinking that Carl might be offended if they left, Jane restrained Duncan with a look of resignation. They both sat down again, and Carl disappeared into the back of the house.

"I thought you wanted to leave," Duncan said under his breath.

"Well, I do, but he's so *nice*," Jane whispered back.

"Careful, Ollie, don't drop it," they heard Carl say in the kitchen just before Ollie appeared, his tongue between his teeth in concentration, as he balanced plates of cake in his hands.

"Ollie, you remember me, don't you?" Jane asked. She attempted to put the boy at ease with a smile.

"Sure," Ollie said. "You're the lady we found."

Carl returned with coffee for the adults and a glass of milk for Ollie. He sat down and Jane decided to keep pursuing information, any information that might help her.

"Do you remember anything at all unusual about that day?" she asked Ollie gently.

He swallowed a mouthful of chocolate cake and shook his head. "It was early in the day yet," he said. "We'd only just got up, Pop and me."

"So I must have been left in the ditch the night before," prompted Jane.

"Yeah, I remember old Jiggers—that's one of our dogs— was missing. We went out early to look for him."

"It took us a while to find him, too. The ambulance blowing its siren ran him off when it came to get you," Carl said with a twinkle.

"We didn't ever find him, Pop. He came home all by himself," Ollie said.

Carl and Ollie got into an interminable discussion about what time Jiggers had loped up to the back porch after his jaunt in the woods.

Jane had nearly finished eating her slice of cake before she could slip into the discussion and ask, "How about the night before? Do you recall any strange cars or lights or anything?"

Carl started to shake his head, but Ollie said, "Yeah, I do remember something! I was out looking for Jiggers—sorry, Dad, I know I was supposed to be in bed, but I was worried about Jiggers and went out after you were asleep. Anyway, I was out looking for him, and I was trying to stay out of the woods, 'cause it's scary in there in the dark. And I was on the other side of the field from where we found you. I saw this van going real slow up by the road."

"Ollie! How come you never told anybody from the sheriff's department about the van?" Carl wanted to know.

Ollie's face flushed and he looked down at his shoes. "I forgot. And even if I'd remembered, Pop, I probably wouldn't have said anything. You told me not to go out by myself after dark."

Carl looked exasperated, but Jane smiled warmly at the boy. "Do you recall what color it was? What make? If it had an Illinois license tag?"

Ollie thought, but shook his head. "I shined my flashlight on it, but it was so dark that it was hard to tell," he said. "The taillights lit up the back of it a little. It was blue, I think. Or green. No, I think it was blue, because my friend's father was looking at a blue van to buy, and we went with him just a few days before. But he didn't buy it, so I know it wasn't him."

"Did anyone get out of the van?"

"I didn't see anyone. Only a van driving real slow. Then it speeded up and went fast."

"How about the license tag?" Duncan asked.

"I was too far away to read it," Ollie said.

Repeated questioning of Ollie turned up no further information, but Jane thought that the van might be a good lead. After Carl told her how to get to the exact spot where she'd been left all those months ago, they thanked both Joneses and left.

It was too dark and cold to examine the ditch near the cornfield that night, so they reluctantly headed back toward the Prairie Rose.

"A blue van—does that mean anything to you?" Duncan asked.

Jane shook her head, but then a picture of a blue van unexpectedly flashed into her mind. They had seen a blue Ford Econoline van on the road yesterday as they were driving out of Chicago, and she had noticed it, had studied it carefully, had even wondered why she was paying so much attention to it.

"Duncan," she said with a kind of darting excitement.

"What is it?" he asked, glancing quickly over at her.

"A blue van. I remember something about a blue van."

"What?" he asked, sounding alarmed.

She squeezed her eyes closed and tried to think. The only thing that appeared was the image of the blue van she had seen riding along next to them on the highway yesterday. She willed the image to disappear, to clear her mind for something else to come through, but it refused to go. A blue van, a blue van . . . something about a blue van hovered on the edge of her consciousness, waiting to be recognized.

"The Coke spilled," she said suddenly.

Duncan braked the car. They were coming into the outskirts of Tyree now, and a bright sign from a local hamburger joint cast a fleeting glow across his face.

"What Coke?" he asked.

"A can of Coke was sitting in one those consoles that fits over the engine compartment in a van. It got knocked over and spilled all over the carpet, and I was angry and wanted to clean it up." She didn't know where the words were coming from, and suddenly her mind went blank.

"*What* are you talking about?" Duncan said frantically. He pulled into the Prairie Rose parking lot and switched off the engine.

She turned to him, feeling as though she had accomplished a major breakthrough.

"I don't know, Duncan, I can't understand what it means, but I *remember*! I *remember*, Duncan!"

He looked startled, but when he saw that she was serious, that she really had remembered something about her past life, he opened his arms and she fell into them.

All Jane could do was say over and over, "I remember, I remember," and soon she was sobbing the words as though her heart would break.

Chapter Twelve

Jane didn't want to be alone. She couldn't be alone. She had to talk, and Duncan was happy to oblige her by listening.

It was much too cold to stay in the car, so he bundled her up the walkway to the motel, making sure she didn't slip on one of the many ice patches.

"It's so strange," she said, heedless of his hurry to get her inside where it was warm. "I have a clear memory of a big van, and it was blue just like Ollie saw, and I know I was sitting in it and the Coca-Cola went all over the floor, and I was angry because it was making a big mess and—"

"Shh," he cautioned as they approached the door of her room. "Someone nearby may be trying to sleep."

She lowered her voice. "So I looked around for something to blot up the Coke, and that's where the whole scene stops."

Duncan unlocked the door of her room for her, and she put a hand on his arm. Her eyes were enormous, and they pleaded with him.

"Don't go," she said. "Please come in."

If he were to be invited into her room at all, he would have preferred the invitation to be couched in romantic terms, but if this was all she could offer at the moment, he wouldn't refuse. They stepped inside her room, and Jane shivered, even though she still wore her heavy coat.

Jane seemed tense, restless, as though she couldn't be still. "It's too cool in here," she said, resetting the controls on the heater built into the wall. After that she seemed not to know what to do with herself. She stared at Duncan for a moment, as though she wasn't quite sure what he was doing there.

"I'd better hang up our coats," she said, and he saw that she had calmed down, but not much. He wondered if he should be concerned about her mental state.

Wordlessly he slipped out of his coat, and she took both his coat and hers and hung them together in the alcove that passed for a closet at the Prairie Rose Motel.

His gaze wandered to the bed, which was an ordinary double bed, but it seemed so large. So welcoming. He looked around for somewhere else to sit. There was only one chair, a stiff plastic-covered armchair, so he sat down on the edge of it. The room was small and intimate; the light from the dim bulb didn't reveal the sparseness or coldness of the standard motel furniture.

Jane returned and hesitated before sitting down on the edge of the bed. Duncan thought it best to return the conversation to her memory of the van.

"You were saying that the Coke spilled," he prodded gently. "Who spilled it?"

Her knuckles bleached white with the force of her grip on the edges of the mattress. She leaned forward in concentration. "I—I can't picture another person," she said finally. "And yet it doesn't seem as though I was alone."

"Were you sitting on one of the front seats in the van? And if so, which one?"

"It seems like I was to the right of the spilled Coke, so I'd be in the passenger side, wouldn't I?" she asked tentatively.

"I suppose so," he said. He felt sorry for her. She seemed fragile and tiny, and the Little Girl Lost quality that had made him want to protect her in the beginning had returned. He wanted nothing so much as to take her into his arms and comfort her, to tell her that everything was going to turn out fine.

To his surprise, she stood up and started pacing the floor. She looked so pretty in the clothes she had made out of Sigrid's discarded fabric; her figure was petite and yet rounded in all the right places. There was certainly nothing wrong with his own memory. Anytime he chose, he could summon to mind a sharp picture of the way she had looked when he stripped off her wet clothes in the old mine and discovered that she was not a girl, but a woman.

Jane stopped pacing in front of him, deep in thought. "I'm sure I was in a van shortly before I was found in the field—it definitely rings a bell. The fact that Ollie saw one late the night before I was found is an important coincidence, don't you think?" she asked. Her eyes were anxious.

"Yes, I do," he said, although it was easier at the moment to think about the unintentionally alluring way she moved than about the blue van.

"And Detective Schmidt might be able to trace such a van," she said. She reached for the telephone. "I'm going to call him."

His hand reached out and stopped her. "It's much too late for phone calls," he reminded her.

"What time is it?"

"It's after ten o'clock. He could be sleeping. Besides, we don't know his home number."

Jane pressed her hand to her temple for a moment and closed her eyes. When she opened them, it was with a rueful laugh. "I forgot about time. I'm so intensely involved in this thing that I don't think about anything else."

"We'll call him in the morning," Duncan said, rising to his feet.

"In the morning," she agreed. She seemed to deflate at the idea that this had to be put off until then, and he could sense her disappointment.

She went to get his coat, and he turned away so that if his longing showed on his face, she wouldn't see it. He would have given almost anything to stay the night with her.

"I'll see you tomorrow," he said more gruffly than he intended, then let himself out of her room. He could have sworn that she said his name as the door closed, and he stood outside listening, in case she spoke again or opened the door, but she didn't.

He let himself into his own room and took in the sight of the tightly made bed with distaste. It was a king-size bed with a mattress that he was sure would be too hard. He wouldn't have chosen a room with such a large bed on his own, but it had been assigned to him by the desk clerk. The size of it would only remind him of how alone he was. He briefly contemplated sleeping on the pull-out sofa that occupied the far wall, then discarded the idea. Those things usually had flimsy mattresses unsuited to his big frame.

As he took his clothes out of the suitcase, he wondered how much longer he and Jane could go on like this. More to the point, he didn't know how much longer *he* could go on like this. This brother-and-sister malarkey was a charade.

He was head over heels in love with her and sure that she wasn't aware of the depth of his feelings. But last night when they had danced, he had been convinced that she had been aroused by their sexual chemistry as much as he had. Dancing with her had been sweet torture, knowing as he did that he could take things no further until she gave him some sort of sign that she was ready. He was honor-bound to be nothing more than her protector until then.

He threw himself across the bed, thumbing through the paperback mystery he'd brought along to read. He couldn't get interested in it, though, because the real-life mystery of Jane Rhodes was so much more absorbing.

He tossed the book to one side and linked his hands behind his head, thinking.

What was Jane's connection to a blue van? And did she really remember spilling a Coke in one? Was it merely wishful thinking on her part? Or perhaps only part of a dream she'd had? He didn't know what to think.

He tried to figure out if he knew how amnesia victims went about regaining their memories. He'd once seen a segment on television's *60 Minutes* about a man who had been missing after an accident where he'd bumped his head, had disappeared from his former life and been absent from home for twenty years or so. After this period of building a new life for himself, he'd been inadvertently hit over the head by the boom on a sailboat, and when he'd regained consciousness he remembered who he was and where he was supposed to be. He'd gone home to discover that he'd been declared dead, his wife had remarried and raised a couple of kids with her new husband.

He turned out the light, rolled over on his side, and tried unsuccessfully to go to sleep. His mind was too active; he kept thinking about Jane in a blue van, Jane in her blue slacks, Jane and her blue eyes. Finally he gave up and turned on the light again. There was no use trying to sleep when he felt so wide awake.

He dressed and went down to the lobby where there was a small display of magazines. In his present frame of mind, he wanted something that wasn't too stimulating, so he bought a newspaper.

He was no sooner back inside his room than he heard a light knock on his door. To his surprise, Jane's voice called, "Duncan! Duncan?" It held a frantic note, and he flung the door open wide to find her standing there in an old flannel robe of his and looking pinched and white.

"Is something wrong?"

Much to his amazement, she hurtled into his room and all but fell into his arms. He steadied her with one hand, closing the door with the other.

"I thought you had left. I came over to knock on the door and you didn't answer and I was afraid you had gone," she said all in one breath. Her eyes were dark with alarm.

"Left?" he exclaimed incredulously.

"Gone home. To the ranch." She clutched his arm tightly.

"I would never do that," he said in gentle surprise. He saw her pulse beating in a pale blue vein at her temple, and realized that she really was frightened.

"But you weren't here," she said in bewilderment, and he slid his arm around her shoulders, to discover that she was trembling as though she was very cold.

"I went downstairs to buy a magazine," he explained. He pointed to the *Reader's Digest* on the table.

"I don't know what's wrong with me," Jane said, her teeth chattering. She managed to calm herself slightly. "I know you wouldn't go off and leave me here alone, it's a completely irrational fear, but it's all I could think of when you were gone," she said, attempting a smile.

"Shh, it's all right," Duncan said as—against his better judgment—he pulled her close. He felt her heart beating beneath the thin robe; the beat slowed as he stroked her hair. He could only imagine the terror in her heart; he had never been alone in the world as she had. That kind of experience was sure to leave its mark, and even though she had come so far since the night he had found her in the mine, she still had a long way to go before she felt totally secure.

Slowly his hand found its way under her long hair and settled on her neck. His touch seemed to have a calming effect on her. She heaved a great shuddering sigh and moved closer, resting her head upon his chest. And that was when *his* heart started to beat louder.

It was a moment of great tenderness between them, and Duncan cautioned himself not to ruin it. He wondered why she had come across the hall to knock on his door while he was downstairs.

Presently Jane lifted her head and asked unsteadily, "Would you mind if I had a glass of water?"

He pulled himself away, though he hated to do it, and went to the sink where he ran water into a glass. She followed him, taking the cup from him after he'd filled it and holding it between both hands as she drank the way a child might.

"Thanks," she said after taking several big gulps. She looked somewhat revived and put the cup back on the edge of the sink. When she turned around again, he saw that the front of her robe gapped slightly, and he averted his eyes.

"Why did you come over to see me?" he asked.

"I remembered something else. When I was in the van—when the Coke spilled—I was worried about some things in the back. Whatever they were, they belonged to me, and I have a vague memory of hoping that nothing happened to them."

"What kind of things?" Duncan said. He was interested, but she was very beautiful, very intense, and he kept thinking of how soft and warm she had felt when he comforted her in his arms.

"Oh—personal belongings. And something else." She wrinkled her forehead in concentration.

"I wish I could help," he said, feeling helpless in the face of her obvious anguish at not being able to recall what she needed to know.

She pulled herself out of her thoughts and focused startled eyes on his face. "You wouldn't have had to get involved in any of this," she said. "You are helping. You *have* helped."

"Not as much as I'd like," he said.

"I can never repay you enough," she said, her voice low and troubled.

"When you get a job—" he began, deliberately misunderstanding.

"I don't mean the money," she returned quickly. "I was talking about the moral support. Being there. It means a lot."

Duncan knew that Jane was sincere, but they seemed to be dragging this conversation out between them. He tried to think of some way to ease her exit. It wasn't what he wanted to do, but he thought she'd better leave before he said or did something stupid.

"I'd better go," she said with that uncanny faculty she had of reading his mind.

He started for the door, but then she raised anxious eyes to his and said in a low tone, "But I'd rather stay."

"Stay?" he inquired.

"Just—to not be alone," she replied. In her eyes he read the message, *Don't get the wrong idea.*

His mind ran off on a couple of tangents. She wanted to stay—but didn't want it to go too far. She was lonely. She was afraid, for some irrational reason that was the result of her background, that he would somehow disappear. She was struggling with a memory that was foggy and unreliable.

In other words, she wanted to spend the night with him, but wasn't looking for anything more than comfort.

Duncan wavered, one part of him wanting to put her out of temptation's way by gently telling her that she should go back to her own room. The other part of him was more human: he didn't relish being alone, either.

"Never mind," Jane said resolutely, correctly reading his uncertainty for what it was. She turned, but he reached out and caught her shoulder. She spun around, her quickness taking him by surprise.

"I overstepped my bounds," she said stiffly. "I'm sorry."

"No," he said, desperate that she understand.

"I'm going," she said, twisting so that he had to capture her in his arms to make her stay.

Her face was no more than five inches from his as he held her there, and he could have kissed her if he'd wanted to. Instead he chose to hold her eyes with his for a long moment, and the communication delivered almost as much impact as something more forceful.

"I want you to stay," he said. "I'm lonely, too."

"Please, I—"

"Nothing will happen that you don't want to happen," he said firmly. "You can sleep on the couch. It makes into a bed."

She only looked at him, and slowly he released her from the circle of his arms. She was breathing hard, as though she'd just run a couple of miles, but so was he. In order to regain control of his emotions, he walked over to the couch and opened it out. It was already made up with sheets and a blanket, so he took a pillow from the other bed and tossed it onto the thin mattress.

When Jane saw that he was serious about her sleeping there she hesitated for a moment, but then she walked around the end of the couch and crawled under the covers without taking off her robe.

Duncan got into bed—the big bed that seemed even lonelier now that she was only a few feet away—and switched off the light.

"Good night," he said softly into the darkness.

She shifted slightly, and he heard the springs creak beneath her.

"Good night," she answered, and when, after half an hour or so of staring into the darkness he levered himself up on his elbows to see if she was awake, she didn't move. She was already asleep.

JANE WOKE UP before Duncan the next morning and lay quietly, trying to determine exactly where she was. The draperies with the splashy print, the thin mattress, the king-size bed and the nightstand attached to the wall on the other side of the room... It took her a few moments to recall that she was in the Prairie Rose Motel in Tyree, Illinois.

And Duncan was asleep in the bed across the room.

She might have a faulty memory, but she certainly remembered the events leading up to her being there in this sleeper sofa in the same motel room with him. He must think she was crazy. First going all to pieces when she remembered the blue van and the Coke spilling in it, and then rushing over here like a wild woman last night and practically accusing him of running off and leaving her. Her behavior embarrassed her.

She heard a noisy group of guests tramping down the hall and slid upward against the back cushion of the couch so that she could sneak a look at the sleeping Duncan.

He lay on his side, his hands pillowing his cheek. He didn't look much different now from the way he did when he was awake. More peaceful, maybe, but that wasn't saying much because Duncan was one of the most peaceable men she'd ever known. Not that she had known many men, but she doubted that most dealt with the other people in their lives the way Duncan did, accepting them as they were and going out of his way to help them, if that was what they needed. She liked that about him.

He stirred in his sleep, and she quickly slid out of bed. She didn't want him to open his eyes to find her inspecting his face so closely. She groped in the pocket of her robe for the key to her room; it was still there. Carefully she unlatched the chain lock and slipped out, closing the door silently behind her.

A man stepped into the hall from the room next door. He was carrying a newspaper and a suitcase, and seemed taken aback when he saw her standing there in her robe with her hair mussed. Then he smiled conspiratorially, and Jane flushed deeply as she realized what he must be thinking. With shaking hands she unlocked her own door and closed it securely behind her.

She had the satisfaction of knowing that what their neighbor was thinking wasn't true, then realized that it might have been true if Duncan were another kind of guy. He could have taken advantage of her in the state of mind she'd experienced last night. What if he *did* want more? Was she prepared to give it?

Shaken by her own thoughts, she went into the bathroom and ran the shower until the water was warm enough to get in. She adjusted the flow of the shower nozzle, her body slowly coming to life. As the soapsuds slid down her neck, into the crevice between her breasts and past the cleft between her legs, it was easy enough to think about the way she'd felt when she and Duncan had danced. The attraction between them that night had definitely been physical.

She was rinsing off the last of the soap when the phone rang. Wrapping a towel around herself as she walked, she hurried to answer it.

"Jane," Duncan said. "I was worried when you weren't here when I woke up. Are you all right?"

"Oh," she said, "sure. I came back to my room to take a shower. I didn't want to wake you."

"It's time to get up, anyway. Let's meet for breakfast. Say, in half an hour or so? We can try the coffee shop attached to the motel."

"Okay," she agreed, and they hung up.

He had said nothing about last night. She knew from experience that he probably wouldn't. He would go out of his way to avoid embarrassing her.

She dried herself on the big towel and studied her assets in the mirror. She was small-boned and delicate, and her skin tone looked alabaster pale in the harsh overhead light. Legs: slender. Hips: could be narrower. Breasts: small but well proportioned to the rest of her. All in all, she wasn't bad. Duncan thought she was beautiful. Was she? She certainly couldn't compare with any of the women on the soap operas she'd watched, but didn't think she was impossibly ugly, either. *Beautiful.* A bountiful word, and one that she was pleased to have applied to her by someone like Duncan Tate. She dressed quickly.

When she met Duncan in the motel coffee shop, it was business as usual.

"Since it's still too early to call Detective Schmidt, I want to ride out to Carlton Jones's field and see if it jolts my memory," Jane told Duncan as they finished eating breakfast. "I'd like to see it early in the morning, which is the same time of day that I was found there."

His eyes searched her face. "Are you sure you really want to go?" he asked.

"I *have* to," she told him, and he nodded slowly in silent acceptance.

After Duncan paid the check, they climbed into the rental car and headed out of town. Duncan drove competently, sure of the way to the field where the Joneses had stumbled across her so many months ago. Jane stared out the window, trying with all her might to remember something, anything about this place.

Snow glistened on either side of the blacktop highway, and as they left behind the town of Tyree, they drove past widely scattered houses with smoke curling from the chimneys. Not many people lived on this highway, Jane observed as she studied the landscape. No wonder there weren't any witnesses to what had happened the night she was left in the ditch.

Duncan slowed the car as they passed the Jonesdale Farm sign. Carl had told them that the place where Jane had been found was about a mile down the highway, just south of a small red billboard. Sure enough, there was the billboard, and as Duncan pulled the car off the road, Jane stared at the billboard long and hard, hoping that its message would mean something to her.

"Anything look familiar?" Duncan asked, reaching over and squeezing her hand.

She shook her head, not trusting herself to speak. Coming here was something she felt that she had to do, and yet it was shaping up into an emotional ordeal. Here was the place where she had effectively left her identity behind; here was the place where Jane Rhodes, aka Jane Doe, had come to be. She was surprised to feel a great revulsion for this field and the ditch beside it. She didn't want to get out of the car.

"Jane?" Duncan was saying in a tone of concern.

She bit down hard on her bottom lip to keep it from quivering.

"Jane," Duncan said more forcefully, and she heard a great roaring in her ears, as though she were losing consciousness. She saw spots whirling before her eyes, and thought, *I shouldn't have come here.* Then Duncan's voice pulled her back to reality.

"Are you all right?" he asked anxiously. He was still holding her hand.

She threw him a panicked look. "I—I'm not sure," she said finally.

"Want to leave? We don't have to do this," he said.

She stared at the ditch, its contours rounded by drifts of snow, and let her gaze roam the field beyond. A small straggly wood stood to one side of the field, and the leafless branches of the trees rattled in the wind.

"I want to get out of the car," she said unsteadily.

Duncan hesitated, then squeezed her hand again. "All right," he said finally, slid out of the car and came around to open the door for her.

They walked to the edge of the ditch and stood there. The wind was blowing briskly, twitching the ends of Duncan's scarf. Jane dropped his hand and walked slowly along the edge of the ditch, willing her mind to stillness in readiness for some sort of impression to form. Her boots crunched in the snow, the sound echoing eerily back at them from the woods on the other side of the field. When she had walked about twenty feet, she stopped and peered down into the gentle white contours of the ditch.

Was it here that she had lain in the night, bloody and unconscious? Or had she been conscious part of the time, trying to scratch her way up the steep sides of the ditch? She tried to home in on a memory of that night. Surely she must remember it; how could she go through an experience such as that one and not remember it? She clenched her hands into fists in frustration.

"Well?" Duncan said.

She turned to face him, a bleak smile on her face. "I can't recall anything about this place. I might never have been

here before. Funny, isn't it?" Her words shattered the stillness surrounding them.

He shook his head and walked over to her. He touched the
sleeve of her coat. "No, it's not funny. It's sad."

She wasn't ready to be comforted yet; somehow she
wanted to experience this place for a little longer. And she
wanted to be alone.

"I'm going to walk over toward the wood. Maybe something will occur to me," she said.

He understood that she didn't want him to walk with her.

"I'll go back to the car," he told her.

He dug his hands deep into his pockets and walked
quickly toward the highway, his head bent against the wind.
He could only imagine how hard this was for her. He
stopped once and turned, watching her as she picked her
way in the direction of the wood, a small forlorn figure in a
coat that was too big. His heart went out to her; he would
have made everything all right for her if he could have, but
he couldn't. No one could.

Jane stopped at the edge of the wood and looked back
across the field. Of course, snow wouldn't have been on the
ground at the time of year when she had been found; it had
been autumn. She must have been cold, lying there in the
ditch. Why couldn't she remember?

She brushed the snow off a fallen log and sat down on it,
hunching her shoulders against the cold. She thought about
the aftermath of being found in the ditch; kind Dr. Bergstrom, that friendly little nurse. What was her name? Rosemary. Rosemary Sanchez. Rosemary had been so helpful in
looking for clues to Jane's previous life, but nothing had
helped, just as nothing was helping now.

She sat on the log until her nose began to grow numb,
then stood up. It was no use, she thought in despair. She
didn't remember anything at all. She might have been
standing in this field for the first time in her life.

When Jane trudged up to the car, Duncan was waiting,
leaning against the fender with his arms crossed.

"It didn't work," she said broodingly.

He uncrossed his arms and put them around her, folding her against his chest. His heart beat reassuringly beneath his coat.

"Let's get into the car where it's warm," he said.

He started the car in silence, and when they were headed back toward town, he turned to her and asked, "Now what?" He was surprised to see that she was silently crying, her small hands clasped and held to her mouth, her shoulders shaking.

He pulled the car onto the shoulder of the road, nearly getting annihilated by a tractor-trailer rig in the process. When the car had bumped to a stop, he left the engine on and drew her into his arms.

"I can't help it," she cried, weeping against his shoulder. "I want to know who I really am. And I don't know if I'll ever find out."

"Shh," he said soothingly, stroking her hair away from her face. "It doesn't matter. It doesn't matter."

She swallowed and pulled slightly away. "Of course it matters," she said. "That's the whole point of this search."

"What I mean is that you'll still be the same to me, even if I never know your real name. Why, even if I found out that your name was Mehitabel or Wilhelmina or Esmeralda—"

"Esmeralda!" she exclaimed, wiping her eyes.

"—or whatever, I'd still feel the same way about you. I'd want to—"

She lifted stricken eyes to his, and placed a gentle fingertip over his lips. "Please," she said. "Don't talk about—about feelings."

He shook off her hand. "Why not?" he demanded. "I want you to know that I do have feelings for you, that I do care about you."

"You shouldn't care too much," she said brokenly.

Duncan stared at her for a long moment. Jane self-consciously resettled herself on her side of the seat. Figuring that he'd be better off not to say anything at all, he threw the car into gear and pulled back onto the highway.

Considering their uncertain future together, he couldn't say she was wrong.

But it was possible that she wasn't right, either.

And as far as caring too much went, he'd been doing that all along, hadn't he? And now when he'd finally found the knack of talking about the way he felt, she didn't want to hear about it.

At that moment he would have agreed with Rooney. Women were strange creatures.

Chapter Thirteen

Later, over lunch, Duncan said, "Do you still want to talk to Schmidt?"

Jane, who hadn't been able to summon up much appetite, stirred the vegetables at the bottom of the bowl of soup she'd ordered and thought about it. Since her visit to Carl Jones's field, she'd had an urge to do something else this afternoon, and figured it might be a good idea to follow her urges.

"I think it's important to check on blue vans—for instance, we need to know if there were any traffic tickets given on that night to a van like Ollie saw. Or if anyone in this county owns one like it. Or—well, Detective Schmidt will know how to check it out. But what I really want to do is pay a visit to the hospital. I want to see Rosemary Sanchez again."

"Then I'll call Schmidt. Unless you'd rather do it yourself later."

"If I go to the hospital now, I might not be able to get to Schmidt until tomorrow. I think it would be best to explore every area we can in Tyree as soon as possible and then, if our search isn't productive, I'll feel free to move on to someplace else. Although where, I don't know."

"Perhaps Rosemary or that doctor who treated you will know something," Duncan said, mostly to be encouraging. This elicited a more hopeful look from Jane, and on that note they parted, he to pay a personal visit to Detective Schmidt, she to return to the hospital where she had been treated and released into her new and ultimately unhappy life.

The hospital was an easy walk from the Prairie Rose, so Jane set out at a fast clip. She was surprised at how alone she felt as she made her way down the street past the city park and the grocery store. Lately she'd begun to think of Duncan and herself as a team, a partnership. A twosome. She shook her shoulders, trying to rid herself of that feeling. If she was to survive on her own later, she couldn't keep thinking that way.

The low red brick building that was Tyree Township Hospital hunkered behind a parking lot full of cars. She slowed her steps as she walked up the curved driveway to the main entrance and went inside. Funny, she didn't remember this part of the hospital. She had been taken to Emergency when she was admitted, and her life here had been lived on the ward and in its environs.

She approached the receptionist on duty behind the wide desk, hoping for a sign of recognition. When she realized that the receptionist was a new one whom she didn't know, she asked if Dr. Bergstrom was in the hospital.

"Sorry, but Dr. Bergstrom is out of town and won't be back for two weeks. Can someone else help you?" The receptionist regarded her with an expression that said, "Haven't I seen you somewhere before?"

Jane didn't feel like taking time to explain who she was and what she was doing.

"Um, no thanks," was all she said, and when the woman was distracted by a ringing telephone, Jane followed the directional arrows on the wall until she arrived in Wing A, the place where she had first come to think of herself as Jane Doe.

"Rosemary?" she said softly when she stood in front of the nurse's station.

Rosemary Sanchez, the little nurse who had been so kind to her, looked up from a patient's chart. For a moment she stared as if confronted by a ghost. Then her face flushed with pleasure.

"Jane!" she exclaimed. In a matter of seconds, Rosemary had rushed around the desk to administer a quick hug. It felt good to be welcomed so warmly, but Jane had a sensation of not being able to get her bearings. She clung to Rosemary for a minute, then took a deep, shaky breath and laughed self-consciously.

Rosemary patted her arm. "I'm about to take my break," she said to Jane as another nurse, someone Jane didn't recognize, arrived behind the desk. "Come with me into the solarium," Rosemary suggested with an encouraging smile. She entwined her arm through Jane's and propelled her along the corridor.

The solarium was a big round room with windows looking out over what Jane recalled was a garden in warmer months. Now the fountain was dry and the narrow paths were bordered by piles of snow. Still, the scene reminded Jane of a winter wonderland; icicles in the bare-branched trees had melted and formed stalagmites of ice on the snowy ground. They sat down on a small sofa, and Rosemary squeezed her arm and said, "Tell me all about yourself. Did you manage to get a job? Did you find out who you are?"

For a moment Jane contemplated telling her the truth, but she couldn't bear to destroy the warm light in Rosemary's eyes. She was struck with the realization that when she needed help, Rosemary might have been her friend. No, she corrected herself, Rosemary *definitely* would have been her friend, but she, Jane, had been too sick and too wrapped up in her own problems to realize that then.

"Things didn't work out in Apollonia," Jane managed to say smoothly. "I moved to Chicago. Lately I've been staying in Wyoming, and I hope to live in California before long. I still don't know my real name."

"You poor thing!" Rosemary said, her eyes widening in dismay.

"That's why I'm visiting Tyree. I was hoping that you might remember something about me, anything at all. I'm trying to get some ideas about where I came from, or where I was going when I landed in that ditch," and she went on to relate Ollie's new information about the blue van.

Rosemary pursed her lips in thought. "I don't know anything about a blue van in connection with you, Jane. I mean, I don't know much about cars. And as for anything else—well, I'm sorry, but I draw a blank."

"Was there anything I mentioned while I was here, or that I seemed to be interested in, or something that didn't seem important at the time that might make a difference now?" she asked.

"I'm sorry, but I don't think so. It was so long ago," Rosemary said helplessly.

Jane felt as though she had reached an impasse. "If you think of anything about me that seemed the least bit unusual, will you let me know?" She told Rosemary that she was staying at the Prairie Rose, and gave her one of Duncan's cards with the Wyoming address in case she needed to reach them after they'd left town.

When Jane made it clear that she had to leave, Rosemary said, "I'll walk you to the lobby. I feel so awful that I haven't been able to help."

Jane smiled at her. "You were a big help when I was a patient here, and that's what counted then," she assured her.

They reached the front door of the hospital, and when Jane turned to say goodbye to Rosemary, she saw that her forehead was knotted in thought.

"There was just one thing," Rosemary said slowly.

"Yes?"

"That purse you carried," she said.

"Purse?"

"It was handmade, like something you might buy at a crafts show. I noticed it because I have an aunt who used to have an old loom at her house. It belonged to my grandmother, and Aunt Frances knew how to use it. I still have a blanket she wove. Your purse reminded me of that handwoven blanket. The same kind of pattern."

"I don't have the purse anymore," Jane said. Still, she remembered it well. The handbag had been large and rectangular and had been woven of variegated shades of dark wool with a wide fringe at the bottom. Even though it had grown old and worn, Jane had kept it until the night of the snowstorm; she must have lost it in her flight from the truck driver. There was no telling where it was now.

Rosemary's face fell. "Well, it's not much of a clue, I guess. But you did want to know if there was anything about you at all that was different, and that purse was the only thing. I know we looked inside it when we were trying to figure out who you were, but it was empty. There wasn't even a label on it, which is another reason that I thought it was probably handmade."

Jane bade Rosemary goodbye, and as she slowly walked back toward the Prairie Rose, she tried to figure out if the purse was a real clue. She'd lived with the purse until she lost it, never thinking that it might signify something important about her past life. It had been old and out of style, and the reason that she'd kept it had been that it was so big that she could carry many of her belongings in it when moving from place to place.

Duncan arrived at the Prairie Rose shortly after Jane, and he looked hopeful.

"Schmidt's going to use his resources to try to uncover any irregularities involving a blue van around the time that you were found," Duncan said. "He says that even though whole cases have pivoted on information like that, then again it might not mean a thing."

"What should we do now?" Jane asked.

He touched her shoulder. She looked drained. "Let's see if we can turn up any information about that blue van ourselves," he suggested.

They spent the rest of the day riding from one service station to another both in Tyree and Apollonia, asking questions about a blue van. Several people told them that they had let too much time pass before looking for such a van, and others gave them a quick brush-off. When they returned to the Prairie Rose that evening, both Jane and Duncan felt discouraged.

Jane was quiet over their dinner of Salisbury steak, mashed potatoes and lime Jello in the Prairie Rose's coffee shop, and Duncan tried to lift her spirits.

"It must have made you feel good when Rosemary Sanchez was so happy to see you," he prompted.

"Yes, but . . ." She bit her lip.

"But what?"

"I couldn't help but think what a difference it would have meant in my life from the time I left the hospital until the time you found me, if I had felt free to go to her for help. I mean, I knew she liked me, but I thought it was a professional interest."

"It probably was, but she would surely have helped you when you were down-and-out if she could have. Don't you think so?"

"I didn't at the time. I was sick, you see, and—well, the loneliness was awful. I was sure that no one in the world cared about me."

"I can imagine," he said evenly.

Her eyes searched his face. "Can you imagine it? Really?" she asked softly.

"Oh, yes. I've been lonely. Not the way you have, of course, because I've always had a home and enough to eat. But—well, it wasn't easy for me after Sigrid left. And before I married her I didn't have anyone except Rooney, and the ranch is so isolated that I didn't often have visitors."

"You and Rooney are such good friends," Jane said.

"Yes, and once I thought that the only true friendship existed between man and man or between woman and woman. I didn't know it was possible for men and women to be friends."

"And now?"

"You've shown me that it's possible for men and women to develop close bonds, something that I couldn't have imagined before. What we have feels like a real friendship to me, Jane. I have to thank you for that." His eyes were clear and steady upon her face.

Jane didn't know what to say. She looked down at her plate, embarrassed. But she found his words singularly beautiful.

"Have I said something wrong?" he asked quietly.

She shook her head. The tears in her eyes had begun to blur her vision.

"What's the matter, Jane?" he said.

"You give me all the credit for our friendship, when you should be the one," she said in a quavering voice.

"Me?"

She blinked the tears away and lifted her head. He was regarding her with all the care and concern that she had grown to expect in his dealings with her. There was no doubt in her mind that she could count upon Duncan's help, no matter what the situation. She had angered him, lied to him, borrowed and even stolen from him, and yet he had always treated her in the same fair-minded way.

She had known, for instance, that she couldn't really count on Rosemary Sanchez when the chips were down. Rosemary might have cared, but not enough to do anything about the circumstances in which Jane found herself—on the streets, out of a job, and down to her last dime. On the other hand, when Duncan cared, he cared with his whole heart. Thinking about it, she realized in that solemn moment that Duncan Tate was her best friend in the world.

"You see people as basically good, Duncan. You saw me that way, too, even though I was—well, maybe acting up the way Mary Kate does, except that my actions grew out of the wish to survive in a hostile world. You were almost too good to be true, and I couldn't quite believe that you were real. I had to test it.''

"I cared about you from the beginning," Duncan told her.

"When you cared, it was with all your heart. Not halfway."

He looked stunned, then his features softened. "You say it so well, Jane. I can't improve on it. I still care with all my heart. More than you know."

She was overcome with a great certainty that whatever had gone wrong in her life, it was about to be corrected.

"I do know," she said with growing wonder. "I think I've always known."

"You've always known that I love you?" he said in surprise.

She stared with astonishment into his dark eyes, his endearing face. "Yes," she said. "Yes."

THERE WAS NO WAY that either of them could finish eating dinner. In fact, they were oblivious to everyone and everything except each other, and as they left the restaurant, Duncan barely remembered to pay the check.

They stood outside on the sidewalk, shivering in the chill.

"What now?" Jane asked. "I'm not sure I know how to act."

"Where can we go? I wish we were back at the ranch," Duncan said.

She smiled at him, knowing how he felt. "I'm sorry about the—the inappropriateness of our surroundings. It's definitely my fault," she commented.

He laughed but immediately became serious. A man stopped his car in the street and hurried to the newspaper-vending machine outside the coffee shop; he took a newspaper from inside it and released the door with a loud clang. Duncan lowered his voice so that the other man wouldn't hear. "I would very much like to kiss you," he said. "But not here."

"Not here," she agreed, and smiled again. It seemed that she couldn't stop smiling.

Above the vintage neon sign of the coffee shop, the sky was velvety dark and slitted with stars. Duncan found Jane's hand at the exact moment she reached for his. An air of expectancy hung between them almost as tangibly as their frosty breath.

"Do you want to go for a drive?" he offered.

"Let's walk," she suggested impulsively. "There's a park down the street; I passed it on my way to the hospital today."

They headed down the main street of Tyree. Not much traffic was out, and with the exception of a few passing cars, they were alone.

It seemed to Jane that she could feel the warmth of Duncan, even though a wide space separated them. Perhaps he felt it, too, because he put his arm around her and pulled her close.

"We fit together walking," he said with satisfaction.

She laughed. The notes of her laughter sparkled in the clear cold air.

"It's important to fit together walking," he assured her seriously, and she laughed again, which seemed to please him. When she looked up at him, her face was alive with happiness.

Around them the park was peaceful and serene under its snowy blanket; the snow shimmered like crystals in the light of the street lamps. But his eyes were all for her. "How lovely you look," he murmured.

They stopped walking, and slowly her hand went up to touch his cheek. It was warm to her touch, and she laid the flat of her palm along it, soaking up his warmth. But that was what she had always done, soak up his warmth. Now she knew that it had been something more, perhaps from the very beginning.

"Duncan," she began, overwhelmed by the force of her feelings for him.

"Shh," was all he said. "Don't talk." And then he took her into his arms, drew her close and brought his lips down to hers.

His lips were sweet and demanding, and Jane ached with the knowledge that she had been missing this during all the past weeks. She touched her fingertips to the strong line of his jaw, felt the smooth texture of his skin, the rough abrasion of his beard. All of it so familiar and yet so new, and she wanted to memorize everything about him, to hold him in her heart forever and ever.

He pulled her closer, unwilling to allow even a small space to widen between them. "You needed time," he said. "I knew that."

"But you were my best friend! Do people often fall in love with their best friends?"

"I don't know, but they should," he said, smiling down at her.

"I wasn't ready to be in love with anyone before," Jane said. "It still seems odd to have found the other half of myself before I've even found my real *self*. Maybe I'm not ready for this."

"Well, if you're not, is it all right if I go on being your best friend?' Duncan asked lightly, and she looked up to find that he was grinning at her in good humor.

She took heart from this and pulled slightly away. "We should talk about this," she said gravely. The last thing she wanted to do at the moment was talk, but she knew it was necessary. And she knew that although Duncan might not agree with her, at least he would listen.

"You're serious, aren't you?"

"Very," she said. "I'm having problems coming to grips with knowing that what I feel for you is love. I had your role in my life all figured out; you were my friend. And now—"

"And now that notion is shot all to blazes, right?"

"Right. And it puts everything—living at the ranch, conducting this search—in a new perspective for me."

"Which affects me," he said.

Full of doubts, she lifted her face to his. "I suppose it's asking a lot to expect you to be patient. But—" She made a little gesture of helplessness with her hands, finding her thoughts hard to put into words, as she had so often since her accident.

He waited patiently. She finally got a grasp on the idea she was trying to get across, but that still didn't make it any easier to say the words.

"It's just that I don't feel right about—about—" Jane stammered.

"About making love when you don't know if you're free," Duncan said in a low voice.

She glanced up at him. "Yes," she replied.

He sighed and she glimpsed a trace of sadness in his eyes. "I knew you felt that way before we started out. The possibility of a hubby and a couple of kids waiting somewhere for you to come home and put on the coffeepot is the reason you wanted to learn your true identity. So this isn't exactly news," he said with grim irony.

She realized that she was shivering. "We'd better go back to the Prairie Rose and tackle this. It's getting colder out here," she said.

He kept his arm around her shoulders as they walked past tattered remnants of snowdrifts in the park, and she thought, *Maybe I should throw caution to the wind and let our love take its natural course.* It would be so much easier to do that; she wanted to lie in his arms all night, to make love with him and to wake up where she would be the object of his first smile in the morning.

They had reached the motel, and he held the door open for her. They traipsed through the lobby under the bored eyes of the desk clerk, and when they reached their hall, Duncan pulled out his key. Jane dug deep into her pocket and found hers, too.

"So I guess it's separate rooms, right?" he said.

She offered him a shaky smile, painfully aware of her own strong need to be with him. But she knew that it would be harder to leave a lover than a friend if she found out that she was indeed part of another compelling life somewhere without him.

"Duncan," she began, feeling her uncertainty like a sharp pain in her heart. If only she could get all of it over with and be free of the weight of her forgotten past!

"I understand," he said heavily. He took her key from her and started to insert it into the keyhole in her door, but her hand stayed his.

"No," she said. "Is it possible—I mean, do you think—?"

"You mean, can we sleep together the way we did last night?" His eyes burned into her.

She caught her lower lip between her teeth and, her eyes never leaving his face, she nodded, once, twice. She remained perfectly still.

He closed his eyes and pulled her close to him. Could he occupy the same room with her all night and not touch her? And if he touched her, if he needed her warmth and softness, could they restrain themselves from the ultimate act?

It was a chance they would have to take. He wanted to be with her for now and for always, and he would respect her decision in this matter as much as he respected Jane herself.

"Whatever you want," was all he said.

She pulled slightly away, and, her eyes never leaving his face, took his key from his hand. Then she led him across the hall to his own room and unlocked the door.

THEY OPENED OUT the couch bed, looked at each other over its expanse of white sheets and blue blanket, then without a word folded it back up again.

Jane went with him to the big bed, and he walked around to one side while she stood on the other. She felt confused;

overlaying her very real desire for him was a kind of constriction. It pinned her down, made her motionless. She didn't know how to go about this.

Duncan made it easy for her. He came around to her side of the bed and kissed her gently on the cheek. "Come to bed," he said softly, easing her down beside him and turning off the light.

They lay in the dark, both of them unwilling to move. Through the thin walls they could hear the occupants of the room next door moving about, conducting their bathroom ablutions, talking.

Duncan turned over and punched his pillow; Jane lay stiffly, staring up at the ceiling and thinking that this had been a mistake. Duncan muttered something, but she couldn't make out the words.

Time passed. It might have been minutes, it might have been hours; she had no idea how long it had been since they got into this bed together. She counted sheep, she named all the colors of the rainbow, she named all the cast members of *Luck of the Irish*. Still she did not sleep.

"Duncan?" she asked, her voice sounding higher and more timid than usual.

"I can't stand this," he observed abruptly, reaching out and yanking the chain that turned on the bedside lamp. The room was filled with light, and Jane pushed herself up on one elbow.

"I'd better leave," she said. "This isn't going to work. I can't sleep, you can't sleep, and it wasn't a very good idea. It's my fault."

"Don't be so quick to take the blame," Duncan said. "I agreed to the arrangement."

"I should have known better," she said, making as if to get up, but he reached for her and pulled her to him. She let herself be drawn toward him, resting against his chest.

"That's better," he said comfortably. The sounds from next door quieted, and Jane sighed. It was so pleasant to be close to Duncan this way, she thought, nestling into the warm curve of his body.

"I think what was wrong was that we were both trying too hard not to touch each other," Duncan said. "We both want to, but we're afraid that one thing will lead to another and that we wouldn't be able to stop."

"Exactly," said Jane, drawing the word out to its full length and growing drowsier as she said it.

"So let's not try too hard. I promise that nothing is going to happen until you want it to," he went on.

She shifted in his arms, intending to tell him to turn out the light, but suddenly they heard the rhythmic squeak of bedsprings from the room next door. Her eyes flew open.

Duncan groaned. So did someone on the other side of the wall, in a slightly different tone.

"Oh no, not that," Duncan said in disgust.

Jane started to laugh. She muffled her laughter against Duncan's chest, and the hair on his chest tickled her nose. Soon he was laughing, too, and they couldn't stop, no matter how hard they tried.

Finally the sounds next door subsided—and so did their laughter.

Jane ventured a look at Duncan. His face was red, but his eyes were bright.

"Duncan, I love you," she said.

"And I love you. Now can we please get some sleep?" he demanded.

"Turn out the light," she said, and when he did she swiveled her head and kissed him.

That night she slept fitfully, her back against his, bracing herself against him the way she would against a strong, solid tree trunk.

Chapter Fourteen

Waking up the next morning with Duncan beside her should have been heartening. Jane should have felt supported and strengthened by their declaration of love, but in truth all it did was worry her. If her past life required it, how would she find the strength to leave him? She loved him, and she should have been happy. Instead she lay beside him in the gray morning light, not merely listening to his breathing but feeling him breathe. That was the difference between friendship and love—with friendship, you merely listened. With love, you felt.

She didn't want to feel this love, not on this particular morning when she was so tired and worn out by the uncertainty of her life. She would have liked to be free of it, relieved of the doubt, fear and vulnerability. Instead she must get up and smile at Duncan, be the receptacle for the caring and compassion that he heaped upon her, unable for the sake of their love to express her negative thoughts. This morning all she could feel was the awesome responsibility of love.

After breakfast she sat on the bed in the motel room while Duncan called Detective Schmidt and learned that he had been able to uncover no news about a blue van in relation to Jane's appearance in the ditch.

"Ollie Jones seems to be the only person around town who saw a blue van that night," Schmidt offered in an apologetic tone.

"But *I* remember a blue van, too!" Jane said when Duncan related the conversation to her. "Doesn't that count for something?" She was so disappointed; she had been sure that the blue van was an important clue.

Duncan shook his head. "I guess not, Jane. I'm sorry." They both knew that her brief memory of the blue van meant nothing unless Jane somehow managed to recall something more about it.

Jane nibbled on a thumbnail and stared into space. A blue van. What did it have to do with anything, anyway? What did it mean? Who had been in the van with her? She reached into the far recesses of memory and came up with—zip—zilch—nothing.

Duncan interrupted her thoughts. "Well, Jane," he said. "It looks like we're stymied. What do you want to do now?"

"I'm packed," Jane said abruptly. "Let's leave Tyree."

"Is that what you really want to do?"

"Why not?" she replied, her tone sharp.

He wavered for a moment, not sure if leaving was a good idea. Jane seemed very much on edge this morning, but, considering the circumstances, he supposed that this wasn't surprising. "I guess there's no reason to stay," he admitted. "It's just that I was hoping we'd learn more while we were here." He made his voice relax, hoping that it would calm her.

"So was I," Jane said. She had begun to take on the air that he recognized as her stubborn look, the one where she got a mulish glint in her eyes like Quixote when he got his dander up. If she hadn't been so strung out this morning, he would have taken her in his arms and attempted to kiss the mood away.

Later, he promised himself as he gathered up his shaving gear and tucked it into a corner of his suitcase. *Later.*

"Let me get that," Duncan was quick to say when they stepped outside the motel carrying their luggage, but as usual, Jane refused his help, marching ahead of him across the icy parking lot with an air of determination.

From where he stood, he spotted the slick patch of ice, and cried out at almost the same time as she stepped on it. And then, heart in mouth, he watched helplessly as her feet flew out from under her and she lost her balance, landing on her back.

Heedless of his own safety on the icy asphalt, Duncan set off at a run and reached her in a matter of seconds, his pulse pounding in his ears. He thought he would never forget his fear as he stared down at her motionless body.

Jane, he thought, and bent swiftly to touch her, to wipe the spot of dirt from her pale cheek, praying that she was not hurt.

A man who had seen her fall rushed across the street.

"Everything okay?" he asked anxiously.

Jane forced herself up on her elbows. She felt nothing; her whole body was numb. And then feeling began to seep into her limbs, bringing with it a huge buzzing that filled her ears, and she couldn't hear what anyone in the small gathering crowd was saying. She had eyes only for Duncan, whose stricken face expressed all the love and caring that she knew he felt. Her head—how it hurt!—but she had to let Duncan know that she was all right, and so she tried to speak, tried to get the words out, but none would come.

"She's had the wind knocked out of her," she heard someone say, and with that she realized that the buzzing in her ears was receding. Her elbow ached; she'd have a big bruise there, she knew.

Duncan's hand was supporting the back of her neck, brushing her cheek, and when at last she could speak, she said with more confidence than she felt, "I'm okay. Really. I'm fine," and warmed to the relief in Duncan's eyes.

"Can you get up?" he asked, and she surprised him by sitting up and taking hold of his arm, hanging on to it as someone gave her a boost from the back.

"I'm all right," she repeated, and the man who had run across the street left, and the woman who had stopped her car nearby got back into it and drove away, spewing plumes of exhaust in her wake.

They were alone in the parking lot, Duncan's arm encircling her waist. She leaned on him for a moment, glad to have him for a protector.

"Do you want to check back into the motel? You may be sore later," Duncan said. He was still concerned; she had a kind of glazed look about her.

"I'm ready to leave Tyree," she said, summoning the strength to speak firmly. "I may have a bruise or two, but there's no serious damage. Honestly," she added when she saw how disbelieving he looked.

Reluctantly and at her own urging, Duncan settled Jane carefully in the passenger seat of the car. She leaned her head back against the headrest while Duncan was stowing their suitcases in the trunk. What an awful fall it had been! She had hit the back of her head on the pavement. She was sure that the fall wouldn't have happened had it not been for her ragged nerves and too little sleep, and knew she was lucky that she hadn't been hurt more seriously.

Duncan shot her a worried look when he slid in behind the steering wheel.

She smiled weakly. "Duncan, don't look at me like that," she chided. "If I wasn't feeling ready to travel, I'd tell you."

"You still seem a little dazed," he said.

"You would, too, if you'd fallen as hard as I did. Besides, I think I bit my tongue," she said, but didn't mention the headache that was burgeoning right behind her eyes. She couldn't recall having headaches since she'd arrived at the ranch, and hoped that the fall hadn't precipitated their return.

To set Duncan's mind at ease, she tried to carry on a conversation as they left behind the outskirts of Tyree.

"I wonder if we really accomplished anything here," she said softly as Duncan accelerated to a comfortable fifty-five miles an hour on the open highway.

"It was a start," he told her, and she was pleased that he seemed willing to forget the fall she'd just taken in the parking lot.

Her head didn't stop hurting all day. If anything, the pain was aggravated by their many stops as they related Jane's story and left Duncan's business card in several gas stations and convenience stores. Jane surreptitiously took two aspirin, but they afforded little relief. She refrained from mentioning the pain in her head to Duncan, knowing that it would only worry him. Instead, she tried to concentrate on their task.

Surprisingly, the people to whom they spoke had often heard about Jane and knew of her initial search for her identity during the time when she was a patient in the hospital in Tyree, but they were able to shed no light on the mysterious circumstances of her appearance in Carlton Jones's ditch.

Sometimes when they'd had a chance to study Duncan's business card for a moment, they expressed more interest in the llamas than they did in Jane.

"I'd better talk to Rooney about hauling a bunch of llamas to southern Illinois," Duncan joked after they'd left a store where the woman behind the counter had become overly enthusiastic about llamas, but had paid scant attention to Jane and her plight. "I bet we could sell quite a few around here."

"You haven't phoned him since we left the ranch, have you?" Jane asked.

"No, and I'd better. I'll call tonight," he said.

That night found them staying in a motel in a small town not far from the Indiana state line, and after dinner, during which they each unsuccessfully tried to bolster the other's hopes, Duncan called Rooney.

Jane, still fighting her headache, tugged at his sleeve. "Don't forget to ask about Mary Kate," she urged in a whisper.

Duncan surprised her by asking after Mary Kate as soon as Rooney answered the phone, and as he listened to Rooney's reply, his expression immediately become more serious. "She did?" he asked sharply. "Are they all right?"

Sensing something amiss, Jane sat up straight. It sounded as though Mary Kate was in trouble again.

"Well, it doesn't surprise me that Dearling stayed around. She's a tame one. Yeah, it's a good thing none of them wandered over by the highway. Okay, I'll call you again soon. Right. Goodbye, Rooney."

"What has Mary Kate done?" Jane asked with a certain sense of foreboding.

Duncan looked angry. "She left the gate open on the pen beside the barn and the breeding females got out. Fortunately, Rooney's managed to round all of them up. That Mary Kate! Why can't she behave herself?"

"She can't help it," Jane sighed. "Anyway, the latch on the gate isn't particularly reliable."

"It's reliable enough when the rest of us use it. Mary Kate is the only one who seems to have trouble with it," Duncan said angrily.

Jane tried to soothe him. "Mary Kate might be in need of attention right now. With both of us gone, Rooney is busy running the ranch. Mary Kate didn't want me to leave in the first place, and now she's probably very lonely."

"Lonely or not, she has no business letting my llamas out. Above and beyond what could happen to them, her carelessness could have cost us thousands of dollars. Many of my breeding females are pregnant, and their offspring are potentially worth quite a lot of money. Mary Kate had better thank her lucky stars that nothing happened to those llamas."

"I'm sorry, Duncan. I'm glad they're all right."

"So am I. Rooney says he's going to devise a severe punishment for Mary Kate."

Jane's heart sank. In her mind she pictured Mary Kate's defiant face the last time Rooney had imposed punishment by restricting her contact with her beloved Dearling. She knew that it was only right that Mary Kate face the consequences of her irresponsible action, but nevertheless her heart ached for the child.

Both Jane and Duncan were exhausted by their busy day, and the troubles at Placid Valley Ranch weighed heavily upon both of them. The bruises she had suffered in her fall kept Jane from falling asleep until late, and when she woke up, she still had a nagging headache.

Although neither of them had slept well, they struck out early that morning, determined to pay a visit to a newspaper in nearby Terre Haute that had published a story about Jane when she had still been a patient at Tyree Township Hospital. Jane thought that the sympathetic reporter who had written the story might be interested in writing a follow-up, and they both thought that any publicity would aid their search.

They had stopped for gas in a Terre Haute suburb and Jane got out of the car to stretch her arms and arch her stiff back. As she was about to get back in, she was almost blinded by the glint of bright sun on the chrome bumper of a car in front of theirs. At first she held up her hand to shield her eyes, but she felt such a sharp pain in her head that she decided to look for a water fountain so that she could take two more aspirin.

Her head swam, and even the cold outdoor air didn't clear it. She headed toward the gas station where Duncan was studying the snack vending machines, but found herself turned around going the other way. The pain throbbed inside her head, and she couldn't see where she was going. She heard a shout and felt the breeze from the passing of a car too near, but she was confused and didn't know which way to go and turned around again, looking for Duncan.

"Lady, get out of the way!" somebody yelled. She dug her fists into her eyes because they hurt so much, and when she took her hands away, there was a pink dress in a store window, and she wanted to buy it for Mary Kate. Then she crashed headlong into a solid object and rebounded. She heard herself sobbing, and the next thing she knew, a woman was holding a cool cloth to her forehead and saying, "There, there, you'll be all right. Just a little dizzy spell, wasn't it, dear?"

Jane swallowed and felt someone squeeze her hand. She pushed aside the cloth on her forehead to see Duncan looking pale and worried. She summoned the strength to smile at him.

"Jane, you scared me half to death," he said.

"What happened?" she asked, bewildered. She had never seen this woman before, and as for the plaid couch on which she was lying and the room where she found herself—well, nothing gave her a clue. Where was she, anyway?

"This nice lady, Mrs.—"

"Alice Beasley," the woman supplied as she returned with a hot cup of tea.

"Mrs. Beasley was in the window of her shop, arranging the merchandise, when you came reeling across the street in front of a car, and when a bicycle on the sidewalk almost hit you, she opened the door and brought you inside," Duncan explained.

"I couldn't see," Jane said, remembering how the reflection of the bright sun on the chrome had affected her.

"I knew something was wrong," Alice Beasley said with great certainty.

"My headache's gone," Jane said in a tone of amazement.

"You never said you had a headache," Duncan said accusingly.

"I didn't want to worry you," she said.

"You should have seen a doctor after that fall. I knew it," he said.

"Don't be angry, Duncan. I feel better now. I know it sounds silly, but I'm fine." Indeed, she felt a resurgence of energy, and the cloud of depression that had hung over her that morning seemed to have disappeared.

"Now listen to me, Jane. If you've started having those headaches again, you must see a doctor," Duncan said.

"I know a good one. Dr. McKelvey. He's been my doctor for over thirty years. I'll call and make an appointment with him, if you like," Mrs. Beasley volunteered.

"Yes, that sounds like a good idea," Duncan agreed.

"No," said Jane.

"Jane—"

"I'll just drink this tea and we'll be on our way. And that pink organdy dress in your window—what size is it?"

"A girl's size twelve, dear. But should you be thinking about that? Shouldn't you see how you feel in half an hour or so?" Mrs. Beasley's face wrinkled into a maze of concern.

Jane surprised them both by swinging her feet off the couch. She felt more energetic than she had in days. Weeks, even. She wasn't sure just what had happened to her, but there was no doubt in her mind that it had been beneficial.

"I want to see that dress," she said firmly.

Duncan and Mrs. Beasley exchanged looks. Finally, as though she were humoring an invalid, the reluctant Mrs. Beasley said, "Well, I'll take the dress out of the window, dear, but if I were you, I'd rest."

Jane paid no attention. Instead she followed Mrs. Beasley to the window and stood entranced as the store owner divested the mannequin of the pink dress.

"Wouldn't that be perfect for Mary Kate?" she asked Duncan.

Duncan, who wasn't sure that Jane was entirely well, eyed the dress doubtfully. It had large puffed sleeves, a satin sash, and dainty white lace edging above the hem. He couldn't for the life of him imagine such an exquisite dress on a child whose knees seemed to be permanently skinned, whose hair hung in limp clumps, and whose fingernails were more often than not rimmed with dirt. Anyway, did someone as careless as Mary Kate deserve such a fine present? As exasperated as he was with her irresponsible behavior, he didn't think so.

"You've got to be kidding," he said. He stood close to Jane in case she became dizzy again, although he had to admit that she looked perfectly healthy. In fact she looked wonderful. He couldn't imagine what had come over her.

Jane was enthusing over the dress. With its delicately embroidered bodice and its petal-pink petticoat sewn of the finest batiste, it was even lovelier than she had thought, and it looked close to Mary Kate's size. What else had Mary Kate said? Oh, yes. The dress was required to have transparent sleeves. These, made of organdy, would fit the bill.

Jane turned to Duncan. She was pleased that she could move her head without feeling that awful dull ache behind her eyes. "Duncan, you don't understand. Mary Kate asked me to bring her a pretty pink dress, and I promised I would. It may be a little too big for her, but with a few tucks here and there I could make it fit," she said.

"This dress was handmade by one of our consignees," Mrs. Beasley told them. "In fact, all of the things in my shop are handmade. Do you do crafts as well as sew?"

"I'm a weaver," Jane said without thinking, then was astonished at the words that had come out of her mouth. Duncan stared at her, unable to move.

She looked at him, still stunned and scarcely believing what she had said. She was a weaver! Not merely a spinner of yarn, but someone who wove it into cloth!

The edge of a memory fluttered somewhere on the outskirts of her mind, and she tried to draw it toward her. But no matter how hard she tried, she couldn't grasp it. It kept eluding her.

"Well, dear," Mrs. Beasley went on in a conversational tone, unaware of the astonished but silent byplay that was going on between Jane and Duncan, "since you're a weaver, you really ought to stop by Shanti Village while you're here. If you feel up to it, of course. I notice from your car license tags that you two are from out of state. Well, I always tell visitors to go to Shanti Village. It's kind of an attraction around here. They have all these crafts people who live and work there, and sometimes you can go right into their houses and watch them work."

"Shanti Village," Jane said. Suddenly a flash of memory, no longer than a second or two, flared in her head. It was of a smiling, deep-voiced, deep-breasted woman who wore a gold Egyptian ankh charm on a chain around her neck, whose laugh was not only frequent but loud, who worked at a loom while her baby slept in a rush basket on the floor beside her. *Moonglow,* Jane thought. *That woman's name was Moonglow. And we used to ride together in a blue van when we went grocery shopping.*

"Yes, I'd be happy to give you directions to Shanti Village, if you'd like. Now, how about the dress? Would you like me to wrap it up for your little friend?" asked Mrs. Beasley.

"Yes," Jane whispered, the way she uttered the word drawing sharp looks.

"Maybe you'd better lie down in the back room again," Alice Beasley said solicitously.

"I—I'm fine. And I do want the dress. Only—only could you tell me how to reach Shanti Village? Here, I'll pay you for the dress, and you can wrap it and we'll pick it up later." Jane fumbled with her purse.

"I'll pay for it," Duncan said, whipping cash out of his wallet, while Jane turned toward the window and stared out at the street, as though she had seen a ghost.

"Shanti Village is about thirty miles north of here on the highway. You'll see a sign on the side of the road right after the railroad tracks," Mrs. Beasley said, clearly confused.

The words were no sooner out of her mouth than Jane was out the door, walking at a fast pace.

Fortunately, the street was miraculously devoid of traffic. Duncan managed a few disjointed words of thanks to Mrs. Beasley, then sprinted after Jane, his long legs barely keeping up with her shorter ones as she clipped smartly along to their car, parked across the street at the gas station.

"What was that all about?" Duncan asked, trying to get a good look at her face.

"Shanti Village. I've *been* there, Duncan! I know a woman who lives there. She's a weaver, like I am. And this street—it seems so familiar!" She kept walking, apparently propelled by the strength of her own convictions.

Duncan was amazed at this revelation. "Jane, what is this all about? Are you sure you're feeling okay?"

"I haven't had a loom since I first became Jane Doe, and maybe if I had, I wouldn't have known what to do with it. But I know now. I used to spend my days at a loom, working in a rhythm, a certain rhythm that was as natural to me as the ebb and flow of the tides is to the sea. How could I not have known that about myself? And I'm certain that I must know other people at Shanti Village besides Moonglow. I *know* it! Oh, Duncan, don't you see? It's coming back to me, something's making me remember!" Her eyes sparkled up at him.

"Moonglow? Is that a person?" he asked, feeling at a loss to cope with all of this information at once.

Jane got into the car and pressed her hands to her cheeks. "Duncan, she's a friend of mine, and she lives in Shanti Village. I'm feeling chills run through me, just thinking about seeing her again. She's somebody I knew, Duncan! Don't you see what a breakthrough this is?"

Duncan pulled her hands down from her face and kissed her. He couldn't help smiling back at her, she looked so happy. And he was happy, too. It didn't matter how or why she remembered. All that mattered was that she remembered. He could only hope that at last they were on the right track.

He started the car and pulled onto the highway.

"What brought all of this on, anyway?" he asked.

"I don't know, it's like a—like a light suddenly went on in my head, illuminating all the dark corners. I must have lived at Shanti Village, Duncan, don't you see? Because I remember my loom! It was set up in the same room as Moonglow's, we used to talk about the patterns we were weaving and I would spin the wool that we both used, because she used to hate to spin, but I was good at it, and—oh, Duncan, that handbag I had! The one that Rosemary Sanchez mentioned? I made that, and I must have made dozens like it! I sewed little labels in them and sold them."

"Why wasn't there a label in the one you had? Didn't Rosemary tell you that there was no identification in it?"

"I remember that handbag and why I had it! It was a reject, one that wasn't good enough to sell, and I kept it for myself. That's why there wasn't a label in it! Those labels were expensive, and I didn't use them on things I made for myself."

"What about this—this *Moonglow*? How did you meet her?"

"I don't know. I only remember that I liked her a lot. And she was having some kind of trouble, some difficulty and—and because of that I moved in with her. What was it—what was wrong?" Jane racked her brain for some sense of Moonglow's trouble, but she couldn't think of it. Finally she gave up and focused on her friend, whose face she could see clearly in her mind. "Moonglow has long dark hair, and there's a baby, too. A tiny blond baby who sleeps nearby while Moonglow works at her loom. We knew each other well, so well that we used to go shopping for food together in my blue van. *My* blue van, Duncan! The blue van is mine!" She clasped her hands together to keep them from trembling and watched the road unfurl in front of them. But it was different from all the other roads she had followed—this one led to Shanti Village and to Moonglow. And it led to her past; she knew it.

"Who was with you when the Coke spilled all over the floor of the van?" Duncan asked.

Jane frowned and bit her lip. "I don't know," she said. "I can't remember that, just like I can't remember my own name. But Moonglow will know. Surely she will, won't she?"

Duncan curved an arm around her shoulders. "I certainly hope so," he said quietly.

Jane stared out the window, willing the memories to surface, trying to recall her name, trying to figure out why she had been in a blue van when Coke had been spilled, but when she thought about it, all she got was a strong feeling of anger and foreboding, of something amiss. It was akin to the emotion she had felt when she had revisited Carlton Jones's field and tried to remember the events of the night when someone had dumped her into the ditch. But this time she refused to despair. She would find some answers soon.

Before long, they crossed railroad tracks and came upon a fancifully lettered sign that pointed in the direction of Shanti Village. They set off on a narrow road that passed several farms and then curved through a patch of woods. And when they came out of the woods, Shanti Village lay before them.

It consisted of a neat clump of houses gathered around a large central hall, and at the end of the street was a gaily painted building with a sign designating it the Shanti General Store. Two children pulled another on a bright red sled in the distance, and several people hurried along the sidewalk. Jane scanned their faces to see if she knew them. If she did, she didn't recognize them, nor did anyone recognize her.

Duncan pulled the car to a stop in front of the store. "Want me to go in with you?" he offered. He wasn't sure that it was a good idea to get their hopes up about this place or about Jane's sudden memories of this Moonglow person, whoever she was. Jane's memory might very well turn out to be unreliable. She had, after all, been acting strangely.

"I'll just run inside and see if anyone knows Moonglow," Jane said, and he winked reassuringly, hoping for her sake as well as his that this was a real lead.

Jane went inside the store, which was deserted except for a man sitting behind a counter watching a game show on a small television set.

Jane barely glanced at the batik wall hangings, the hand-quilted bedspreads, and the woven blankets draped over a stair rail.

"I'm looking for someone named Moonglow," she said to the man.

He cast her a brief look. "You a friend of hers?" he asked.

She nodded, her throat feeling dry. She felt a need to explain but didn't want to waste the time. She wanted to find Moonglow now, right away.

"Third house on the left. The yellow one," he said, returning his attention to the TV set.

Duncan, waiting outside, drummed his fingers impatiently on the back of the seat. He couldn't help the sensation that things were moving too fast. All this talk of someone named Moonglow and Shanti Village—where would it lead?

All at once he recalled the story of the man who had lost his memory due to a blow on the head and regained it only after a second head injury many years later. He was struck with the certainty that Jane's recent fall was a factor in the sudden return of her memory now.

"Any luck?" he asked when she slid back into the car.

Jane felt jittery and on edge. "The man inside says that Moonglow's in the third house on the left," she said tersely.

"Hey, are you sure you want to do this?" Duncan asked.

"I'm scared," she admitted. "What if she doesn't know me? What if it's the wrong Moonglow?"

"How many people named Moonglow have you known in your life?" Duncan grinned as he started the engine, and with that Jane relaxed slightly. He *did* have a point.

When Duncan drove up in front of the yellow house, she hesitated.

"Would you mind coming with me this time?' she asked him.

"Of course not," he assured her, and they walked up the path to the house together.

Jane took in every detail about the place: the window boxes that must have held flowers in the spring and summer, the green shutters and white trim, the uncurtained windows hung with small stained glass sun catchers. If Moonglow had been her friend, wouldn't she remember this place?

And then she did remember. The house hadn't always been painted yellow. Once the clapboards had been white. But the porch floor had always been painted dark green, just as it was now. And—

Duncan rapped sharply on the door.

"Come in!" called a voice, a familiar husky voice. Moonglow's voice.

"Should we?" asked Duncan, and Jane found that her legs felt rubbery and she was clinging tightly to his hand.

"I said, come in!" the voice said more impatiently, "I'm changing a diaper."

"She's a trusting soul, letting in people she can't even see," Duncan muttered as Jane reached out a trembling hand and turned the doorknob. He was nervous, too, although he never would have admitted it.

Inside, the sweet fragrance of sandalwood incense hung in the air, and it was overlaid with the aroma of freshly baked gingerbread. *Gingerbread—it's one of Moonglow's specialties,* thought Jane. A complacent white cat jumped off the windowsill and proceeded to wash her face under a loom in the corner, and the word *Lotus* appeared unbidden in Jane's mind. It was the cat's name.

"Lotus?" Jane said tentatively. The cat stopped washing, the tip of her pink tongue protruding from her mouth, and Jane smiled. She and Moonglow had always laughed at Lotus when they caught her with her tongue hanging out.

"Be with you in a minute!" Moonglow called from somewhere down the hall, and Jane knew that she would be standing at the old dresser that they had converted into a dressing table for Moonglow's baby. Somehow it heartened Jane to think that she hadn't been gone long enough for the baby to be toilet trained yet.

Then she heard brisk footsteps on the hardwood floor, and Moonglow Everlight, the familiar gold ankh at her throat, stood at the entrance to the room.

They stared at each other. Moonglow's face drained of all color. Jane didn't know what to say, could have said nothing, even if she'd tried.

And then Moonglow gasped, "Celeste! Oh, Celeste! You've come back!" Bangle bracelets jangling, long brown hair afloat, Moonglow hurtled headlong into Jane's arms.

Chapter Fifteen

Celeste. Jane's real name is Celeste, Duncan thought as he watched the two women embrace. And then he thought, I would have never pegged her as a Celeste.

"Where have you been all this time? Do you know how hard I've tried to get in touch with you? Why didn't you call or write or something? I've been frantic!"

Jane, still in shock over finding someone who actually seemed to know her, gently disengaged herself. Suddenly she found herself in the position of having to explain, and she knew that it wouldn't be easy. There were still so many blank spaces.

"I think we need to talk," she said, and Moonglow, after a curious glance at Duncan, drew them over to a couch where they all sat down and, in sudden embarrassment, kept looking from one to the other.

Jane was the first to pull herself together. She introduced Duncan, and then she began to relate her story. At first Moonglow was incredulous, but as the story progressed, she had to dab at her eyes with a tissue more than once.

"I can't believe that someone could get so lost," she kept saying, even though Jane and Duncan assured her that it had really happened exactly as Jane had said.

"So," Jane said, finishing up her story, "I'm here to find out about my life. I don't know if I have a family, or children, and only today did I figure out that I was a weaver. Please tell me everything you know about me."

Moonglow reached out and gave Jane an impulsive hug. "I just can't believe that you're sitting here beside me after so long," she said apologetically. "And you are my best friend and I know a lot about you, so it's going to take a long time to tell you everything."

"Please," Duncan said. "Tell us."

So Moonglow told them that Jane's real name was Celeste Norton, and that she and Moonglow had both been weavers in this small community of craftsmen before Jane disappeared.

"You had a disagreement over policy with the community leaders," Moonglow said. "They wanted to turn this place into a tourist attraction in the summer months, with an amusement park for children, a petting zoo, and even a miniature train that would circle the village and feature cowboys and Indians jumping out of the woods. We both felt that the prime purpose of Shanti Village was to give artists a place to create, not to provide fun for tourists. The people who were in favor of this amusement park concept argued that it would bring more people to the village and thus provide more customers for our crafts, but you said you didn't want them turning this place into a circus."

"I didn't like that man—what was his name? He had a beard and I used to joke that he looked like a pirate," Jane said, recalling him with a shudder. He had tried to make her life miserable here, she recalled. She had led the group that opposed him.

"His name was Fenton Murdock, and I'm happy to say that we voted him out of the village council shortly after you left," Moonglow told her. "In fact, he and most of his followers left. He's driving a cab in Newark these days, I hear."

Both she and Jane laughed, and Jane's heart warmed to Moonglow's familiar, throaty laughter.

"Anyway, Fenton used to assign you to work extra hours in the village co-op's store, and when you objected and told him that serving those additional hours meant you had less time to spend at your loom, he called you a troublemaker. You were outraged and appeared before the village council, calling for equitable scheduling. That made Fenton really mad, and when some of those handbags you used to make disappeared from the store and turned up in a boutique in Urbana, Illinois, you suspected that he had stolen them and passed them off as his own, pocketing money that should have been yours."

"I *remember*," Jane said excitedly. "One of the boutique's owners called here and asked to speak to the person who made those big woven handbags, and when I called her back I realized what had happened. The man she described as the creator of them was Fenton Murdock!"

"You and Fenton had a big row, and you said you couldn't work here anymore. You said you knew of a colony of weavers in Ohio where you could work in peace and where there was a ready market for your work. So that very night—you wouldn't even wait until morning—you sat here and took your loom apart, and you packed it and everything you owned into the back of that blue van of yours, and you rode away, promising to let me know where I could reach you. And that was the last I saw of you." Moonglow's eyes brimmed with tears again.

"A loom! That's what was in the back of my blue van, Duncan! I was so worried about it that night, the night the Coke spilled!"

"The Coke spilled?" Moonglow looked confused.

Quickly Jane told her about the brief memory of Coke spilling on the carpet of her van, and how she recalled trying to clean it up and being worried about the things stowed in back.

"Of course I would have been worried about my loom," she said. "It was my livelihood, the way I made my living. I was afraid that if something happened to it, I wouldn't be able to support myself."

"Can you remember when I left here?" Jane asked Moonglow.

Moonglow thought a moment. "It would have been in November of that year," she said.

"I was found in the ditch on November 3," Jane told her.

"I was so worried because November 10 came and went without a word from you. Sun-One was three months old on that date, and you promised to call because it was her three months' birthday."

"Sun-One," breathed Jane. "The baby. May I see her?"

Together the two of them tiptoed into the small nursery. It had, Jane realized, once been her own room. But her twin bed had been pushed into a corner and was piled with pillows like a couch, and Sun-One's crib was where the bed used to be. And asleep in the crib was Sun-One, sucking her thumb.

When they were back in the living room, Jane clutched Duncan's hand excitedly. "The nursery used to be my room, Duncan. I remembered it! And Sun-One—she's beautiful, Moonglow. I helped deliver her, didn't I? You wanted a home birth, and I was the one who went to get the midwife."

"In a pouring rain," Moonglow agreed, finishing her sentence with that laugh of hers. "And you coached my breathing."

"It was why I moved in here, wasn't it? Your husband ran away with another woman, and you needed someone to help you pay expenses because you were going to have a baby. And I moved here from—" Jane faltered and couldn't remember any more from that.

"From one of the studio apartments over the general store. There was a waiting list for them, and we both thought it would be a good idea for you to live with me, because it would make the studio available for someone else. As you said, I needed the help, and you were going to help me bring up the baby. You always loved babies, Celeste."

Jane grew suddenly quiet. "I can't get used to being called Celeste," she said.

"It's the only name I've ever known for you," Moonglow told her. "I remember when you came here, fresh out of a dead-end office job, so eager to make a living with your weaving, which is the thing you love to do most."

"Me? In an office job?" Jane could manage only a vague recollection of a huge office furnished with row after row of gray metal desks, and glaring fluorescent lights overhead, and people who spent their lunch hours comparing their bowling scores. She had never fitted in.

"Yes, and there was nothing to hold you there, no relatives except that old aunt of yours, who practically turned you out of her house when you told her that all those old newspapers piled up inside were a fire hazard and that she ought to get rid of them."

"Aunt Hildegarde," Jane said, calling to mind a sparrowlike woman who had insisted that Jane come to live with her after her parents died, and then had proceeded to make Jane's life miserable with her irrational outbursts.

"You got a letter from her doctor after you left here. I opened it, because when I saw the doctor's name on the return address, I thought it might have something to do with your disappearance. She died in a nursing home. I didn't know how to let you know," Moonglow said.

Jane was silent for a moment, wishing that she could have done something to help her aunt.

"I'm sorry," Moonglow said softly.

Jane shook her head. "It's okay," she said with a sigh. For so long she'd wondered if she had any family, and it was a deep disappointment to know that Aunt Hildegarde was gone, even though the two of them had never liked each other much.

"Look at me, forgetting my manners. I've just baked fresh gingerbread," Moonglow said. "You'll have some, won't you?"

It wasn't an offer that Duncan was about to turn down, so they trooped into the kitchen and sat down around a round oak table, eating as they pieced together Jane's story.

"What I can't figure out," Duncan said, "is how Jane got into Carlton Jones's field."

"I think she was somehow abducted on the road," Moonglow hypothesized. "Somebody hit her on the head and left her for dead."

"But then where is her van? It's hard to hide a big blue van, you know," Duncan said.

Jane tried in vain to remember driving away from Shanti Village in the van, tried to recall if she had stopped anywhere along the way. It was no use. She couldn't remember anything about the trip.

"If I was going to Ohio, I was a long way from there when they found me outside Tyree, Illinois," she reminded them.

"Whoever kidnapped you headed in that direction," Moonglow offered.

"If only I could *remember*," Jane said. Her memory loss was even more frustrating now that she could recall so many other things. She wondered if she would ever find out exactly what had happened in the time between the moment she left Shanti Village and the morning that Carlton and Ollie Jones found her in the ditch.

One thing she did know after talking with Moonglow. She was not now nor had she ever been married.

"You almost got engaged once," Moonglow filled her in. "It was to a man who worked in that office with you. Only he didn't have any appreciation of your weaving, and you finally decided that you couldn't spend your life with someone who admitted that the highlight of his year was watching the Super Bowl on TV. That was one of the reasons you sought us out at Shanti Village."

Jane glanced at Duncan; he had gone limp with relief. She smiled at him, and he rewarded her with a wide grin. He reached over beneath the table and squeezed her hand.

Moonglow wouldn't hear of their going out for dinner; instead she prepared a vegetarian meal in a wok, and even though Duncan had misgivings about eating it, he managed to down two full plates. Afterwards, still hungry, he tried to recall if there was a steak house on the highway back into town.

And later Jane played with Sun-One, marveling over all the words she could say, and Sun-One, now a bouncing twenty months old, brought all of her favorite toys out of the closet and laid them one by one in Jane's lap until Jane was almost hidden under a heap of rubber duckies and fluffy stuffed animals. Duncan thought how lovely Jane looked with her face pressed against the baby's silky hair, the tiny clutching fingers wrapped around her thumb.

At that moment he was supremely thankful that Jane had no husband and children to whom she must return because he, he wanted to be the one to give her children. He could imagine it—little replicas of Jane and himself leading llamas around the ranch. That reminded him that he was supposed to call Rooney. He asked Moonglow if he could use her telephone.

His conversation with Rooney left him worried; Rooney sounded overwhelmed by dealing with the problems of running the ranch as well as holding the headstrong Mary Kate in check. It was, he knew, time to go home. He made reservations for the next day on a flight to Cheyenne.

Jane and Moonglow parted tearfully after Jane promised to write and to call, leaving the Placid Valley Ranch address in case Moonglow needed to reach her.

"I'll be there until spring," Jane promised Moonglow.

And beyond, Duncan thought to himself, imagining Jane in summer, with her hair bound back by a yellow ribbon, riding along beside him on Diggory, the horse that he had decided should be hers. He tried to catch Jane's eye, but she was handing Sun-One back to her mother and didn't see. He couldn't wait until they could be alone.

Duncan found a hotel in Terre Haute where he checked them into the best room in the house and, still hungry after his experimental foray into vegetarianism, ordered a steak from room service. He ordered one for Jane, too, thinking to celebrate the end of their search. But when they sat at the table across from each other, the candle that the waiter had lighted with such a flourish casting a golden glow on their faces, she appeared distant, thoughtful. *She seems,* he thought with a certain amount of disbelief, *like someone I don't know very well.*

The thought, once it wormed its way into his consciousness, wouldn't go away. Maybe it was because today he had

seen Jane in a place that was totally different from the surroundings—his ranch—where he had first come to know
her. Shanti Village was a rarefied kind of environment, a
place for artsy-craftsy people, the kind of people with whom
he had never associated. In fact, all that talk about Fenton
Murdock and selling handbags to boutiques seemed to have
little to do with the Jane Rhodes he knew.

The *Celeste Norton* whom he knew, he corrected himself. Only he didn't think he would ever be able to call her
by that name. To him she would always be Jane. Dear,
sweet, wonderful Jane. He smiled at her across the table, a
little light-headed from the champagne he had ordered. But
she wasn't smiling. Now she was talking animatedly about
the day's events, hardly noticing his own silence.

"After all this time, it's amazing to find the place where
I belong. It felt so right sitting there in Moonglow's house,
playing with her baby," she said, alight with excitement.

Duncan stopped in midchew and forced himself to swallow. This was a development for which he wasn't prepared.
"You don't have any urge to return to Shanti Village, do
you?" he asked, the words catching in his throat.

"I don't know," she said. "It's all so new."

The faraway light came back to her eyes, her mind clearly
drifting elsewhere. All her tension seemed to be vibrating at
a new and higher frequency; her sensibilities were focused
on Shanti Village, he could tell. He hadn't realized that the
place had had such a strong attraction for her.

Suddenly Duncan couldn't eat any more. "You're coming back to the ranch with me tomorrow, aren't you?" he
said.

The air fell deadly quiet, and it seemed like an eternity
until her eyes lifted to his.

"I don't know," she said again.

He set down his fork and pushed back his chair from the
table. He missed the barn, his usual refuge when things
weren't going right, and he felt as though he might be sick.

He went to the window and stared out. They had left the
draperies open, and the lights of the town twinkled up at

him. Car headlights crawled along the length of the bridge across the river. His own reflection stared back at him, and he blinked.

Jane's reflection slid into place behind him on the darkened window. She wore a bleak expression, and for once he was tired of it. Tired of always putting her first, tired of constantly thinking of her well-being, tired of the pressure they had both been under for days, even weeks. What about his needs? He loved her. He loved her!

"Duncan," she said, touching his arm.

If they had been at the ranch, he would probably have slammed out of the house and walked over to the barn to cool off. But they weren't at the ranch; they were having a late supper in some hotel room in Terre Haute, Indiana, with a table set with gleaming silver and a rose in a silver bud vase, and a candle flickering mellow light over all of it. A *candle* for Pete's sake, and it was supposed to be romantic, but it wasn't! That made him angry.

"Damn," he swore softly under his breath.

"Duncan, I just don't *know*," Jane said brokenly.

"Well," he said, "just when will you 'know'?"

She responded to the unexpected sarcasm in his tone by drawing back as though he had struck her, and uncertainty flickered in her eyes.

"What I mean is, now we've found out all the information you wanted, whether you have a home and a family, who you are, where you lived, even right down to old Aunt Hildegarde, and you don't *know*? What else is there to find out, Jane?"

"I—"

"Let me answer that," he said, turning around to face her. He took in the eyes widened in surprise and hurt, the fingernails bitten to the quick, and hardened his heart. He had waited long enough; what he wanted now was commitment.

"I'll tell you what there is to find out," he went on. "Just one thing. And that is if you love me or not."

He watched her as color suffused her face. The hurt in her eyes almost broke his resolve, because he hated to see her hurt. He worked to control his emotions.

"Of course I love you, Duncan, but it's all so hard to deal with. Finding out that I have a real name, that I apparently had a satisfying life at Shanti Village, that I'm fully capable of earning my own living as a weaver—it's a shock." She stopped when she saw the vein pulsing at his temple, then drew a deep breath and went on.

"And the ranch—of course I'm grateful to you for letting me stay there and helping me get on my feet, for believing in me when no one else did. Just because I've found out who I am and where I once lived doesn't mean that the quest is all over for me. I'm still searching. Trying to figure out where I fit in. If I go back to the ranch with you now, you'll be on my mind every second, I'll live only for you. How will I know who *I* am? I'd always wonder if I could have made it here on my own. If my previous life was the one I should have chosen." Her chest heaved, and her hands were clenched into tight little fists at her sides.

"I never dreamed that you might want to stay here," he responded, unnerved by her words.

Her voice fell into a gentler cadence. "Would you rather I pretended that everything is okay? That would be as bad as lying, and you know how I feel about doing any more of that."

For once Duncan wished that she'd never developed her penchant for telling the truth. Lies could be so much simpler—for a while, at least.

"Duncan?" she said, waiting for him to speak.

Duncan's anger subsided suddenly. He saw her point. He ran a hand through his hair and sighed. The anger had been replaced by an ache in the vicinity of his heart.

"I was going to make love to you tonight," he said. "It wouldn't be such a good idea, would it?" He risked a look at her agonized face.

She looked as though she might cry, and he hoped she wouldn't. His jaw clenched in resistance. If she cried, he'd want to comfort her, and that would lead to something more, and all at once he yearned to feel her cool hand against the back of his neck, her soft lips against his.

Although he stood motionless and, he liked to think, stolidly, she reached up and put her arms around him. He forced himself to think of something else, anything else, anything but her small body pressed against his.

But then she pulled his head down, his arms involuntarily circled her and tightened so that she drew even closer, and as she found his lips with hers, his detachment dissolved entirely.

She began to unbutton his shirt, and for a moment his hand stayed hers, but she brushed him away impatiently and kept unbuttoning. He kissed her more deeply, a long, passionate kiss, and by the time it was over he was completely undressed and she was feathering her fingers across his back, something that always excited him.

Somehow he managed to get her clothes off, she was telling him over and over that she loved him, and they fell back onto the bed.

They had shared a bed before, but never like this, throwing back the bed covers, tangling in them, expressing all their pent-up passion. Her ardor surprised him, and he was amazed at the way she abandoned herself to pleasurable sensation. He touched her breast, reverently at first, then cupping it to his mouth so that she moaned and then sighed his name. And when he lifted his head she was smiling at him, a smile full of love. Then he knew that it was real, that she really did love him, and that he loved her more than he had even admitted to himself.

If he had thought she would have said yes, he would have asked her to marry him there and then. For that was what he wanted, to live with her forever at Placid Valley Ranch, and there was no doubt in his mind that it was meant to be. But he had done all he could to help her; if she wasn't sure what she wanted now, perhaps she would never know. And, as she had once said about his relationship with his wife, it was better to have had something than nothing; now they would have this night.

The light from the bedside lamp was shining full into his eyes, and she reached over to turn it out, the vulnerable slender white underside of her arm brushing his face for a brief moment. When it was dark he tumbled her over and slid his thigh between the gentle softness of hers.

As his eyes adjusted to the glow from the candle on the table, she seemed to float beneath him, light and buoyant, and then he was part of her, being absorbed into her body, knowing her, *knowing*.

Now it didn't matter if there were things that she still didn't know, that there were uncertainties, because for all time he would know, would know *this*. And for the moment, it was all he wanted.

HE DROVE HER to Shanti Village the next morning. She sat close beside him, her face pale and drawn, her lips swollen from their lovemaking the night before.

"I'll call you," she promised as they stood on Moonglow's doorstep beside her suitcase.

"I wish you'd come with me," he told her.

She tried to smile. "I know," she answered, and bent to lift the suitcase.

"I'll stop by Mrs. Beasley's store and pick up the dress to take to Mary Kate," he told her, wanting to postpone his leave-taking as long as he could.

"Thank you, Duncan. For everything," she added. She wished she knew what else to say.

"It's all right." Icicles were melting off the roof overhang. One fell and broke with a tinkle on the porch railing. He tried to make a joke. "This place is a far cry from California, wouldn't you say?"

"Yes," she said. "I guess it is."

"You'd better go in," he said. He didn't know whether to kiss her out here or not.

She nodded, then put the suitcase down again. "Oh, Duncan," she said, and went into his arms.

As he tried to memorize the way she felt in his embrace, he remembered the first time he had held her. It had been the night he found her in the mine, and she'd lain naked in his arms all night long. Like last night, except that on that first night she had slept. Last night neither of them had slept much. There had been other things to do.

"I won't say goodbye," she said. "It seems so final."

"All right. Give Moonglow my regards."

"I will. Tell Rooney hello, and tell Mary Kate—" Here her voice broke. She swallowed and began again. "Tell Mary Kate I love her," she finished.

Duncan nodded, backed down the steps, then turned swiftly and walked to the car. He drove away without looking at her, and when he summoned the strength to glance into his rearview mirror, the porch was empty.

He stopped to pick up the dress for Mary Kate, evading the questions of the kindhearted Alice Beasley. He hand-carried the package all the way home but didn't give it to Mary Kate. That was something for Jane to do.

If she came home. *No,* he corrected himself. *When* she came home.

Chapter Sixteen

Jane and Moonglow moved Jane's old bed into Moonglow's room, and Jane settled into the household routine. Up early in the morning, breakfast with Moonglow and the baby, scheduling time on Moonglow's loom so that they each had a turn. She took to wearing loose jumpers over tights and high-topped shoes, the way Moonglow did. She bundled up her bright hair in a snood. When she looked in the mirror, she seemed to have become someone else, someone she didn't know very well.

It was a life that Jane—Moonglow called her Celeste, but somehow she still thought of herself as Jane—that Jane remembered, but it didn't seem quite real to her. It was as though this was a movie she had seen and liked a long time ago, not a real life.

And if some mornings she woke up and expected to see the yellow walls and flowered draperies of her room at Placid Valley Ranch, well, maybe that, too, was a movie she had seen once. With a real-life hero who had rushed to her rescue, who had treated her with unfailing kindness and consideration, and who loved her. Now that she was caught up in life at Shanti Village, her life at Placid Valley Ranch sometimes seemed more like a dream than a movie.

She wove an afghan and sent it to Duncan, thinking that it would warm him on cold nights when he sat reading in his chair by the fire. He called and thanked her for it, but communication between them was stiff and awkward. They had many such conversations, and Duncan was always terse; he seldom told her anything that was happening at the ranch. She always hung up the phone feeling sad and missing the warmth and happiness she had felt when they were together.

"Why don't you go back to him?" Moonglow asked once when they were having one of their frequent heart-to-heart talks.

"Because I don't have a real sense of who I am yet," Jane said, staring at the floor.

"If you love each other, you should be together," Moonglow said firmly.

"If only it were so simple," sighed Jane. "You see, when I came into Duncan's care I was lost and angry and defiant, and he let me know that he cared about me, so all I wanted to do was to be like him. It worked for me then. But now I've learned that I had a life before that, and I want to live it for a while. Then I'll know if I can go back to the ranch and pick up where I left off."

"What about California?" Moonglow asked.

"Going to California was a dream I had. Maybe it wasn't realistic, although it kept me going through the hard times. Oh, I don't know. All I want right now is to live here and do my work, and I'm so grateful to you for letting me stay."

"Nonsense," Moonglow said as she swung Sun-One onto her lap. "This is your home, too."

Many of the people who lived in Shanti Village before the Fenton Murdock faction came into power had moved away and were now moving back; Jane quickly reacquainted herself with the ones she knew, and they were eager to accept her once more. They held potluck suppers every Tuesday and Thursday night, afterward lingering for long talks over coffee, during which the villagers engaged in mutual support of their endeavors. A warm, convivial feeling enveloped the place, and Jane's work went well. She began to produce handbags for the boutique market and learned to weave new patterns, as well. She was happy enough.

But she missed Duncan. All she had to do was hear his voice on the phone and it would send her into a blue funk for days. She would think about the way he laughed with her over lunch at the ranch, the way she could tell by the set of his shoulders when he came in from the barn how tired he was, about how he looked with Mary Kate settled into the crook of his arm as he read her the Sunday comics with Amos purring in snatches at their feet. And she would wonder if he missed anything at all about her—her attempts to cook the same foods that his mother used to make, the hum of her spinning wheel as they kept each other company in the living room on those long winter evenings, the way they had made love that last night in Terre Haute.

The lovemaking had exceeded her expectations. She hoped it had lived up to his. And now that she had had a sample of it, her body ached with wanting him.

As if all that wasn't enough, during her third week there she received an incoherent phone call from Mary Kate, who had found her telephone number scribbled on a notepad in Duncan's house.

When the phone rang, Jane picked it up and immediately heard someone sobbing on the other end. It only took her a few seconds to realize that this was a long-distance call and that Mary Kate was the caller.

"Mary Kate? Mary Kate, now listen to me. Calm down, honey. Calm down and tell me what's wrong," she said. The sound of the child's crying made her frantic. She didn't know if something had happened to Amos, or Duncan, to Rooney or Mary Kate herself.

"J-J-Jane," was all Mary Kate could say, and this made Jane even more worried.

"Mary Kate, honey, can't you tell me what's wrong?"

Mary Kate struggled to contain her crying, and after a moment, she hiccuped a few times. "D-Dearling," she managed to stammer at last. "They s-sold her."

Jane felt only shock. *"What?"* she gasped, incredulous.

"They sold her. My Dearling. She's gone!" Mary Kate began to sob again.

Jane tried to get a grip on the situation. Dearling sold! But Duncan wouldn't do such a thing to Mary Kate. He'd been angry about her letting the breeding females escape, but he wouldn't have done this.

"Tell me about it," Jane said apprehensively, not really wanting to hear. She still couldn't believe it.

"G-Grandpa did it. He sold her. He's punishing me. But I miss her so much! Dearling won't be happy anywhere else," Mary Kate said all in a rush.

"Oh, Mary Kate, I'm so sorry," Jane said. A deadening depression began to seep through her; she felt helpless to do anything to make Mary Kate feel better.

"You are not! If you were sorry you'd come back here. You promised! You *promised*! And then you didn't come back and didn't come back, and now you're never coming back!" She began to cry again, tears of anger and despair and frustration, feelings that Jane recognized because they were all too familiar.

Mary Kate was right. She *had* promised. In the aftermath of discovering her lost identity, her promise to the girl had dimmed in importance. She felt sick with guilt.

"Look, Mary Kate, may I please speak to Duncan?"

"He's not here," Mary Kate said coldly, then slammed down the receiver.

Moonglow happened to walk through at that moment, leading Sun-One by the hand. "Bad phone call?" she asked with interest as Jane slowly set the receiver on its cradle.

"Very bad phone call," Jane agreed. Trying to think, she sat down on the floor and leaned her head against the wall.

"Problems, I gather," Moonglow said, dashing down the hall to retrieve Sun-One as she toddled away.

"Sit down here, Moonglow, and help me figure this thing out," Jane said, patting the bare hardwood floor beside her. So Moonglow brought Sun-One and set her down to play nearby while Jane outlined the situation.

"If I were you I'd get myself back to Wyoming," Moonglow said when Jane had finished.

"If I go back, I won't want to leave," Jane said.

"So what's wrong with that?" Moonglow asked, rolling her eyes and getting up to chase after Sun-One again.

"I'm just starting back to work, and I do like it here, and—"

"And you've been mooning after Duncan Tate ever since he dropped you on my doorstep. Now I ask you, does it really make sense to stay here when you're head over heels in love with the man?"

"I didn't know it was that obvious," Jane said ruefully.

"You can't talk to him on the telephone without going all fluttery, and afterward you're no fun to be around, believe me. And he's obviously crazy about you. Go for it, kid. As a woman alone, I can tell you that it's no picnic. If Duncan Tate was in love with me, I'd snap him up so fast it would make your head spin."

Jane digested this, then thought about Mary Kate again. "I can't believe they sold Dearling," she said under her breath.

"Sold what?" Moonglow said.

"Dearling. Mary Kate's pet llama. I just can't believe it. Oh, I've got to talk to Duncan and find out his version of the story."

She picked up the phone and dialed Duncan's phone number in the barn, which, according to her calculation, was where he would be at this hour. No one answered.

"I'll call him at the house later," she said.

But when she tried to reach him just before her bedtime, the phone rang and rang, and she finally decided that Duncan was out. She called the Rooneys' house, and Mary Kate answered. She sounded as though her nose was stopped up.

"Mary Kate," Jane began.

"I *don't* want to talk to anyone," Mary Kate said before slamming down the phone.

"Poor Mary Kate," Jane said brokenly.

"She sounds like a real pain to me," Moonglow observed.

"You don't understand. Mary Kate's had a hard life. She needs lots of love and nurturing and—oh, if only I were there," Jane said, burying her face in her hands.

"Then why don't you go?" Moonglow urged.

"It's not exactly around the block, you know," Jane said.

"I know, but you could fly out of Indianapolis and be there in a few hours."

"I'll sleep on it," Jane said, pulling the bed covers up over her head.

She didn't sleep well that night. When Moonglow made Cream of Wheat with cinnamon and brown sugar for breakfast, she hardly ate any.

"Look, this is ridiculous. Why don't you try calling Duncan again?" Moonglow suggested a few hours later when she saw Jane sitting motionless, staring at her idle loom.

"I did," Jane admitted. "Twice. And I called Rooney's house and the office in the barn. There's no answer there, either."

"Bruce Hodges is driving into Indianapolis this morning to pick up supplies. Want me to call him and see if he'll give you a ride to the airport?"

"I'm not ready to leave."

"Get ready, then. Look, you love Duncan. You love these other people. It doesn't make any sense for you to be here if they're having trouble. You belong with them."

"You're right," Jane said, lifting her eyes. "They helped me when I needed it."

"Exactly," Moonglow replied. "That's what it's all about, isn't it? Letting your lives spill into each other, taking from someone else's cup when yours isn't full enough."

"I was going to California because I intended to find a life for myself and people who would love and care about me. But I found all that at Placid Valley Ranch, didn't I?" Jane stood up.

"Shall I call Bruce Hodges?" Moonglow offered again.

"Please. And where did you store my suitcase, Moonglow?"

Moonglow looked as though she would have jumped up and clapped if she hadn't had a baby in her lap. "It's in the closet in Sun-One's room," she called as Jane rushed down the hall.

Jane packed in record time. She hung the loose jumper borrowed from Moonglow in the closet and put on her gray slacks, along with one of Duncan's favorite sweaters. When she looked into the mirror, her first impression was that she looked like her old Jane self, not the new Celeste self she had become since moving back to Shanti Village. She was discovering that she preferred her old Jane self, the self she had become at Placid Valley Ranch.

"Goodbye, dear friend," Moonglow said, hugging her before she left.

"I'll see you again soon," Jane promised, kissing Sun-One on her dimpled cheek.

"I doubt it," Moonglow said, laughing through her tears. "I expect you'll stay a while once you get there."

"Come see me if I do?" Jane asked.

"Maybe. Does that Duncan of yours have a brother?" Moonglow asked hopefully.

"No, there's only Rooney," she said.

Moonglow made a face. "I'm not interested in a man who would sell a kid's *pet*," she sniffed.

At the airport, Jane discovered that air traffic was backed up due to weather problems in the west, but she added her name to a waiting list for flying standby to Cheyenne and spent her time nervously pacing up and down the concourse by the gate from which the plane would depart. She hoped she would get a seat on it; if she didn't, she would wait here until another flight left.

She had no idea what she would say to Duncan when she saw him. She had no idea what he would say to *her*. She thought up imaginary conversations in her head. Instead of the usual platitudes like, "How have you been?" and "I'm fine, thanks," they would get right down to the central issues.

"I was stupid," she would say, looking him right in the eye. "We had something special going, and I didn't realize how good it was until I didn't have it anymore."

"I forgive you," he'd say. "And besides, it was really out of character for me to get angry that last night in the hotel in Terre Haute. It's you who should forgive me."

Then they would fall into each other's arms, never to be separated again.

At least that was the way she pictured it, the way it would happen on *Restless Hearts*. But by this time she knew that real life hardly ever followed the approved script.

Finally, when the tension of waiting became almost unbearable, she sat down in a seat near the gate and forced herself to read a newspaper that someone had thrown down beside her. Moonglow didn't get a newspaper at Shanti Village; with no television set, either, Jane had often felt cut off from the world while she was there.

She read the front page first, then tried to read the comics. Nothing held her interest, until she spotted a headline in a story across the bottom of a page of state and local news. She bent over the newspaper, scarcely believing what she was reading.

Van in Pond Is Clue in Jane Doe Case

An irrigation pond on the property of Tyree farmer Elwood Merck yielded valuable information in Tyree's mysterious "Jane Doe" case, according to Detective Bill Schmidt of the Tyree County, Illinois, Sheriff's Department.

"Mr. Merck was draining his pond in preparation for the growing season, and at the bottom of it was a blue Ford Econoline van registered to Ms. Celeste Norton, who is known to this community as 'Jane Doe,'" Schmidt said.

The Jane Doe cited by Schmidt captured Tyree's interest seventeen months ago, when a young woman bearing no identification was found lying in a ditch on the farm of Carlton Jones. She was suffering from a head wound, Schmidt said.

The van found in Merck's pond contained a handgun that was traced to a convicted murderer, Harry Milton Furgott, Jr. Furgott is presently serving time in the Indiana State Prison.

Schmidt says that Furgott has admitted to abducting Ms. Norton near Indianapolis seventeen months ago.

"Apparently Harry Furgott had just broken out of jail on that date, and he saw Ms. Norton's van at a service station, where she was filling it with gas. When she went inside to pay for the gas, he hid in the van, and when she reentered the van, he held her at gunpoint and forced her to drive to Illinois," said Schmidt.

Schmidt says that Furgott told authorities that Ms. Norton became angry when he spilled a can of Coca-Cola in her van, and he struck her on the head with the butt of the gun. He panicked when he thought she was dead and tossed her out of the van into a ditch.

"After that, he was in an agitated state and drove around Tyree and its environs trying to figure out what to do. The night was exceptionally dark, and he wandered off the main roads, becoming lost and by accident driving Ms. Norton's blue van into Mr. Merck's pond. He had to swim for his life, but managed to hitchhike out of the area after walking to the highway," Schmidt said.

Furgott was recaptured two weeks later near Des Moines, Iowa, and returned to the Indiana State Prison.

Schmidt added that Furgott will probably be charged with kidnapping and assault with intent to kill.

JANE LET THE NEWSPAPER DROP to her lap. She felt a rage of murderous proportions. After all this time of not knowing what had happened to her, now she knew. She could dredge up no actual memory of Harry Furgott or his act, but the knowledge of it, sharp and corrosive as acid, hit her hard. She allowed herself to feel anger, to feel hate, to feel disgust for someone who would hurt another human being. For he had done more than hurt her physically; he had robbed her of her past, left her with no present, and jeopardized her future.

The drone of the public address system speaker directly over her head jarred her out of her thoughts.

"Passenger Jane Rhodes report to Gate Two, passenger Jane Rhodes report to Gate Two," the voice said, and Jane, feeling slightly nauseated, stood up. At the last minute, she scooped up the fallen newspaper and stuffed it into her purse. She would want to read the article again.

"You may board Flight 832 to Cheyenne," the ticket agent told her, and she hurried through the jetway to the plane.

As she sat in her seat waiting for the plane to take off, her mind flowed with replays of her life since she encountered Harry Furgott on that fall day seventeen months ago. The hospital, kind Dr. Bergstrom, and that awful social worker who had been supposed to help her. The shelter for battered women, and her job in the little restaurant in Apollonia. Her bewilderment at being forced out onto the street, and the bus stations and shelters where she had slept. Finding Amos and hiding him in the recesses of her coat in the Chicago library, where she had so often gone to keep warm. Losing her coat in Saint Louis, and the truck driver who had given her a ride in Wyoming. She was overcome with the unfairness of it all. But finally she'd found Duncan. Oh, how happy she would be to see him again!

But what about this man, this Harry Furgott, who had virtually stolen seventeen months of her life? He had certainly wronged her. She was amazed to discover that she felt no malice toward him. The huge surge of anger that had hit her after reading the article was gone. Even when she looked deep inside herself, she could dredge up none of the earlier rage.

Harry Furgott would surely be brought to justice for his crime. And she—she had a future again. She had no intention of jeopardizing it by hanging on to her anger. It was best to let it go; she already had.

The flight to Cheyenne seemed mercifully short, and Jane was surprised when the captain of the plane spoke to them over the plane's public address system and told them that they were landing just ahead of a powerful snowstorm that was sweeping out of the west. She edged forward in her seat to look out the window as they descended. The sky was the color of lead.

Her heart sank. She knew all too well from personal experience how severe a Wyoming snowstorm could be. By the time she had claimed her luggage, no one was leaving the airport. Visibility was near zero.

Gazing out the airport window at the blowing snow, Jane told herself stoically that at least it looked as though it would be a long time until spring. Duncan wouldn't insist that she leave until then; that had been their bargain, and he was a man for keeping his word.

At first she held out hope of being able to contact Duncan at Placid Valley Ranch, but long before nightfall it became apparent that this was impossible. No vehicles were leaving or arriving at the airport. She soon learned that all hotel rooms in the area were booked by delayed passengers, which meant that she spent the night arranged across several hard plastic seats in the airport. She slept better than she'd expected, but then there had been many a night in her past, the past she was so eager to forget, when she'd found worse accommodation. If it hadn't been for the snores of the woman on the row of seats beside hers, she would have had a good night's sleep.

In the morning she tried calling the ranch again, but there was still no answer from any of the three telephones.

When someone told her that the roads would soon be clear enough for buses to get through, she elbowed her way to a counter and managed to buy a ticket for a long-distance bus that was bound for Rock Springs on I-80. Perhaps she could talk the driver into letting her off near Durkee.

The bus was crowded, but in spite of the storm, or perhaps because of it, a holiday atmosphere prevailed, and someone offered her a chicken leg from his sack lunch, which kept her from being too hungry. Two lanes of the interstate highway had been cleared of snow, and although their progress was slow, it gave Jane time to watch out the window for wildlife. Her seatmate, an elderly man, pointed out rabbit tracks at the side of the road, and twice they saw deer turning tail and leaping away over the snowbanks.

Even though he was reluctant to do it, the bus driver let her off at an interstate highway rest stop not far from Durkee, and Jane plowed through the snowdrifts to reach a pay phone. It alarmed her when there was still no answer at Placid Valley Ranch.

"Duncan Tate?" said the caretaker at the rest stop, when she asked him if he knew how she could get to the ranch. "I know him. Happens my sister went to elementary school with Duncan. You want to go out to the ranch?"

Jane assured him that she did, and he rubbed his chin and allowed as how he could take her there when he got off his shift in an hour or so, if she didn't mind riding in his pickup truck with the heating system on the blink.

Jane said no, that wouldn't bother her at all, and for the next hour she huddled against the tile wall in the women's rest room, turning the hand dryer on from time to time for warmth from the heated air.

They set out from the rest stop at a crawl, and Jane thought they would never reach the Placid Valley exit. They kept passing abandoned cars, dark hulks barely visible beneath the snow. Her anxiety grew; it worried her more and more that no one had ever answered the ranch phones.

The highway past the ranch entrance had been plowed, and they were able to increase their speed. The heater in the pickup kept switching on and off with a thump, and Jane frequently blew on her hands for warmth, eliciting profusely apologetic looks from the man who was giving her the ride.

When they finally reached Placid Valley Ranch, Jane was pleased to see that although the mailbox at the entrance of the driveway was mounded with snow, the driveway had been plowed. She got out of the truck, pulling her suitcase after her.

"If you want me to drive you down to the house, I will," said the man, peering anxiously out the crack in his side window at Jane, who was hopping from one foot to the other trying to keep warm. But the pickup's engine had developed an ominous knock, so Jane waved him off and, carrying her suitcase, began to trudge resolutely toward the house.

In the distance the mountains shadowed blue-tinged billows of snow, and the roof of the barn peeked over the trees. It seemed so long since she'd walked this road, so long since she'd seen Duncan! Her heart began to beat faster at the prospect. She wondered if he would welcome her with a kiss, or if the love he had felt for her had changed. She didn't think it would have died, not so soon, but she knew very well that it could somehow have taken a different shape, could have cooled into a feeling more akin to friendship. For friends were what they had been before they became lovers. Best friends. And she knew that friendship was not all she wanted now.

When she was halfway there, she set down her suitcase on the packed snow and rubbed her aching hands together. A puff of smoke from Duncan's chimney wended its way lazily up through the trees, and she took heart. Someone was home, someone was here; despite the unanswered phones, nothing could be wrong if there was a fire in the fireplace.

At the front gate she abandoned the suitcase and ran, mindful of icy spots after her last fall, to the front door of Duncan's house. She knocked, quietly at first, then more loudly. *Duncan,* she said to herself. *Finally I'm going to see Duncan.*

He opened the door. He was wearing his old flannel shirt, a familiar one with a frayed collar. And he wore his boots, so that he seemed even taller than she remembered. He stared down at her, nonplussed. He shook his head slightly as though he couldn't believe she was really there.

"It's me," she said quietly, all the meaningful things she had planned to say scattering to the four winds. "I'm home."

He didn't say anything, only opened the door wider and engulfed her in his arms. And then she was laughing, he was smiling and she was sobbing, and Amos came and twined himself around their ankles, purring so loudly that Jane wiped her eyes and bent to pick him up.

"I'm beginning to enjoy snowstorms. They usually bring you," Duncan said, wrapping his arms around her. Amos was crushed between them, but he seemed not to mind.

"Oh, Duncan, they found my blue van," she told him as he drew her inside where it was warm, and then she told him about the newspaper story that named Harry Furgott as her assailant.

"Schmidt called a couple of days ago, and I tried to call and tell you about it, but our phones have been intermittently out of order because of the storm, and I gave up trying to dial long-distance," Duncan told her.

"That explains why I couldn't reach you," she said as they sat down together in front of the fire.

"Why didn't you wait to come when it would be easier to travel?" he asked, holding tightly to her hands, as though he expected her to disappear if he didn't.

"I hadn't heard about the storm when I left for the airport in Indianapolis. All I knew was that I had to get here. I was worried, Duncan, because of a phone call I got from Mary Kate," and she related how Mary Kate had called and told her that Dearling had been sold.

Duncan's eyes became solemn. "I would have stopped Rooney if I could have," he said. "By the time I knew about his selling Dearling, he had already clinched the deal. Dearling's new owner is a fellow over in Scottsbluff, Nebraska. He wrote and said he suddenly had a hankering to have a llama for a pet, and Rooney called him up and told him he had a nice, tame, trainable llama available. They agreed upon a price over the phone, and the guy showed up right away and hauled Dearling away in a van.''

"Mary Kate is heartbroken," Jane said.

"I know, and there's not a thing I can do about it. Rooney is punishing her for letting the llamas out of their pen."

"But such a cruel punishment! Dearling was everything to Mary Kate," Jane said.

"I agree. It's a shame. I'd personally give my right arm to get Dearling back, but there's no way. Anyway, I couldn't have overruled Rooney's decision. He was disciplining Mary Kate."

"Mary Kate needs love and attention, not harsh punishments," Jane said with conviction.

"I agree with you, and even Rooney admits that he was wrong. He'd like to get Dearling back as much as anyone, if only to improve Mary Kate's disposition." Duncan said. He paused and studied her carefully. "Is Mary Kate the only reason you came back?" he asked.

Jane stopped scratching Amos's chin. "No," she said. "No, it's not. I missed you, Duncan. Terribly."

She was gratified when he enclosed her in his arms. She inhaled his familiar pine scent and closed her eyes as he stroked her hair. They sat like that for a long time, and then he stood up, gently took her by the hand and led her upstairs to his bedroom.

"We'll move your things in here, okay?" Duncan said, murmuring against her temple.

She pulled away. "I've just thought of something, Duncan. I left my suitcase out by the gate!"

He laughed, a low rumble deep in his throat. Then he unbuttoned the top buttons of her sweater and impatiently pulled it over her head.

"We'll get it later, my love," he said. "Much later."

Then he took her to bed.

Chapter Seventeen

The next morning when Jane was passing by her old room, she noticed a large box on the bed, topped with a big pink bow. Curious and wondering if it was for her, she investigated, only to discover from the sales slip tucked under the bow that the package was from Alice Beasley's shop near Terre Haute.

No doubt the package was the dress that Duncan had picked up to bring back to Mary Kate. Jane had assumed that he had already given it to her.

"Duncan," she called when he passed the door of the room. "I thought you'd already given this to Mary Kate."

He stopped, leaned against the door and looked down at the floor. "Well, I didn't," he said sheepishly after a moment or two. "I thought it would be best if you did. When you came back."

"How did you know I would?" she asked in surprise.

"I didn't. But I was hoping," he said. He crossed the floor and kissed the top of her head.

She turned and circled her arms around his torso. How well they fitted! She was still glorying in their physical proximity when he said, "Look out the window. You're going to have a chance to give Mary Kate the present right away."

Outside, Mary Kate was working her way along the tamped-down snow path from Rooney's house. Only this wasn't a bright-eyed, exuberant Mary Kate. It was a Mary Kate on whose sagging shoulders the world had settled.

"Oh, she looks so unhappy," Jane said, going to the window so that she could wave if Mary Kate looked up. But Mary Kate didn't. She kept her head down, and dragged her feet when she walked.

Jane ran downstairs and met Mary Kate at the back door. When she threw the door open, she said, "Surprise!" and a startled Mary Kate's mouth fell wide open.

"You came back," Mary Kate said flatly.

"Yes, and I've been wanting to see you," Jane said, overjoyed to see her young friend again.

"Well, you didn't come over."

Mary Kate's cool welcome deflated Jane only momentarily. She was determined to make the child feel loved. With so much love in her heart now, there was plenty left for Mary Kate.

"I would have stopped over at your house in a few minutes, but you've beaten me to it. Come in, Mary Kate, you're so cold, you look as blue as a Smurf."

"I think I'll go home," Mary Kate said, still resisting her overtures.

"But Mary Kate—"

"You're here, but you might not stay. And then I'll be all by myself again. Without Dearling. Or you," she said pointedly, her face shut against the world.

Jane refused to assign importance or credibility to this statement. "I'm going to bake something special for Duncan's lunch," she said. "It's gingerbread. A good friend of mine, the one I was visiting in Indiana, gave me her recipe. I was counting on you to help."

"Gingerbread?" Mary Kate asked. Jane detected a note of interest.

"Yes, and it'll be the best you ever tasted, I promise. Hurry inside, Mary Kate, or you'll freeze out there."

Mary Kate reluctantly came inside and tossed her coat over a kitchen chair.

"The coat goes in the closet," Jane pointed out as she busied herself finding pans, measuring cups and flour sifter. She watched out of the corner of her eye as Mary Kate grudgingly carried her coat to the closet and hung it lopsided on a hanger.

"I made an F on my geography test yesterday," Mary Kate announced as though it was something to brag about. "What do you think about that?"

Jane saw the challenge but rose to it. "I think it's awful. You should have studied.'

"Ha! I don't care about dumb old Africa or dumb old Asia. I don't care about my dumb old teacher, either. He says he's going to have to ask Grandpa to come in for a conference." Mary Kate energetically greased the cake pan, dropping a wad of Crisco on the floor in the process.

Jane quietly cleaned up the Crisco with a paper towel, then washed her hands again. "Well," she said while drying her hands, "maybe that's what you want."

Mary Kate slanted a grudgingly respectful look in her direction. "Maybe," she said.

"All right, now we have to sift the flour. Would you like to do the honors?" Jane asked, and Mary Kate nodded. She managed the chore without spilling much, and Jane began to measure out the other ingredients.

"I don't think Grandpa has ever gone to a parent-teacher conference," Mary Kate volunteered as she swung on a cabinet door.

"Why not?"

"Never had to, I guess. Maybe he'll have to now. He'll have to go get the teacher out of the teachers' lounge, I'll bet. That's where he stays all the time."

Jane privately thought that if she had a student like Mary Kate in any classroom where she was in charge, she'd probably take up permanent residence in the teachers' lounge, but thought it might be better to change the subject.

She handed the bowl with the batter in it to Mary Kate and said, "How about stirring that for me? Seventy-five stirs, and try to keep the batter in the bowl," she cautioned before running upstairs to get the present.

When she returned, Mary Kate was counting, "Sixty-one, sixty-two, sixty-three," and Jane let her count all the way to seventy-five before she produced the beautifully wrapped package from behind her back. Mary Kate was so surprised to see it that she almost dropped the bowl.

"Wow! Is that for *me*?" she gasped. Jane deftly removed the bowl of batter from Mary Kate's hands before slipping the box into them.

Mary Kate's eyes were as wide as saucers as she unceremoniously tore the ribbon and paper off the box.

"Oh!" she exclaimed as the dress spilled from the box in a flutter of pink organdy. "It's my pink dress!" She held it up and danced a madcap dance from one end of the kitchen to the other.

"Do you like it?" Jane asked anxiously. Mentally she was running up darts in the bodice and shortening the skirt to fit Mary Kate.

"Do I! It's the most beautiful dress in the world, Jane. The *very* most beautiful. It has sleeves you can see through and everything."

"I'll have to alter it to fit you," Jane said, holding the dress up to Mary Kate's bony shoulders.

"That's okay. You're a good sewer. When can you do it?"

"After we put the gingerbread in the oven," Jane said.

"I'll go show Amos my dress," Mary Kate said, and ran to rout Amos from his napping place on the living-room couch.

Duncan came downstairs and watched Mary Kate as she twisted and turned in front of the mirror beside the front door. "I take it from the squeals I heard as I was coming downstairs that Mary Kate likes the dress," he said.

"She loves it," Jane said as she tucked the pan of gingerbread into the oven. "I'm so glad I bought it for her. It only needs a few alterations here and there to fit her perfectly."

"I was thinking," Duncan told her, planting a kiss on her cheek. "Since the loom you owned is presumably water-logged after spending a year and a half under water inside your blue van, we'll have to get another loom for you. Why don't you order it?"

"I will. And do you know that I received three more orders for my llama wool from hand knitters back East? Not only that, Moonglow says she wants to try it. If I get some of the fiber artists at Shanti Village interested in llama wool, that's a good, steady market."

"Duncan, look at my dress," Mary Kate demanded as she twirled by.

"Mmm. You'll look like a fairy-tale princess in it, no doubt about it. Would you mind telling me where you're going to wear such a gorgeous outfit?"

"For my birthday party next month. Grandpa said I could have one. *If* he doesn't change his mind," she said with a frown.

"Tell you what, Mary Kate. If he changes his mind, you come to see me. Jane and I will change it right back again," Duncan told her. He had already extracted the admission from Rooney that he wished he could get Dearling back but could think of no way to do it.

"Let's go upstairs and get started fitting that dress," Jane suggested, and as she ushered Mary Kate out of the kitchen, she turned and mouthed silently to Duncan, "Ask Rooney when Mary Kate's birthday is." She knew he understood when he answered with a wink.

"I WANT TO DO something really special for Mary Kate's birthday," Jane told Duncan that night as they were lying in bed.

He traced idle circles on her shoulder. "Like what?" he asked sleepily, his chest vibrating as he spoke.

"Like doing something with the llamas. The other kids will love it."

"Like doing *what* with the llamas?" Duncan asked, slightly more awake now.

"Oh, maybe a pack trip. And didn't Mary Kate say something about llamas pulling a cart? Couldn't we give the kids rides or something?"

Duncan hooted. "Her birthday is only a few weeks away, sweetheart. On April 25, in fact. And we still have snowstorms here at that time of the year. Why, I remember last year when—"

"Snowstorms? In April?"

"This is Wyoming, Jane. Not Chicago. Why, Chicago's weather can be *tropical* compared to Wyoming's. So I don't think we should plan a pack trip, and as for pulling a cart, Mary Kate was going to train Dearling to do it. But Dearling, unfortunately, is gone."

Jane sighed. "She misses Dearling terribly. I walked out to the barn to get more llama wool out of the closet today, and do you know what I found in there? Mary Kate, sobbing her heart out. I don't see how Rooney could have been so heartless."

"He thought he was doing the right thing at the time. He'd like to atone for his mistake, which is why I think he'll agree to have this big birthday party for Mary Kate. He wants to make it up to her."

"Nothing can ever make up for the loss of Dearling," Jane said with great certainty. "Nothing. Not even a party."

"You're right, of course. Now don't you think it's time to go to sleep?"

She thought about her own feeling of loss when she was separated from him; but they had come together again in the end, and she was glad. She reached out to him, marveling at the tautness of his muscles, the warmth of his skin.

"Of course I think it's time to go to sleep," she said as he responded to her touch. "But not just yet."

JANE SET UP HER NEW LOOM in the bedroom that had once been hers, and she began to weave llama wool into blankets. Llama wool was less elastic than sheep's wool, and she experimented with mixing in ten percent sheep's wool as she spun her yarn. She was pleased with the results, and after providing samples, Moonglow asked her to send more. She also sent a check representing the proceeds from the sale of Jane's creations in the boutique in Urbana and at the Shanti General Store.

Jane put away the check, biding her time before mentioning it to Duncan. Once it would have paid her way to California, but now she wasn't sure what the future held. Her dream of a new life there seemed unnecessary at this point; it had served her well when she needed it, but now she knew that she had no desire to enroll in a computer training program. She was well able to provide for herself through her spinning and weaving. She had proven it.

But what about the future? Duncan had said nothing about his expectations, and she didn't want to bring it up. She was happy. So was he. Right now it suited their purpose to live one day at a time, enjoying their new relationship.

It was Jane who answered the telephone when Dearling's new owner called. She was tying up the treadling sequence on her new loom one day when the trill of the phone interrupted her, and she didn't want to answer it. But Duncan and Rooney had both gone into town, and Mary Kate was at school, so there was no one else. She rushed to pick up the phone and was out of breath when she answered.

"No, Duncan Tate isn't here right now," she said, pushing Amos away when he tried to play with the phone cord. "May I take a message?"

When she started to write down what the man was saying, she realized with a jolt that she was talking to Dearling's new owner.

"Like I say, the llama looks like she's ailing. Nothing major, you know, but I thought I'd call."

"Is she eating? Drinking?" Jane asked in alarm.

"I can't say. I travel a lot, and I got her for my boy. He's kind of lost interest in her. She stays in the barn and well, he's an average boy. Interested in baseball and girls. The llama's a novelty, but he doesn't pay much attention to it."

"I'll ask Duncan to call you," she told the man, and hung up feeling dismayed.

When she told Duncan about the call, he appeared concerned. After phoning the man and talking with him, he seemed even more so.

"It doesn't sound good," he told Jane. "In fact, it sounds like the worst way to treat a llama. Llamas are herd animals, and they like to have others around. I suggested that he get another llama to keep Dearling company, but he scoffed at that. He said that he wasn't about to go out and buy another one when his son didn't pay attention to the one he already had."

"Dearling was such a tame llama, used to a lot of petting. She's probably pining away from lack of love."

"I gave him some suggestions. All I can do is call at the end of the week and see how Dearling is doing," Duncan said on a note of apprehension.

They waited out the week, but didn't mention Dearling's troubles to Mary Kate, who would have been even more heartbroken to know that Dearling's new owners didn't appreciate her. When Duncan came in from the barn that weekend after calling to check on Dearling, his lips were set in a grim line.

"It's worse," he said. "In fact, he wants to get rid of Dearling, he said."

"You mean sell her?" Jane asked.

"I guess so. He says he's got money tied up in her that could be used for better things."

Jane put aside the wool she was carding and went to kneel beside Duncan's chair. "Duncan," she said quietly, "I want to buy her."

"Buy her? Are you serious?"

"Definitely. Because I want to give her to Mary Kate."

"Well, I suppose I could give him a refund," Duncan said slowly.

"I don't mean that. *I* want to pay for her. With my own money. I have money, Duncan, enough to buy Dearling. It's from selling my wool and my shawls and handbags and blankets and—well, once I would have used it to start a new life in California. But now I know that the best thing I could do with it is to buy Dearling back as a birthday present for Mary Kate.''

He saw that she meant it, and cupped her chin in his hand. Her eyes, a deep, dark blue, gazed back at him with a candidness that he knew he could trust. His heart spilled over with happiness.

"I'll call him and tell him that's what you want. If it really is," he said.

She let the vision of palm trees and aquamarine swimming pools, of computer classes and friends who sported deep suntans, slip away forever. That dream had never been real to her, had only been a stopgap solution. And it had never offered the safety, security and love that she had found here at Placid Valley Ranch.

"It's really what I want," she said, and reached up to kiss him lingeringly on the lips.

THE TWENTY-SIX FIFTH-GRADERS, members of Mary Kate's class at the Placid River Elementary School, milled around the kitchen, dining room and living room of Rooney's small bungalow.

"Now who wants to play Pin-the-Tail-on-the-Donkey?" Rooney shouted into the melee. No one paid the slightest attention to him.

Nine or ten children watched the cartoon video he had rented for them. Three were having a popcorn fight. Another was energetically grinding kernels into the carpet, and one boy was sound asleep under the kitchen table. Five were stuffing cake and ice cream into their mouths and occasionally someone else's. Mary Kate, wearing a pointed gilt cardboard hat, was arm-wrestling the class bully.

"Nice party," Jane said as she poured Kool-Aid into glasses.

"Nice party, my eye," Rooney grumbled. "When I was a kid, we all sat around the dining-room table and kept quiet until the birthday kid opened his presents. Then we all went home.''

''But I bet you didn't have half as much fun,'' Jane observed.

Rooney grinned. ''You're probably right,'' he said.

''I wonder where Duncan is,'' Jane said, tilting the blind at the window so she could see up the driveway.

''I don't know, but I wish he'd get here pretty quick, so we can clear these kids out of here soon,'' Rooney said, before rushing to pry apart two boys who were rolling on the rug and trying to poke out each other's eyes with their fingers.

Jane had gone to assist Rooney when she heard the rumble of Duncan's truck rolling across the cattle guard at the end of Rooney's driveway. The truck pulled a small trailer, and Duncan parked so that the trailer was directly in front of Rooney's front door.

She signaled to Duncan with an Okay sign and went into the living room.

''Mary Kate,'' she said over the din, ''there's a package for you outside.''

Mary Kate brushed her bangs out of her eyes and trod across the cake crumbs to the door. Her eyes widened when she saw the pickup and trailer.

She sent Jane a puzzled look.

''Go ahead,'' Jane urged gently, and by this time several of Mary Kate's classmates had gathered to watch.

Mary Kate pushed open the front door. Suddenly shy, she hung back when Duncan, smiling broadly, held out his hand.

''Come open this trailer door for me, Mary Kate. It seems to be stuck.''

''*You* open it,'' Mary Kate said in a choked voice. ''I can't.''

Behind Jane, Rooney snorted. ''Seems to me you're pretty good at opening gates and doors and that kind of thing. Seems to me you know how to *leave* them open, too,'' but he said it in a joking tone.

Mary Kate said, "Oh, Grandpa, hush."

"What's in the trailer, Mary Kate?" asked the boy whom she'd beaten at arm wrestling. A girl said, "Just wait and see," and soon everyone was clamoring to know what surprise was waiting for Mary Kate.

She walked slowly up the ramp to the trailer door and fumbled with the latch. Then it sprang free and the door swung open. Finally there appeared a dazed Dearling, who, appearing somewhat startled by the watching crowd, lurched into Mary Kate's arms.

"Dearling! Oh, it's my Dearling!" Mary Kate cried, and the little llama nuzzled her cheeks, seemingly puzzled by the salty tears that now flowed freely down Mary Kate's face.

"She's a birthday present from Jane," Rooney said, pointing to the huge red ribbon around Dearling's neck.

As the group of awed children gathered around Mary Kate, Duncan slid an arm around Jane's slender shoulders and drew her apart from the group. The snow on the ground was thawing into mud, but he walked her over to the fence behind Rooney's house, where they stood looking out over the pastures and at the mountains beyond.

"That was a good idea you had, buying Dearling back," he told her.

"Dearling's all right, isn't she?" Jane asked anxiously. "I mean, she's not sick or anything, is she?"

"I expect she'll make a full recovery. She was suffering from a broken heart, and that, in this case, is easily mended."

Jane leaned on the fence and inhaled a deep breath. "I smell spring on its way," she said, resting her head against Duncan's shoulder.

The sun was bright and golden, chasing the tail end of winter, and on the snow-covered mountain ridges, dark rivulets heralded the thaw. Soon the pastures and the mountainsides would burgeon with the gentle greens and yellows and pinks of spring.

There was something so optimistic about spring, Jane thought. No matter what went before, no matter how cold the winter or how many snowstorms it brought, you could count on spring coming along to make everything fresh and new. And after spring, summer, that golden flowering time when life seemed infinitely precious and beautiful.

"It was just this kind of day I used to dread," Duncan said, gazing down at her. "I thought you would leave in the spring."

"I'm not leaving, Duncan. Ever. Not in spring, summer, winter or fall."

"Of course you're not. You're going to marry me," he said comfortably, fitting her into the curve of his arm.

"Soon," she agreed.

"And we'll raise children," he said.

"And llamas—"

"And we'll live happily ever after, Jane Doe. You're home at last."

Mary Kate called them back to the party, and from where they stood they could see that the pink sash of her organdy dress was trailing in the mud. They looked at each other and laughed.

Then, hand in hand, they walked back through the melting snow toward a future as new as spring, as bountiful as summer, and bright with the radiance of the rest of their lives.

Harlequin American Romance.

Gull Cottage

The sun, the surf, the sand...

One relaxing month by the sea was all Zoe, Diana and Gracie ever expected from their four-week stay at Gull Cottage, the luxurious East Hampton mansion. They never thought that what they found at the beach would change their lives forever.

Join Zoe, Diana and Gracie for the summer of their lives. Don't miss the GULL COTTAGE trilogy in Harlequin American Romance: #301 CHARMED CIRCLE by Robin Francis (July 1989); #305 MOTHER KNOWS BEST by Barbara Bretton (August 1989); and #309 SAVING GRACE by Anne McAllister (September 1989).

GULL COTTAGE—because one month can be the start of forever...

GULLG-1

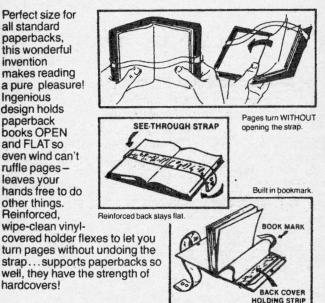